# GREY LADIES
# AND
# MOONSHINE

# PETER THOMAS JACKSON

*World War Two 1943/1944*
*Merchant Navy Company*
*Kingston Upon Hull*
*East Yorkshire*
*England*


**Shipping Company clerk Lask is plucked from his duties to utilise his skills in the organisation of volunteer seamen who will crew converted gunboats for a S.O.E. ( Special Operations Executive) secret operation under the guise of the British Merchant Navy which will sail through enemy controlled seas to.......................................................**

# GREY LADIES AND MOONSHINE

## BY
## PETER THOMAS JACKSON

January 8<sup>th</sup> 1943.

Light was dim in the office as Lask worked through the accumulated paperwork that war had produced.

The clock on the wall struck eight.

Instinctively he looked at his watch checking for any error.

Watch and clock agreed.

He decided he would leave at eight thirty and allowing for the unexpected he would be home by nine o'clock.

Silence was only broken by the tick of the clock upon the wall and the distant sounds of trains and ships shrieking sirens.

His work was repetitive, shifting and sorting and filing large amounts of inter related pieces of paper necessary for running a large shipping company in time of war.

Even Lask, the humble clerk was important, at least that's what he told himself. He wondered how his wife was coping with the blackout and the boys, aged eleven and nine and growing fast.

Sorting through the mercantile papers he worried about the future, his own future and his ability to cope, but he knew he was no exception, everyone was in the same position, everyone had concerns, worries which varied in predicament and intensity.

He had volunteered for active service but had been rejected because it was thought his expertise was an invaluable asset to the Company. He felt neighbours looked at him with envy as he had a regular, stable and relatively safe job which was almost guaranteed for the duration.

' *How did he wangle it ?*', he imagined people saying and though his wife was delighted with his position he sometimes imagined she and the boys harboured similar thoughts, especially when they heard of the war exploits of fathers of their friends.

Not far away from the office, just over the railway bridge, the docks were busy in the bleak January dampness and the sounds broke into his lonely, maudlin introspection and he changed thought, imagining he was on the bridge of a Company ship ordering the helmsman to turn the wheel two points to starboard. He felt a tension , the excitement as the bows of the ship cut into the swell of the sea .

He wiped imaginary sea salt from his brows as his eyes focused on his desk and he heard the familiar tick of the clock upon the wall.

Nearly eight thirty.

He smiled in quiet satisfaction at the order he had made out of chaos. Suddenly the door burst open.

A loud gruff voice shattered into the room.

' *Lask just the man I want to see, caught you just in time* ', barked the authoritative voice of Captain Turnbull whose frame appeared dark and sinister in the half light with tiny droplets of condensation sparkling in his full black beard.

Nervously Lask  looked up towards the over crop of eyebrows that sheltered the wide penetrating eyes of this powerful man, and he stuttered as he answered that he had almost finished for the day and he firmly hoped that he had.

' *If you're sure you've finished Lask, I'll give you a lift home, I've got the car outside. Ready are you ?* '.

Lask , taken aback, nodded vaguely and nervously as he put the finishing touches to the order of his desk and as he reached for his overcoat  the burly Captain paced impatiently around  puffing clouds of cigar smoke into the small office.

Lask knew Captain Turnbull only vaguely after infrequent visits to his disorganised and unkept office, but he knew his reputation, and he had a feeling of unease, as he followed the Captain.

Lask, a tidy man, a man of nervous energy and organisation, in his early thirties, clean shaven, five foot eight, slight physique whose grey eyes, fine features and thinning brown hair described and disguised the man.

He compared himself to the man he followed out through the impressive revolving doors into the darkness feeling a sense of regret at the contrast he perceived between  himself and the Captain.

The Captain opened the door of the car and fell into the driving seat giving a side wards glance at the tentative Lask and sighed with resignation.

' *Don't worry Lask. Tell you the truth I can never see where I'm going in the black out. Hit a tree last week. Car survived. Tree didn't. Thing is it was in someone's garden* ', and his laughter rebounded with demonic resonance within the confines of the car.

The tentative nervousness of Lask was replaced with an acute physical unease as the Captain started the engine and the car began to move forward in uncertain directions.

' *Still its only a Company car, serves 'em right for bringing me ashore, putting me in that dammed office. Where do you live, off Anlaby Road is it ?* '

The Captain crunched the gears, swerving to avoid an obstacle in the blackened, uninhabited streets.

' *Third car I've had since I've been ashore, smashed the other two, bloody drivers, don't know the basics of navigation* '.

The car swerved violently as Lask gave precise instructions to Captain Turnbull who acknowledged with grunts as the engine grated and he concentrated on the road.

Perhaps it was his eyes which provoked the thought in Lask that the Captain didn't like to be given instructions by a lesser mortal as himself, but the thought was overtaken as the car slowed down.

Captain Turnbull turned to Lask.

' *I should be at sea you know. Terrible being at home all the time. The wife says I'm an irritable old man. Can't wait to pack to pack my kit bag. I don't know Lask, I just don't know* '.

As the car accelerated Lask became increasingly apprehensive and impatient to know where all this was leading.

' *Nearly there Captain, first on the left, past the pub, then second on the right, number twenty three* '.

Mounting the pavement the car came to an abrupt halt.

Though it was bitterly cold, Lask was sweating.

He pushed open the door to his darkened house and from the shadows his wife Joan emerged looking sternly at the unexpected visitor and for a moment the Captain felt awkward, but shuffled about and found composure.' *Ere, evening Mrs Lask, 'er just a spot of business with your husband. Company business.Shouldn't take long* '.

Joan looked sharply at her husband and began to mumble incoherently, then her words formed with accusative clarity.

*' Whatever is the matter Herbert Lask, what have you been up to ?'.*

She switched on the hall light and the full bearded face of the Captain animated with bellicose laughter and a mischievous glint appeared in his eyes as he half sought to reassure her.

*' Well Mrs. Lask I don't know what he's been up to, but I do want to have a chat with your husband '*, he paused, his expression changed and the glint in his eyes vanished, replaced by a hard penetrating stare and his voice became cold and official.

*' Company business. Will not take long ! '.*

Lask gestured their visitor into the front room and Joan made sure the curtains were firmly closed before she switched on the standard lamp and she asked the unexpected visitor if he would like some tea, but the Captain was dismissive.

*' Tea !, anything stronger ? Scotch perhaps !'.*

Lost for words she retreated to the kitchen followed by her husband who opened the larder in search of the bottle of Scotch, and as he found it and dusted it down he wondered just how long it had been there.

*' Ah here we are Captain, don't drink much myself '*, and he poured two large measures.

*' Good man, good man, by the way what is your first name ?.*

*' Herbert '*, answered Lask.

*' Is it. Ah well. I think I'll stick to Lask if you don't mind. Now down to business. You've been running that office for some time I undersatnd and apparently you do it very well, but in these times we all have to be adaptable. Look at me shuffling around the docks when I should be on the bridge of a ship in a stormy sea. Ah well ! This whisky is good. Now Lask have you heard of the Commodore '.*

*' Vaguely, didn't he have something to do with Operation Performance. Secret wasn't it ? '.*

Lask began to warm to the Captain as he refilled their glasses. The bulky figure tipped half a tumbler of whisky down his throat, lit a cigar, threw the match into the empty grate, inhaled the smoke, grunted and flicked ash on the carpet.

Lask began to realise why the Captains wife wanted him away to sea.

*' Mister Lask it couldn't have been much of a secret if you knew about it '.*

*' Well Captain things get around the office '.*

*' Lask, what I'm going to tell you is secret, I repeat secret, in fact top secret . Understand ! '*

Lask understood and adjusted his physical stance to fit the occasion, standing alert and at attention with whisky glass in hand.

*' The Commodore is going to organise an operation using converted gunboats to carry cargo. He wants these boats to be crewed by our men and to fly Company flags. This is where you come in Lask. You'll be a coordinator, a liaison man, between the Company and the other parties involved. You'll be dealing with the crews and unfortunately working alongside me. Long and irregular hours. You'll need an office, a car and a telephone. Start tomorrow. Will you do it ?'.*

Lask realised he wasn't been presented with an invitation and the Captain took the answer for granted as he drained his glass and made for the door.

*' Good man, good man, as I've kept you up late, have a bit of a lay in tomorrow but be in my office by nine o'clock. Well must be off, say goodnight to Mrs. Lask for me. By the way there will be a few extra bob in your pay packet. Thanks for the drink. Goodnight Lask '.*

He gave Lask a long lingering look.

Then the door closed and the sound of the engine of the battered car spluttered slowly then roared off into the night and Lask poured the last of the whisky into his glass.

Joan came in looking pensive and worried.

He ignored her, though not on purpose as he was embroiled with the events of the last two hours as he began to realise he'd been singled out to be part of something special.

Joan wasn't to pleased.

*' What's all this Herbert Lask, talking business, bombs one minute, drinking whisky the next, in our front room and, and, there's a war going on out there, what about the boys, bet they've been listening in, at this time of night, do I get to know Herbert Lask, do I get to know ?'.*

Lask was oblivious to his wife, he was lost in the excitement of the moment as he speculated about his future.

*' Herbert, Herbert Lask  I'm talking to you !'.*

Lask answered in hushed, nervous, serious tones.

*' Ah yes Joan, secret work, secret '.*

*' You, secret work,  they're not sending you away to sea are they ?'.*

*' No nothing like that, but it's a new job, I'm to be a coordinator,  we'll get a telephone. A telephone and a car and an increase in pay ',*

He drained the last of the whisky from his glass and he looked into her eyes as he spoke.

*' It's an important job, very important, I'll be doing something worthwhile at last '.*

Joan shook her head from side to side.

She was angry.

*' What the devil have you been doing up to now I ask you, what's the hours of this new job, irregular , you hardly see the boys as it is '.*

She sighed and angrily, swept up the heap of ash left on the carpet by the cigar smoking Captain Turnbull, but she hadn't finished yet.

*' I suppose war is all about drinking to much whisky and big noisy hulks like him flinging ash all over the place, the boys not knowing what time you're going to be in, the black outs, the rationing. Oh Herbert Lask I'm so fed up with it all '.*

She threw the ash into the fireplace.

She banged the dustpan on the hearth.

Lask looked away and breathed deeply .

*' I know Joan, but don't forget the others, others are worse off, perhaps this operation will bring the end of the war  a little closer and if  there was any more in the bottle I'd pour another to celebrate '.*

Shocked by her husbands new bravado she snatched the empty bottle and stared at him through tired narrow eyes and she spoke very softly.

' *That's enough Herbert, you'd better get to bed or you'll not be fit for work in the morning* '.

Lask didn't answer, nor did he move, he just stood there in there in the middle of the room.

He wasn't tired . He was excited

Though he had hardly slept Lask was up early and feeling
exhilarated by the prospects of the day.

Joan was busy providing hearty breakfasts as the  boys filled the
house with irritating noise and were asking questions about his new
job and eating porridge and toast at the same time and then they left
for school leaving behind a welcome silence.

Lask smoked a cigarette and Joan cleared away the dishes.

She could cope, but the continuous dreariness, uncertainty, the ration
book and the bombs had its ' snapping' effect. '

' *I'm off Joan'*, and as he struggled into his overcoat she came close
to wishing him good luck with a hug and then she returned to the
dishes in the sink.

' *Show 'em what you're made of Herbert Lask. No drinking whisky and
don't be late home* '.

With his orders ringing in his ears he walked apprehensively into the
cold morning air and as he passed the bombed out bakery his senses
recalled the delicious aroma of freshly baked bread that used to be
part of the everyday and on any other day the passing scene would
add another layer to the misery, yet this morning wasn't just any
other morning.

It was eight o'clock when he knocked on the door of Captain
Turnbull's office.

The huge voice bellowed out, ordering him to enter.

' *Thought I told you to have a lay in, couldn't  sleep eh, know the
feeling, like taking on a new ship. Lets get to it Lask* '.

He quickly took off his coat and looked around the office which had a
similarity to the devastation of the bombed out streets he'd just
walked through.

The Captain beckoned him and led him across the room and
gestured Lask to take a look.

' *Right old son, this is your office. As we are working together and  I
have it on very good authority that you are a very orderly man,  you can
start and sort my office out while I rustle up some tea* '.

Lask surveyed the two offices.

For a moment he had second thoughts about his new direction, but when he saw three telephones, two black, one red and a large world map upon the wall he was reassured.

He busied himself, carefully organising papers into piles, separating engineers specifications, damage reports, cables and directives.

Soon Lask had created space and the door creaked open as the Captain shouldered his way in.

A long delicate finger of ash jutted out from the half smoked cigar clenched in his teeth and clasped in his hands were two pint pots of steaming tea.

*' Ah Lask, good, good man. Looking better, never one for paper work, myself. Now Lask drink ya tea man, drink ya tea '.*

Lask sipped his tea, but it wasn't what he was used to and when the Captain asked him if the tea was agreeable, he smiled, realising he would have to develop a taste for it.

He viewed the Captain with a certain amount of awe and trepidation as here was a worldly Master Mariner bringing him, Mister Lask, tea.

*' The place is looking better already, never one for paperwork myself. Can't beat a strong pot of tea. Can't abide piddling cups. Well what do you think ? '.*

Captain Turnbull perched himself on the edge of a desk and with a benign expression looked Lask straight in the eye.

Lask felt uneasy.

Apart from the tea he began to realise he would have to get used to a different way of life working alongside the Captain .

He told the Captain he wasn't sure what was expected of him.

The Captain coughed, put his pot on the table, lit another cigar, stood up and stretching his legs, puffed blue smoke into the office while giving Lask the enigmatic look, then he spoke.

*' Lask, I'm in the same position as you. All I know is what I told you last night, but I'll tell you this, the Superintendent came to see me saying he wanted me to work on a special operation and I might adtelling me that I had to work with you. Tell you the truth I'd never heard of you before '.*

Suddenly he regretted his words.

His eyes blinked nervously.

He stroked his beard as he thought his way out of his verbal indiscretion, fumbling his words as he backtracked.

*' Well I mean to say, I knew you worked in the office somewhere, but you see paperwork isn't what I do , '* his voice rose as he stood up and concluded,

*' I'm about ships. Understand Lask '.*

He looked down at the floor as he inhaled breath through his teeth making a grating sound.

*' I think the Superintendent thinks you as a stabilising influence on me. Anyway we'll find out what this operation is all about at eleven fifteen. Briefing in the Superintendents office.'* So Lask we can do a bit more here, making the place ship shape', he laughed heartedly , ' you tell me what to do, you be the Captain, well for just a moment at least '.

Lask acknowleged the Captain and thought all this was very strange but to his surprise the burly figure began to respond to his directives. After a short while the Captain stopped, sighed and looked around with a tired look of bewilderment as he stroked his beard,

*' Lask I told you this isn't my cup of tea. But I suppose, yes I suppose '.*

Then the two men worked quietly together.

The Captain responded to the diplomatic instructions of Lask who wondered why a Master Mariner of such reputation should be ashore where he was so out of place and hankered for the sea as if he were in exile. However, there was work to be done, and Lask needed things to interlock, to have form, logic and his working methods only made sense when he could see tangible results from his efforts.

Within a relatively short space of time the offices offered space.

Documents could now be identified, ledgers had found their niche, maritime manuals stacked on shelves and in order as the two offices were made one and thought to be functional for the business in hand.
At ten minutes to eleven the Captain beckoned to Lask.
Both men dusted themselves down and straightened their ties and Captain Turnbull led the way, swaying from side to side, clouds of cigar smoke bellowing from his head, mumbling about a dog seeing the rabbit as doors seemed to open for him.
His personality seemed to intoxicate.
Lask was under the influence.
They came to the top of the building, walking along a dark panelled corridor towards the inner sanctum of the Company.
On approaching the large solid door the Captain stood aside and gestured Lask to knock.
Seconds passed, then from within a commanding voice ordered their entry. The office was large, rectangular with a panoramic window overlooking the railway that led to the docks.
In all his working life Lask had never been this close to the heart of the Company and he was mesmerized by models of ships past and present in glass cases sitting on polished tables, then there was the Superintendent.
A big man, with thinning grey hair, attired in a well tailored crisp dark suit, starched collar, an immaculate knot in his tie, firm and straight.
He looked at both men with steely blue, grey eyes.
Now Lask felt uncomfortable.
After the Captain, now the Superintendent.
*' Morning Turnbull, Lask, sit down, sit down, smoke if you wish '.*
The formality began to ease only slightly as Captain Turnbull looked at Lask and Lask realised the Captain felt, if not as awkward as himself, apeared to be  visibly uneasy.
The Superintendent slid an oriental decorated box across the table.
*' Cigars your weakness aren't they Turnbull ? '.*
It wasn't so much a question as a statement of fact.

Captain Turnbull grinned through his beard as he took a long cigar from the box.

Lask took out his Woodbine cigarettes.

*' Have one yourself Lask '*, commanding the Superintendent and Lask put his cigarettes away and fumbled with the cigar as he took a light from the Captain.

*' Drink gentleman ? '*, and without reply he went over to the drinks cabinet, taking out three large crystal glasses, pouring equal measures into each one.

The three men raised their glasses with silent, implicit sentiments of luck and health and then the Superintendent put his glass to his lips, took a sip and inhaled deeply from his cigarette.

*' The Commodore should be here soon. Do you know anything about him Lask ?'.*

Lask threw a glance at the Captain who nodded assurance.

*' Well Sir only what Captain Turnbull told me last night '.*

The Superintendent turned and walked over to the window looking out over the bridge to the docks and the silence of a few long seconds was broken as he turned to face the two men.

In sharp, clipped words, the business of the day began.

*' The Commodore. Interesting man. Knowledge of commerce, trade, steel, an expert on Scandinavia. Volunteered for the Royal Navy. Now works for the Special Operations Executive, if you don't know what that is, you soon will . He was behind two other maritime operations in the last couple of years'.* The Superintendent stopped, looked down at his desk, shuffled a few papers, then continued .

*'One of the operations was successful '.*

He looked at the two men.

*' From now on everything is secret. Understand ! '.*

Captain Turnbull fondled his empty glass, twitched his cigar, and looked at Lask.

The Superintendent continued.

*' The Commodore knows a great deal about the Company, about our ships and our men. Lask do you know anything about Motor Torpedo Boats ? '.*

' *Well Sir I understand M.T.B's are to be converted to carry cargo and to sail into enemy waters, all a bit risky* ', and no sooner had Lask uttered his opinion he regretted his words.

The Superintendent looked across at Lask expressing a smile of little humour as the great room sank into a grey silence of seconds to be broken by a slow, quiet, devastating broadside from the Superintendent.

' *Of course Mister Lask, war is a bit risky* ', and his words grated around in his mouth, '*but then Mister Lask, opening your front door in a morning is a risk, don't you think Mister Lask* '.

This truth fractured the thin veneer that had sheltered Lask from the grim realities of war.

' *Mister Lask, you know well that men in Company ships sail to all points of the compass. Sometimes they don't come back. But to send ships into enemy controlled waters is a risk I'd not readily sanction because….* ', and the Superintendent seemed to become stuck for words.

Lask sensed unease and ventured a hesitant conclusion to the Superintendents remarks.

' *Precisely, Mister Lask, precisely, sailing behind enemy lines, extremely dangerous .These converted gunboats will be crewed by our men. To me this Company is one big family, not always happy I'll grant you that, but still a family, and I have the responsibility for sending men to sea. Sometimes I wish I was facing the same dangers but I go home every night. When I see the widows of those who don't come back I wonder what they think of me. I am responsible* '.

He turned and gazed out of the window as the light of the day turned to grey and in the long following silence Lask and Turnbull held their breath, both knowing they were privy to the Superintendents innermost thoughts.

Angry with himself for his lapse into self revelation he abruptly turned from the window.

Tension was broken by a sharp knock on the door.

' *Come in !* ', shouted the Superintendent. The door opened and an air of culture enveloped the three piece suited man who strode into the office swinging his brief case in his left hand.The Commodore was short, stocky, clean shaven with dark hair immaculately in place and a tight puckish smile  which betrayed nothing as he spoke.
' *Morning Superintendent Watson, good to see you, been a long time, about a year I think* ', and the two men shook hands with an easy familiarity.
' *A year almost to the day. Well Commodore I understand we're going into business, let me introduce you to my men. Herbert Lask, everyone knows him as Lask, desk man, organiser, coordinator and Captain Turnbull. The Captain knows his way around ships and the seas. He gets things done in ways that defy belief, he's our fixer* '.
Having shaken hands and dispensed with the formalities the Commodore took from his briefcase a sheaf of papers, photographs, design specifications spreading them out in order on a nearby table.
' *We've got hold of a few M.T.B's supposed to be for the Turkish Navy but we needed them more. Quite advanced. Three diesel engines capable of twenty eight knots, with a range of twelve hundred miles. For our purposes quite a few modifications need to be made.* '
' *Basically holds fore and aft, capable of taking forty tons of cargo. Amidships, a light plywood deckhouse containing accommodation, galley, shower, radio room, radar shack. Davy Paxmen diesels, experimental. So gentlemen we have, or I should say, we will have five rather graceful boats with rakish bows* '.
' *And I might add an exciting prospect ahead  for any young mariner. To penetrate the sea walls of fortress Europe no less* '.
The Commodore pointed towards specific areas on the plans and photographs as he reeled off modifications to be made with a panache of an expert who relishes imparting every detail to a captive audience.
' *On the foredeck there will be twin Oelikon machine guns and on either side of the bridge box twin Vickers 303 machine guns. Mounted aft of the bridge quadruple Vickers guns. Navigation, gyro and magnetic compass, echo sounder and rather a primitive radar.* '

*' Scuttling charges here and here. So there we are. Five boats to be converted to carry cargo. Very fast.*
*Heavily armed.*
*Now gentlemen I want from you five crews.*
*Volunteer crews you understand.*
*We have eight months '.*
The four men looked at each other with earnest seriousness.

Harry Whitfield lay alongside his wife in the comfort of their bed.
When at sea he'd looked forward to coming home,.
He'd dreamed of his wife and the warmth and security of their home
during the long bitterly cold nights aboard ship in convoy to and
from Russia. But now he couldn't sleep and though he was warm and
snug he felt a bitter chill of the Arctic wind in his bones.
He knew he was lucky. He had made it.
Chilling thoughts of the sea. Memories.
Sudden lacerating explosions. Submarines found their mark.
Exploding ships. Flames, shrieking screams hanging on the edge of a
jagged wind lasting for eternity. Sinking and twisting.
Facts of daily death and life.
Sitting targets for the underwater predatory enemy.
Images and sounds fed his inadequacy, but he wanted to fight back.
His wife awoke and asked if he wanted some tea.
He did and they both went downstairs to the kitchen.
As they sipped their tea his wife slowly coaxed anxieties out of him.
She told him that the Company was looking for volunteers for a
special mission and in a way she hated what she was saying as she
wanted her man home and alive, but she wanted him to be the man
she married before the long treacherous convoys took there toll and
it seemed the mention of a special mission might rekindle his spirit.
She was right. He was interested, very interested, but he didn't like to
hear this kind of information coming from his wife, though he didn't
say. He would have preferred to have heard it down at the shipping
federation and he wondered just how his wife knew of such things as
he knew operations described as special meant highly dangerous and
secret. But the Port was a compact place of merchant seamen and
trawler men and everyone to some extent knew each others business
as the sea and ships was their business.
*' I'll make enquiries later . I have to go to the Office and Federation so
I'll find out then '.*
With the tea finished they slowly climbed the stairs for the second
time that night and slowly Harry Whitfield and his wife drifted into a
warm comfortable sleep.

Shafts of late February light shone through through the grimy
windows illuminating quick shifting expressions of men seeking
sanctuary and relaxation from the tensions of the day in the
Empress public House.

The bar was crowded, noisy, full of men , awkward, large, amiable,
small, grey, boisterous, introspective, expansive, all friends, not
always friends , as arguments broke out and settled in some sort of
way, talking, shouting, cursing, drinking as if there was no tomorrow
and for some the no tomorrow would be soon.

Master Mariners,  Chief , First, Second, Third Officers, chippie's,
sparky's , greasers, monkey men, stokers, cooks and a few hangers
on.  Ordinary seamen, but no one was ordinary in the bar as rank
didn't matter as all specialised in some sort of way. There were
mention of ships, arguments about football, about ladies, of streets,
accompanied by coughing, spitting,  and of indiscretions made and
repaired  and swearing in words which belonged to the sea as bodies
swayed, gesticulated in a great rising cacophony of sound that would
end suddenly.

Then.

Motionless men stood in silence listening to a solitary voice,
telling of  a particular ship torpedoed in the middle of the Atlantic, or
of houses demolished in air raids and when the voice finished there
was silence, as if shared experience demanded reflection until a deep
sigh signalled murmuring at first, then shouting, for drinks, names
calling names, telling jokes and of course laughter as normality
levelled out and the only way to be heard was indeed to shout.

' *Avn't seen Reg about , 'as anybody seen Reg, anybody know what
'appened to 'im  ?'*

' *Reg who ? '.*

' *Reg Sampson ! '.*

' *Oh 'im, broke 'is leg, laid up 'e is '*, answered a red headed, red eyed,
bent backed figure .

' *Ow did 'e do that ? '.*

*' Fell out of bed in a brothel ',* and the smoke filled roomto insane laughter.

Harry Whitfield saw Frankie, a boson of high repute.

Frankie, highly respected for his seamanship, but to be avoided ashore when drunk, but he wasn't drunk yet and Harry decided it was a good time to have a word.

*' Frankie how's tricks ? '*

*' Ar Chief , I'm o.k. We were lucky last trip, you know yourself. Sod it 'av a drink '.*

Frankie couldn't forget men in burning oil, in freezing sea, boys he'd seen grow up, lost before they were men. Frankie, thin faced, small, square shouldered, a wiry crop of black hair that belied his twenty eight years. He grimaced, blue eyes flickering for a moment as if startled by some ghost and then he shrugged his shoulders and laughed. He looked at Harry, he looked at his empty glass and then with urgency he summoned the barmaid

*' Eh Doris luv, two pints, two drams, one f'ya sen, when y're ready !'*

Doris acknowledged and pulled the porcelain pumps filling two straight pint glasses with weak looking ale and then carefully measured out two whiskies.

Knowingly she smiled as she spoke.

*' There you are Frankie, we're running out so don't spill it '.*

Frankie slammed some silver on the bar with one hand and with the other picked up his pint and devoured half in one quick gulp. Then he burped, slurped ale down his shirt, smiled broadly as if everything in the world had been put to rights, and for Frankie, just for a moment, it had.

Then he burped again.

Harry Whitfield sipped from his glass asking if he knew anything about 'special missions'.

Frankie's expression suddenly changed, becoming serious and he put his hand to his mouth to guard the words he spoke.

*' Special missions . Not much. Met Captain, ya know, old Turnbull, shame 'bout 'im, told me Company 's looking for volunteers f ' sum kind of mission.'*

*' Told me to see some bloke called Lask if I wuz interested. Tell the truth, fancy some 'ut different from bluddy convoys '.* Frankies eyes twitched, he tapped his empty glass and looked at the floor.

Harry quickly emptied his glass trying to catch the eye of Doris.

*' I know exactly what you mean Frankie, something different that's the long and short of it. I think I'll see this man Lask ',* but his thoughts were interrupted by the increasing sound of Frankie drumming his fingers on his empty glass which conveyed the message.

*' Frankie same again, yes of course, same again Doris when you're ready '.*

Conversations merged into a commotion of jokes, ghosts, exaggerated tales of women in distant lands, in distant times, as they drank a small portion of time away while thinking of secret missions.

Harry Whitfield and Frankie left 'The Empress' walking briskly side by side through the streets of the old town and in the midday light war seemed far away as they talked about family, old friends, mates and ships.

They arrived at the Company building pushing their way through the revolving doors, going straight through to the general office joining a small group of men all familiar with each other milling around the large notice board, but there was nothing unusual to catch the eye.

A door to the left of the board opened and a tall gaunt figure emerged.

*' Jacko, Jacko over here, here. How are you, how are you ? ',* shouted Harry.

*' Harry, long time no see, good to see you, and how's yourself ?',* asked Jackson whose eyes usually did what words did for others.

*' How's that little lass of yours ?',* asked Harry and Jackson said that she was fine and there was to be another before the end of the year.

*' Congratulations Jack ! ',* exclaimed Harry and Frankie in unison and Jackson seemed lost for words, embarrassed, but then an enigmatic smile appeared on his face and he asked if both men were going to volunteer.

Frankie nodded his head.

Harry said he was thinking about it,

*' We'll be seeing more of each other.*

*Must be off , say hello to your wife ',* and with a nod of his head and a smile Jackson was on his way.

*' Never could figure 'im out. To quiet f'me, 'ardly ever see 'im in the bar ',* mused Frankie who couldn't understand men who didn't drink on a daily basis.

*' He's a family man Frankie ',* said Harry, *'as good as his word, known him for years, play darts with him. So there's one man who is going to volunteer for the special mission '.*

Frankie thought that all Officers stick together but as Chief Officer Harry Whitfield went in search of the man called Lask  Frankie the boson followed.

As the seasons played tricks between winter, spring and summer many men passed through Lasks office working on details of the operation converting gun boats to cargo boats and when their work was done these men would disappear only to reappear sometime later.

Lask was coping well with Captain Turnbull's dictates, his jovial irreverence, irregular hours and his drinking.

With acute shortages of everything, rationing was an accepted irritant, a part of deprived normality, and the shortage of good spirits was a constant challenge taken up by the Captain who needed a daily supply in order to function effectively and Lask  became complicit in mysterious trading in what what was described as ' moonshine '.

Lask had never drank so much, as Captain Turnbull introduced him to the smokey underbelly of the Merchant Navy where other languages were spoken, some without words, and Lask learned fast the nuances, inflections and gestures, and he learned to cope with the hangovers, but more surprisingly he began to like Captain Turnbull's  tea which was no mean achievement in itself .

Lask arranged interviews or what was known as 'vetting' .

Selection was made not only on the basis of skill, adaptability, toughness, experience, but also for the ability to live and work in extremely cramped conditions which the boats would affordSlowly Lask began to get to know Captain Turnbull and the Captain told him how his eye sight was impaired, how he had failed the statuary test, which meant he was unfit to command a ship and so he was forced ashore and had intimated it wasn't very agreeable to him , which was a well known fact.

From others Lask learned of Captain Turnbulls reputation as one of the Companies most popular Masters.

It was said of him that he had the ability to combine an abrasive flamboyant charm with spiky aggression which got things done in an unconventional way.

Men would love to hate him, but they'd do what he asked and they'd do it whatever was asked extremely well.

Lask observed and slowly he adopted some of the Captains traits and mannerisms which began to have an adverse effect on his domestic relationship with his wife.

His sons began to imitate his newly acquired gruff vocal no nonsense manner, with humour, much to the amusement of their friends.

Lask and the Captain shared an office but when problematic situations arose involving officialdom and Company men, the Captain would escape the office to deal with the problem and Lask would not enquire about his whereabouts and the problems would be resolved without much rancour or time wasting confrontations.

It was a known fact that Captain Turnbull got things done.

Lask brought balance, stability, calm and patience to the organisation of the operation  the very qualities Superintendent Watson knew that would augment the blustery, cantankerous, methods of the Captain.

Lask had to learn fast how to recognise the qualities and characteristics of youth, enthusiasm , adaptability, definitive seamanship skills, capability of working in extremely cramped conditions which the volunteers had to have to be accepted for the mission.

Lask was a changed man.

His work load had increased, not that people treated him with the veneration they gave to the Captain, but he was seen in the company of the Captain and he began to feel something he hadn't felt before and his wife treated him differently though she said little, and the boys were now always asking questions and they seemed to be satisfied yet excited when their father, put his finger to his lips, and whispered, ' secret '.

A real tangible bonus and a symbol of  promotion was the car, just a little black Austin, but nevertheless  very visible.

When there was an infrequent Sunday free, weather permitting, he would take the family out for a drive in the Company car and they would find a spot on the coast sheltered enough to make camp, there to eat sandwiches, have tea from the flask and play cricket on the beach which was free of mines but not squawking gulls.
Life had changed.
But for all his new found confidence he felt not quite worldly enough when explaining to volunteers the dangerous nature of the mission as sailors would look at him, utter no words, smile with slight condescension, with expressions that told of survival.
He confided his feelings to Captain Turnbull.
*' How do I tell them of the dangers when every voyage they make is dangerous ? '.*
The Captain shook his head, giving Lask a despairing look and in no uncertain terms told him what to say.
*' Emphasise the bonus . More money more risk more danger don't piss around with them they'll understand '.*
From then on men who came to his office were told straight.
They didn't smile.
They understood as they weighed up their chances of survival in convoy with the Royal Navy in attendance, against a secret mission in a converted torpedo boat.
It was the unknown of the known against the unknown of the unknown which was left to the imagination.
More pay. More pay.
Some didn't bat an eye lid as if extra pay was an irrelevance and they signed up.
Not that a signature was a guarantee of acceptance as Lask would explain they had to pass through the training session before being accepted as a volunteer.

Jackson walked into the bar of ' The Empress ' his tall frame swayed as he took his coat off, hung it on a peg by the door and made his way to the bar.

*'Afternoon Doris can't stand this weather gets right into my bones. Reckon a rum will put me right '.*

Doris shook her head, sighed, and poured the dark liquid into a small glass.

*' You men are all the same, you brave the elements out there on the sea, not to mention the war and then you start moaning about a bit of rain ',* and she handed him his drink and the darts which she knew he wanted.

He wondered were her usual smile had gone as he thanked her and he walked over to the dart board and began to idle time away, smoking cigarettes, throwing darts, improving his game.

As the bar began to fill up Harry Whitfield appeared, hair glistening rain as he shouldered his way towards the bar where he greeted Doris, asking her what was new and as she served him his drink she told him her latest and his humorous expression changed to deep concern as he fumbled a few awkward words and then took his pint pot making his way over to the dart board.

*' Now then Jacko what's new ?'.*

The question didn't disturb Jacko's concentration as he threw the dart and smiled with satisfaction as he walked up to the board, withdrawing the darts and making a mental note of the score.

*' Nothing much Harry I'm winning my game and Doris doesn't seem to be herself today '.*

Harry cast a careful glance towards the bar.

*' She tells me she's lost someone close . Happening all the time '.*

He sat down and looked into his glass as if he was trying to discover the future.

The two men were silent. Their glasses were empty.

Jacko sighed, pushing himself out of his chair he went to the bar, his tall frame dwarfed Doris as she frantically cleaned glasses.

*' Doris two rums please and whatever you're having ',.* her lips trembled, momentarily lost for words, she looked up, then quickly composed herself and she laughed as she picked glasses off the bar.
*' Glasses, glasses, becoming more and more scarce, you'll have to bring your if it goes on at this rate ',* and her voice faltered as she bit her bottom lip and looked down to the floor.
*' You'll have to bring in your own soon '.*
As she gripped the bar, tears welled up in her eyes and Jacko reached across and took her hand with a gentle squeeze and looked into her eyes.

Apart from serving, keeping order and responding to a certain amount of banter, Doris shared and imposed her considerable personality on the bar and made it her own. It was her willingness to listen to the experiences of the seafarers which made her popular and also made her feel special. Amongst this family of men she felt secure , but for the vicissitudes of war, happy.

Medium height, slim,  shoulder length auburn hair framed her soft round face. She had never married.

Though she had many offers, some serious, she was content to be looked after by the men who brought her presents, told her stories and shared with her a part of their lives, and she listened, not always sympathetically to their innermost thoughts during quiet moments. She felt deeply wounded when one of her family didn't come back from the sea.

This was one such day.

She'd heard earlier in the morning and in her private time memories ebbed and flowed.

He was a good man and in her bitterness she asked, ' why him ?'.

She smiled thinly, bringing up the corner of her apron, wiping away the tears.  At the end of the bar two sailors waved empty glasses and she gripped Jacko's hand tightly.

*' Thanks Jack, take care of yourself '.*

The tall young veteran of many dangerous voyages slowly walked through the quiet conversations to the table near the dart board where his friend Harry sat.

Having been selected for the operation he wanted to know if Jacko had been selected but he didn't need to ask.

*' I heard yesterday, the wife was pleased being promoted to Captain and all, but I didn't tell her the rest, not that I know anything, apart from putting to sea in a converted motor torpedo boat, sailing to god knows where. And you Harry ? '.*

Harry nodded his head and the two newly promoted Captains didn't have much else to say to each other and nursing their drinks they sank into thoughts of their recent stormy past and the uncertainties of the future.

Crisp ice edged shards of light shone through the thin curtains
waking Frankie from his alcoholic slumbers and as he rubbed his
eyes he began to piece together time and place, the here and now.
He sat up, yawned, coughed, shook his head and wondered what to
do with another day of shore leave.
Like most sailors he liked to come home, but for him there was a
limit to the time he could be away from the sea. The sea had made
him a hardened sailor who received great respect for his experience
and craft when aboard ship at sea but he knew only to well that he
was a different man when ashore, no more than when he was in the
confines of a small house playing only a minor part and subordinate
to his wife who commanded the house and all things pertaining in no
uncertain terms.
He heard noises in the kitchen.
Uncharacteristically he thought of taking his wife out for the day, but
that thought receded as he rolled himself a cigarette and wondered
what the results of the interview for the special mission he'd
volunteered for would be.
His thoughts were interrupted by shouts from his wife.
*' Frankie  there's a letter. Official looking '.*
 Suddenly he was awake,  alert. Quickly he dressed and was down the
stairs in three moves landing before his wife in the hallway.
He snatched the envelope from her hand and tore it open.
*' Great. Great. Been picked. Special mission I told you a'bout might be
sailing tomorrow '*, he stared at her hoping for a smile.
*' It's different, more money, just what we need '.*
She looked at him with benign disdain waving her hands dismissively
as she turned away.
*' I'm sure it's what you need. I suppose you're off to get plastered now.
You could be more help around the house. It's hard when you're at sea
and when you're home I hardly see you. I don't know I just don't know
what with the......'.*
He grinned awkwardly and for a moment looked innocently younger
than his thirty years as he appealed to her.

*' You're the boss around here. When I try to do summit you're allus telling us off and well you know luv. Right I best be off to the office see what's what '.*

She shook her head from side to side, despairingly, and then in a tone of voice that couldn't be ignored she said.

*' Can't think why I married you Frankie Hebden, like a little boy with a new toy, thought you might, but you never change, go get a shave, smarten yourself up, look a bit respectable. I'll make some breakfast then you can scarper. Understand '.*

Frankie did understand, he kissed her on the cheek, gave her a mock salute and obeyed her.

Soon he was spruced up and ready to go, quickly eating his breakfast, finishing his toast and slurping his tea. His eyes flashed excitedly as he got up from the table in anticipated, as his wife stood inspecting him. She wore expressions of resignation and pride.

As he opened the door he turned, stuttering, searching for words to justify himself and when they came they seemed awkward.

*' Av to find out who I'm sailing with '.*

He opened the door quickly, but the frying pan hit the door frame. He stood still, frozen to the spot, his face expressed half humour, half fear as his wife exploded with venom.

*' Expect you'll cum back drunk, disgusting man, can't think why I put up with you '*, and she rushed to him, straightened his tie and kissed him on the cheek, then she pushed him away and he walked briskly up the street. As he approached the corner he heard his wife shout.

*' Aye bugger off then, I could be up with the angels tomorrow but I can't get drunk '.*

From the safety of distance Frankie looked back laughing as he had to have the last word.

*' Course you can't, you don't drink ya daft thing '.*

Turning the corner, the chill of the morning began to alternate with warmth, but as as he walked he hardly noticed the familiar streets and he didn't notice the elderly couple huddled together clutching a suitcase as they struggled over the rubble of a bombed out building.

He walked on and came to the first of a number of pubs he would
visit by their side doors and with a nod and a wink he asked after
shipmates, then onto the next and then to ' The Empress '.
' *Morning Doris, cheer up lass not the end of the world, pint please* '.
She frowned as she pulled the pump that filled the glass.
' *One pint coming up Frankie, now don't spill it down your nice clean
shirt, your wife wouldn't like that now would she* ', she said with heavy
sarcasm.
Thanking Doris he moved amongst the morning customers, glass in
one hand, cigarette in the other, nodding at faces he vaguely knew
and from a table clouded in smoke and stacked with glasses a voice
called.
' *Eeh up thee Frankie, over 'ere, over 'ere* '.
Frankie recognised the voice which surprised him.
' *Eddie, Eddie Higgins, you've started early* '.
' *Right there Frankie, I've answered the call. Saw that fella Lask. Gave
me me papers. Travel warrant, off tomorrow, destination secret, 'av you
seen what we're lerring ourselves in for ?* '.
Frankie was taken aback.
' *What you on'bout Eddie ?* '
' *Frankie, the great boson ! You, you don't know !* ', Eddie stood up
swaying and leering at the boson, ' *well pal, you tek yasen down to
Amos and Smith's yard, down on docks, 'an y, you'll find out. Ships.
What a laugh, an me a big boat man. ' av a drink Frankie, ' av a drink*'.
Frankie, quickly drained his glass. He was confused with what Eddie
had just said, deciding he would have to take a look he suddenly
took off and as he went though the door the voice of Eddie echoed
ominously ' *small boats on big seas* '.
In Albert Dock, amid the assembly of coasters and trawlers he saw
tucked away against the quay two small gun boats upon which men
worked with an uncommon ferocity dismantling the accommodation.
He was lost in apprehensive brow furrowed thought and as he
examined every inch of the small grey boats a harsh, gruff voice,
broke his concentration.

*' Not much to look at Mister, but they'll be alright by the time you're aboard '*, and Captain Turnbull puffed away on his cigar as he himself surveyed the noisy dock yard industry.

*' So what do you think Mister Hebden, what do you think ? '.*
The wirey boson drew on his soggy cigarette wondering how these small boats could cope with deep seas. He'd sailed on vessels of all descriptions, coasters, coalers, tankers and most of the Company ships, but he'd never put to sea on a boat so small and he was apprehensive and curious.

*' Captain what'll they be like when them lot 'av finished ? '.*
Captain Turnbull looked up at the dark clouds drifting in from the west, feeling the first drops of rain upon his face he directed Frankie's attention from bows to stern.

*' There'll be new accommodation, made from the best plywood we can get '.*
Frankie's jaw dropped as he looked at Captain Turnbull then at the small boats then back at Captain Turnbull again.

*' Plywood, I'm going God knows where in a wooden boat ? '*, exclaimed Frankie in disbelief.
Captain Turnbull seemed to be offended as they walked round the quay to have a closer look . He shouted to the men working aboard the boats and these men, carpenters, shouted back to the Captain, telling him in no uncertain terms just what he could do with his boats, war or no war. The drizzle turned into a down pour and they all swore as they ducked for shelter.

*' Not to worry Frankie we're using the best plywood. You've sailed on worse, I just doubt if they were so small '*, and the Captain roared with a course, sarcastic, sadistic laughter as if he was enjoying seeing the apprehension dripping off Frankie's chin.

Frankie was wet, very wet and he shivered. He wanted to know where they were going to on the mission. He had to ask , knowing that he wouldn't be told and predictably Captain Turnbull shook his head .

From the shelter of the doorway the two men looked out through the haze of rain to the boats which looked even more decrepit.

*' Of course Frankie you can speculate all you want, but you'll be told when time is right. Did I tell you the boats will be powered by three Davy Paxmen Ricardo diesels not that will interest you but you'll be alright lad, you always are. Get yourself to see Lask he'll fix you up, you'll be off tomorrow '.*

Frankie looked at the Captain in disbelief.

*' Sailing in one of those half built speed boats, you're kidding '.*

*' No no no Frankie, you're going to Weymouth, training with the Royal Navy, Lask will give you your travel documents. Training for the operation, the secret mission eh '.*

The rain eased and the two men stepped out of the doorway and walked away from the dock. Unease and apprehension turned to anxiety as Frankie slowly began to realise the seriousness of the operation he'd volunteered for and he made a half hearted attempt to humour himself as he said to Captain Turnbull.

*' Weymouth eh ! A holiday by the sea '.*

*' Aye Frankie a holiday by the sea. Calm before the storm , '* and the Captain slapped him on the back and roared with laughter that disturbed the seagulls flapping overhead.

Then the two men went their different ways.

Frankie picked his way through the wartime litter of the streets with a sense of foreboding recalling his wife's description of him as a boy with a new toy.

He could think of better toys than the boats in Albert Dock but then the rain stopped and he went to see Lask who gave him his travel documents .

The boys had been at school all day and then had been out adventuring, sustaining cut knees and grubby faces until they were hungry and Maam shouted out that it was time for tea.

They waited for their father to come home hoping that he might tell them secrets of the war as they now had a status amongst their school chums and had become agents in their own right.

Disappointed there were no secrets , they were washed and scrubbed and under their blankets. By the light of battery operated torches they read of the adventures of Sextan Blake the detective and as tiredness crept over them they planned adventures for Sunday as they slipped into contented sleep.

With the boys asleep, or pretending to be asleep , Lask and Joan relaxed as they enjoyed the late evening, drinking tea and listening to the wireless .

He reflected on the past few tiring weeks .

Though he was elevated with responsibility and self satisfaction he knew he was only a very small part of the larger whole.

The programme on the wireless and the jolly music of Ivy Benson and her all girl band flooded the room making them both tap their feet and the dullness of the weary street seemed far away.

Joan didn't understand her husbands work but she knew a telephone and a car warranted great importance and she was surprised when he began to tell her about ships, men, and meetings he'd had and special operations. As his words flowed he began to regret revealing so much and he felt he had to issue a warning.

' Now don't go gossiping, I've told more than I should ', he said with a touch of arrogance.

Her attentive mood changed, as her eyes narrowed and her tongue whipped out a tart retort.

' What do you mean by that Herbert Lask ! '.

At once he was on the defensive, regretting his revelations and he smiled weakly as he knew he was on shaky ground.

' Oh Joan a little bird told me ', he said meekly and defensively.

Though he was a changed man with authority he knew that it didn't extend to the family home as Joan demonstrated.

*' A birdie. A birdie told you. Bugger the birdie, sounds as if I'm been accused of something, and who was this little birdie eh ! ',* and he now began to sense something different.

Her daily life was dull, repetitive, just as his own had been until recently, but he had felt a need to impose his self importance upon the family home and his voice rose .

*' Harry's wife, a few weeks ago, she said you'd told her everything that Captain Turnbull said when he came round here '.*

The peace and quiet of the evening had evaporated.

*'It's coming to something when I can't talk to my friends about what you're doing !',* she snapped*!*

*' It's not that Joan, supposing there'd been a fifth columnist in Eubels butchers shop ! ',* and he shook his head defensively.

But she hadn't finished yet.

*' Oh my God Herbert Lask, I know they are of German stock, but there are lots of butchers with German names like Kress and Wagner, been going there all my life, come to think of it Herbert, we haven't got the most British of names have we ?'.*

There was no answer from Lask,

The sudden explosion of tension ebbed away as the last of the evening became distinctly chilly and the wireless talked about the war and Lask thought of the men he had sent to Weymouth and he muttered something about their chances just loud aloud enough for his wife to hear.

Joan's eyes held steady and her words were quick and sharp.

*' Whose chances. Charlie Eubels. Kress and Wagner. The children, yours or mine ?'.*

He shook his head, sighed and tried to explain how he wished he was going with them.

*' Seems to me Herbert Lask all this cloak and dagger business is going to your head, and as for going with them, you're not going anywhere, you're staying right here. Understand !'.*

For the moment Herbert Lask did understand.

There was silence between them for a seemingly long time until Joan shuffled, shivered and got up out of her comfortable chair and said she was going up to bed .

Lask murmured and out of habit made a few safety checks of fire place, windows and doors, then followed her up the stairs.

The morning arrived with Herbert long gone , the boys boisterously breakfasted and Joan made sure they were well scrubbed as she sent them off to school .

Joan wasn't well pleased as the night before lingered .

Lask said it was the demands of war and everyone had to do whatever they could, but this sounded hollow when everyday, everybody did whatever they could and some did more than others.

When Lask arrived home earlier than usual Joan felt something was wrong and when he told her he had to go to Weymouth and would be away for a week or more her anger was mixed with deep resentment, insecurity and pride.

She'd heard about many a man who told their wives they'd be away on harmless sounding missions and she knew of the telegrams informing women of their loss. He had explained at length his work was strictly organisational and when he enlisted Captain Turnbull to allay her fears and reassure her, which he did and to his surprise, she was assurred.

She had given him a ' matter of fact kiss and a take care of yourself hug ', and he felt he needed more, but he reassured himself as he left for the station. But this feeling was soon displaced by an inner excitement fuelled by the exuberant gregarious companionship of Captain Turnbull who had made sure their carriage was some way away from the rest of the noisy volunteer crews.

The journey was fraught by stops, starts and changing trains as the miles went by, revealing different pictures of industry in fields and streaming smoky cities across counties of England and into Dorset. At the M.T.B. base at Weymouth the volunteers were to go through an intensive training programme acclimatising them to the rigours of sailing small, fast, armed craft, through treacherous enemy seas.

Lask and Captain Turnbull would take note and report directly to
the Special Operations Executive in Baker Street, London.
The R. N. Commander offered the Merchant Navy men every facility
of hospitality, though the usual banter between the two navies
became part of the nervous rivalry as the volunteers settled down to
their task with a rough edged pride in their seamanship.
Frankie Hebden felt the treatment they were receiving indicated the
dangers they would face when they had to do the real thing.
Like everyone else he knuckled down to the training with his own
and humour as the Royal Navy endeavoured to teach the Merchant
Navy the ways of small boats in big seas.
Captain Turnbull took the opportunity to get to sea again but when
he found himself in the claustrophobic engine room of an M.T.B.
with engineers and motormen he was dismayed to find himself
struggling to keep his balance as the small craft bounced off rolling
seas and though he wouldn't admit to it felt the need for dry land.
Training was intense involving gunnery exercises aboard boats
travelling at high speed with course changes, resulting in violent
movement on rough seas and all had to have their wits about them.
The sailors trained, they speculated and when Lask was asked he
affected a disturbing, silent, conspiratorial smile but he wouldn't say.
After days of twirling around coastal waters aboard the M.T.B's
firing machine guns, perfecting balance, fine tuning their seamanship
skills the sailors became bored to the point when creative divergence
shaped their behaviour when ashore. Incidents emanated from the
wilder spirits resulting in complaints and the local constabulary duly
investigated. It wasn't that the sailors went out to offend but
unintentionally they did. The real offence occurred when Doctors
noticed their surgery name plates disappear from the doors of their
practises only for them to reappear on cabin doors of the M.T.B's.
For a short time Frankie Hebden assumed the mantle of Dr.
Fitzpatrick M.D. The R.N. base Commander delved into his
diplomatic bag and justice was seen to be done. The offenders were
reprimanded and those who were offended against were appeased.

These incidents didn't appear on the progress reports  sent to the
S.O.E.

Superintendent Watson inhaled deeply from his cigarette smiling as
he thought of brass plates.

He coughed violently.

Next to the telephone the ash tray overflowed.

He'd ignored his Doctors advice, lit another cigarette and paced up
and down his large office glancing fondly at the paintings of ships on
the walls. Out of each painting came men who had performed heroic
deeds on the oceans of the world and done devilish deeds in many a
port.

And now, losses of men and ships etched a few more lines under the
bags beneath his eyes that now concentrated in a distant stare
looking through the large window towards the docks from where
Company ships sailed to Russia, America and the far east.

He'd known many Germans, he hoped he still did and he wondered
how they were.

He cursed.

Stubbing out his cigarette he read reports and learned that the
conversion of four of the M.T.B's was almost complete and reading
between the lines it seemed that the S.O.E. was in two minds about
the operation.

His thoughts were interrupted by a knock on the door and he
growled permission for entry.

*' Ah Lask, how's the wife, keeping well I trust. What news, delays,
breakdown in morale, ah well, the Commodore is due soon then we'll
get to know what's been decided. They tend to keep us in the dark but
that's the nature of their business '.*

Shafts of summer sunlight radiated through the window casting deep
shadows on the floor and intricate patterns on the walls as the
Superintendent momentarily thought of other places, other times
when a forceful pounding on the door banished his innermost
thoughts as the door swung open and in walked the Commodore.

The three men exchanged pleasantries.

The Superintendent took three glasses from the ornate cabinet and placed them on his desk .
Then he took the bottle and poured generous measures of whisky.
Glasses raised contents dispatched,
' *Gentlemen I understand we have a few problems . Have the engineers sorted them out Lask ?* '
Lask, feeling uneasy took a deep breath and then he was able to give the Commodore an up dated report .
He pointed out that the engines were experimental and when he had finished he looked apprehensively towards the two men and he realised they knew everything he had reported.
With a slight yawning resignation the Commodore spoke.
' *I understand the training of the crews in Weymouth led to high spirited escapades, but I gather they came through with flying colours though I might add the Royal Navy was dammed glad to see the back of them* '.
The Superintendent smiled, took hold of the bottle and refilled their glasses. The Commodore savouring the warming liquid nodded his head in appreciation and spoke slowly and quietly.
' *The timing of the operation is crucial, it all depends upon the weather conditions over the North Sea . Low cloud and moon less nights will afford best protection from the enemy. The meteorological experts suggest October* ', the Commodore took a sip from his glass and he looked at the ceiling as he licked his lips , ' *Excellent whisky. Excellent, where is it from ? *' .The Superintendent's expression warmed, recognising a fellow connoisseur.
' *Isle of Islay, quite rare these days, father in law sends me a bottle now and then when he can* '. Though his taste was limited Lask nodded his agreement making a mental note of the Scottish Island for future reference as the Commodore continued.
' *Excellent, now the boats. I've given them the following names. The 'Nonsuch* ', *after the first ship to sail for the Hudson's Bay Company. The ' Hopewell ', the ' Gay Corsair ', the ' Gay Viking ', and the ' Master Standfast ', this last name  to underline and  to propagate our purpose in all this if you understand my reasoning.* '

*' In the ward room pictures of Mister Churchill and Sir Francis Drake just to emphasise the almost, piratical nature of the mission ',* the Commodore smiled a mischievous smile.

The Superintendent was impressed.

Lask felt privileged to be a party to these events in this great office. Hands firmly grasped behind his back the Commodore raised his voice and spoke in quick, clipped sentences.

*' As Commodore I shall be sailing on each of the missions. We have four boats almost ready for sea. Men on standby I understand. It is time for the crews to be called as soon as possible. Have them aboard the boats Wednesday 23rd September 0800hrs '.*

Lask, uncharacteristically, quickly interjected, with concern.

*' But Commodore, we have five crews and only four boats '.*

The Commodore smiled, still savouring the malt whisky and looked into his glass with deep concentration.

*' Yes Lask four boats and five crews. By the way what is your first name ? '.*

Lask, taken aback, mumbled his first name, Herbert.

*' Is it. I think I'll stick to Lask, suits you, good name Lask. The fifth crew will be spread out over the four boats. It'll be a bit cramped, but if I can fly across the North Sea in the bomb bay of a Mosquito aircraft then I'm sure our men can put up with a little discomfort.*

*Now, no mention that this is a training exercise. As far as everyone is concerned this is the real thing . Now lets get these boats to sea '.*

Harry Whitfield finished his tea and went through to the lounge and from the bookshelf he took down Melville's ' Moby Dick '.
Though he wasn't a great reader this one book was of great pleasure to him and as the fire crackled he traded the fear of the U – boat for the comparatively less fearsome, great white whale.
From the kitchen Mrs. Whitfield looked through to the lounge watching her relaxed husband as she traded her long emptiness, when he was at sea  for the warm luxury of being together, distanced only by fireside and kitchen.
She reflected upon the nature of the man who earlier had washed dishes and meticulously put them away in the cupboard. He seemed to do things a lot of men were unable to face and what with the mayhem going on around the world she felt extremely lucky and safe.
In the hall the telephone rang, she went out and answered it , said hello, listened, and looked through the open door to her husband.
*' Harry, Mister Lask for you ',*
She thought pensively about the kit bag, the taxi, the goodbye kiss and a tear came close to appearing.
Suddenly Ahab, long boats and whales were firmly pressed together as Harry took hold of the telephone and listened, he acknowledged, replaced the receiver and went into the kitchen.
His wife read the signs.
Imminent departure.
She knew what he was going to say.
The words were different but the message was always the same.
*' Have to be aboard ship, Wednesday '.*
She  hated this and for a few moments they stood facing each other, their eyes exploring the parameters of their relationship as the past and present fused.
They pottered about putting things back in their place .
Doors were checked and black out curtains made secure.
They climbed the stairs as evening became night and the night became warm and strong, then calm drifting off into the peaceful ebb and flow of sleep.

A quick fresh and cutting edge was in the air as reluctant rays of
sunlight pierced the early morning mist slowly revealing sheds and
ships as spluttering steam winches clattered and crane men swung
dangling cargoes from ship to shore. The sharp, quick and astute
made sure loads would encounter obstacles and crash to the deck to
be scavenged by eager hands as the spilled cargo of tinned meat
conveyed by nods and winks disappeared only to reappear later ,
much later, within, if not a black, then a decidedly grey market .
The dampness, laced the smell of tea and greasy food frying which
drifted from makeshift canteens, galleys, watch men's huts and there
amidst the trawlers, coasters, tankers and barges lay two sleek
freshly painted naval grey boats. Across the dock two others,
identical grey, nestled smart, superior to the rusty, war weary
weather beaten coasters. Small groups of sailors began to assemble
on the quayside, standing by their kit bags, smoking, talking, joking,
shuffling their feet as Lask clipboard in hand moved amongst them,
recognising men and ticking names off his list. He spotted Frankie
Hebden and tried to avoid him but the wiry boson cornered him.
*' Morning Mister Lask, what do you call them ?'* and he pointed to the
small boats.
Lask sighed and smiled with resignation .
He looked the hard faced boson straight in the eyes.
*' What do we call them, we call them the Grey Ladies Mister Frankie*
*Hebden, the Grey Ladies, if that's alright with you ? Is it ? '.*
Frankie was taken aback by Lasks unflinching look and quick reply.
*' Grey Ladies eh !, that sounds all rite Mister Lask, now tell us where*
*we're off to ! You can tell us Mister Lask '.*
Lask, sighed with resignation, then suddenly became serious and
confidentially beckoned the boson closer to him, and whispered in his
ear.
*' Well Mister Hebden, not a word to anyone, understand. ! ',* Frankie
nodded compliance and shuffled closer as Lask's hushed words told
him the secretive information.

*' You'll be sailing under complete secrecy. If anything gets out, God help me ! You'll rendezvous at a secret location off the coast of Spain, there to unload special supplies, then you'll sail to Gibralter '.*

*' Can't tell you anymore. I've told you enough already. Not a word Frankie, not a word to anyone, understand '*

Lask swiftly moved on and disappeared into a crowd of sailors.

Lask had learned a lot from Captain Turnbull.

Frankie stared into space, open mouthed, with a stump of a cigarette hanging from his bottom lip.

He went aboard the Gay Viking and as he found himself a bunk in the accommodation his mate Tom appeared.

*' Eh up Frankie lad, where we oft to then ?'*

He didn't expect an answer.

*' It's secret Tom, I've sworn an oath to that fella Lask, top secret, not a word you understand. We're off to a rendezvous off the coast of Spain then onto Gibraltar '.*

Tom began to change into his seagoing gear, squinting mockingly at the boson.

*' Not like you Frankie '.*

*' Wha d'ya mean ?'.*

*' Mister Lask's spinning y' a yarn, only bloke knows where we're oft to is skipper, must be all the ale you sup, loosing ya'touch. Christ it's cramped, not enough room to swing a cat in 'ere '.*

For a moment Frankie was vacant, non plussed, he grinned and wondered about Lask and agreed with Tom that there wasn't enough room to swing a cat as he began to change into his sailing gear.

Having inspected his quarters Captain Harry Whitfield climbed onto the open bridge smiling broadly as he surveyed his first command, but on reading the crew list his smile disappeared when he saw that Frankie Hebden was his boson , but he consoled himself with the knowledge that he was a dammed good sailor.

Lask now back in his office shuffled papers out of habit.

Above the industrial  noise he heard an unfamiliar deep gutteral mechanical roar from the direction of Albert Dock.

The door of the office burst open to the deeper gutteral roar of
Captain Turnbull.

*' Hear those engines Lask, powerful eh. Wish I was on the bridge of
one of them boats, eh, ah well, can't be helped ',* and the burly
Captains words echoed in Lasks mind as if they were his own.

For a seemingly long time both men looked in the direction of the
sound of the Grey Ladies engines.

They imagined the rakish bows of the four sleek motor cargo boats
sailing in formation cutting through the still waters of the River
Humber as they gathered speed towards the North Sea.

*' Can't do much else now can we !, I'll make some tea '.*

Lask thought about the Captains tea.

*' Captain, I prefer something stronger '.*

Captain Turnbull scratched his beard as he eyed Lask up and down.

*' Good idea, good idea. You never fail to amaze me Mister and you can
take that which way you want. Something stronger, something stronger
lead the way Mister Lask, lead the way.'*

Away from the shore the four boats left the calm of the silver glinting
mud brown river of the Humber estuary heading into the undulating
deep green Northern sea.

Aboard the Nonsuch Captain Jackson squinted into the wind,
gauging the weather with sensitivities developed  over many an ocean
and shivered and said *' God almighty '* to no one in particular.

Thoughts of God were not uncommon amongst the crew as the bows
of the small craft plunged into the sea.

The Captain checked the compass and the S.O. E. Chief Officer took
bearings as the Nonsuch led the line of boats through the coastal
minefields and by mid afternoon they had passed Flamborough
Head.

From the accommodation the Commodore appeared and clapped his
hands together, drew breath as the cold hit his face.

*' Ha, ha, yea gods, not much protection from the elements is there
Captain ',* the tall Captain nodded his agreement as the Commodore
continued.

*' I volunteered for the Royal Navy. Wouldn't have me. Said I was to old. Couldn't understand why. But now by a devious route I'm at sea . This circumnavigation of Britain will be a good experience , good training for the real thing, almost operational conditions '.*

Captain Jackson hoped the Commodore might reveal something of the true purpose of the mission.

But the affable Commodore took out his pipe, filled it with aromatic tobacco and after several attempts the bowl of his pipe glowed and he bellowed smoke.

The S.O.E. Chief officer, a big man with a well trimmed beard which outlined his pock marked face, laughed to himself. The Commodore and Captain looked at him demanding to share in his humour.

The S.O.E. Officer obliged.

*' I heard the boson on the Gay Viking was telling the lads we're heading for Gibralter on a secret mission '.*

The Commodore smiled wondering who could have put that piece of information about .

Light faded as the wind grew fierce picking up the sea.

Exhileration affected every crew man as spray swept over the bows. The bows plunged in and out of troughs making handhold and foothold difficult as they all acclimatised to the dark raging sea.

For those off watch there was no sleep.

They wedged themselves into bunks as the sea reached and tumbled and tumbled and reached. Those on watch, the navigators looked up through the racing clouds for star bearings and there was more than one man who silently sang of the eternal father who was strong to save for those in peril on the sea.

Aboard the Gay Viking there was one man who was in peril not from the sea but from the barbed tongue of his long standing shipmate.

Their watch over, Frankie and Tom lay back on their bunks trying to sleep but without success.

Without no hint of humour Tom spoke.

*' Eh Frankie, I didn't know Spain was North of the Humber '.*

Frankie began to realise Lask wasn't the insignificant pen pusher he thought he was.

Tom rubbed salt.

*' Secret missions to foreign parts, thought Scotland was on our side in this 'ere war '.*

*' Give over Tom, 'ow did I know 'e wuz 'aving us on. Trouble with Company men they tell ya anything. Anyway who told you we're off to Scotland eh ? '.*

*' The stars Frankie, the stars ',* and as Tom closed his smiling eyes he wondered if he'd be able to do a spot of fishing when they reached the Lochs.

In the engine rooms of the four boats the experimental Davy Paxman engines pounded out the horse power under the watchful eye of engineers and motormen with oily rags, wrenches and spanners constantly to hand. The mixture of oil, sweat and noise was augmented by the cursing shouts of encouragement and many jokes about ladies, especially ladies in grey.

Steward cooks previously well balanced on deep sea ships in storms learned quickly new ways to avoid spillage and to facilitate sandwich making from rough brown bread, filled with anything from tins that tumbled from lockers.

Men struggled in the slight space which passed for accommodation and as the bows dipped under each oncoming wave the would be slumberers grabbed the sides of their bunks, cursing and swearing. For some the wild danger of trawling around Bear Island seemed pleasurable to this pounding.

The night became complete and the Grey Ladies became silhouettes to each other as the seas became calm.

News went around the boats that they were entering foreign waters and Edinburgh was soon abeam and as the diesels sped the boats on towards Aberdeen a croaking voice began to sing,

*' The Northern Lights of Old Aberdeen '.*

The words of the song bounced off the deck and drifted across the now settled sea and on other boats men caught the familiar melody and joined in until a sea born choir struggled with a shattered 'G' flat over a resinous bass of the diesels.

On the bridge of the Nonsuch the Commodore hummed a little and turning to the Captain he said.

*' Must make a note Mister not to start singing when we're in enemy waters. Ha ! '.*

The Captain laughingly replied.

*' Well Commodore the crews could learn the Horst Wessel song, give the Germans a bit of a treat '.*

The song and the laughter died away.

Travelling fast the four boats cruised in the freshening breeze of the Moray Firth towards Inverness and the Caledonian Canal .

Entering into the Beauly Firth the navigators checked their positions looking to port for the canal which would take them to Loch Ness.

Ashore the pipe smoking Lock gate man looked through the dirty window of his hut, his blinking eyes focused causing him to mutter aloud to himself at what he saw.

*' Guid gawd what d'wee have here ! '*

Engines purred as the line of four boats edged towards the lock gates with crews on the decks , the suspicious whiskered highlander went about his business of operating the gates while watching through his narrowed eyes the men on the grey boats.

From a nearby granite house a soldier appeared with rifle slung over his shoulder, buttoning up his great coat to meet the chill he made his way to inspect the unusual boats.

The Commodore looked on smiling agreeably at the scene and he called to the soldier and the Lock man.

*' Good morning to you Sir, fine morning. Chilly ! '* and the Commodore made his way from the bridge to the deck and from the deck to the quayside.

The highlander was taken aback by the smiling pucker faced uniformed English man who by no fault of his own evoked historical iniquities of Culloden Field. But these were soon forgotten as the Commodore smartly produced a small flask of malt whisky which was offered and enthusiastically accepted by the lock gate man and this diplomacy effected a sudden friendship which ensued an ease of passage for the four boats through the lock.

Sailors, motor men and engineers with blackened faces sprawled about the decks looking on as the lone soldier walked along the quay inspecting the Nonsuch.

He remembered his orders to be on the lookout for anything unusual and unexpected, and these boats definitely looked unusual as they bristled with guns, yet flew the Red Ensign which baffled the soldier. His thoughts were further confused when he came face to face with seaman Gunner Dobson.

Dobson winked, unnerving the soldier, who nervously effected an officious, official tone as he spoke.

*' What's all this eh Jimmy, 'er, gunboats with Red Ensigns, Cap'n Morgan. Pirates are we laddie. Dunna get many imposters through 'ere. Ya dunna look like real sailors t'me '.*

An engineer glistening in diesel oil shouted.

*' An you don't look like a real soldier to me '.*

In the face of superior numbers the soldier retreated a safe distance shouting defiantly.

*' More of a soldier than you'll ever be '.*

Seaman Gunner Dobson never at a loss for words replied.

*' You're rite there Jock, good job we're sailors !'.*

The Commodore, the Captains and the Chief Officers looked on, mildly amused, as the soldier wandered back to his granite house and the four grey boats slipped through the canal and there wasn't a man aboard who didn't expect to see something unusual emerge from the deep waters of Loch Ness.

Most of the crew were Humbersiders and Company men, though worldly wise, they were insular and suspicious and as the Chief Officers, betrayed by their accents, were outsiders and therefore subjected to rumour and speculation .

Some of the more seasoned men read volumes from the facial expressions of the S.O.E. Chief Officers whose physical demeanour revealed little more than the harsh realities of the present.

But it was said of theses men that they had been a party to death at close quarters.

Nothing of substance was learned of them and their secrets were hidden by their uniforms, but their very presence indicated the dangers of the missions which lay ahead.

Sailors overheard conversations and put two and two together usually making five or seven elaborating on what was heard .

*' He's the brains behind the mission '*, said one sailor as he pointed to the Commodore.

*' ' Eard 'e flew across the North Sea in the bomb bay of a Mosquito '*, said another.

*' Who did ?'.*

*' Commodore that's who '.*

*' I heard he narrowly escaped the clutches of the Gestapo in Norway '.*

*' He's with us now ! '.*

*' Aye but will he be with us when things start ?'*

Stories, scraps of information, half truths were gleaned, polished, chewed over, embellished which enhanced their strengths as the sailors got to know the characteristics of the boats and themselves.

The Nonsuch led the flotilla out of the last Loch and the echelon of Grey Ladies gathered speed, sweeping into the Firth of Larne cutting through short waves which sparkled in the intense light.

The Commodore gazed up at the delicate threads of white clouds hanging in the pale blue sky and he puffed on his pipe in quiet satisfaction.

In the cubicle that went for a chart room the Captain and the Chief plotted their course between islands.

Port side Jurra.

Starboard Colonsey.

Rounding the Isle of Islay the Commodore remembered the Malt he'd tasted in the Superintendents office and he looked at the island with reverence, thinking he would make a visit when the war was won.

The Grey Ladies cut a course through the south channel heading into the Irish sea as the sky gradually clouded and short gusts of wind picked up the swell.

Aboard the Hopewell the shadowy Chief Officer illuminated the lives of the crew with his encyclopaedic knowledge of sea shanties.

As the boat plunged and corkscrewed through the sea towards Anglesey the crews discomfort caused by continuous buffeting was eased slightly by singing along with the Chief.

The sea began to rise.

The sea began to fall.

Increasingly the wind whipped up and gathered a storm as the sailors sang, ' *Blow ye Winds* ', with the bows plunging into and under the oncoming waves, cascading spray over the bridge, and they sang in expectation, ' *Away me lads we're homeward bound* ', but there was much sea to sail before they'd see the River Humber.

Anglesey approached in the darkness.

Aft of the box bridge on the after deck Frankie leaned against the quadruple Vickers guns, a damp cigarette protruding from his weather lashed lips.

Tom stood by his side as the sea calmed and the Viking neared land.

' *Doesn't look much does it Frankie ?* '.

' *As long as it keeps still for an hour or two it'll do me. I heard they speak a different language 'ere* '.

' *They speak Welsh Frankie but you'll 'ave no problem Frankie, no problem at all* '.

The boson, thinking of a pint, belched and his belch turned Tom away saying.

' *You should see someone 'bout that* '.

The Grey Ladies were to be based at Holyhead for nine days during which time the crews were to be engaged in more extensive training including gunnery practise, station keeping and general boat maintenance .

During the evenings the crews made for the pubs and other hostelries.

In the bar of 'The Live and Let live', Frankie leaned against the bar consuming pints at a rapid rate, slurping, belching while telling stories to a captive audience of two.

*'Eh Lads, in Americo, New Orleans, was in the bar, lady comes up t'us did I wan a good time. Ha !, did Frankie Hebden wanna a good time ?'*
The young barmaid scurried to the safety of the back room as the audience of two increasingly unable seamen encouraged Frankie on.
*' Wore 'appened Frankie '.*
*' Wore did ya do ?'.*
*' Bet ya fell over ! '.*
Frankie slurped, belched, drew on his cigarette , farted and continued with his story.
*' We wen up stairs inta 'er room. She locked it and ',* laughing to himself , he fumbled his words into an incoherent jumble of obscenities which so interfered with the local atmosphere that the faces of the locals began to turn crimson. Frankie managed to form words into sentences .
*' She 'er, she, she, took off her !, 'onest lads , and she 'er.... '.*
The faces of the locals began to turn red and then crimson and downing his ale Frankie just held onto the bar as he swayed, his eyes glazed over vaguely seeing Tom in the distance.
The two sailors urged Frankie on.
*' Go on Frankie, wore 'appened, wore 'appened '.*
Frankie slouched belching and just caught hold of the bar.
The barmaid appeared with eyes blazing.
Tom anticipating, jumped out of his chair, moved quickly to rescue Frankie.
*' Come on Frankie, that's enough f ' tonight, don't want to upset these good people do we, don't want to blot ya copy book do we '.*
Frankie fell into his mate and as Tom dragged him towards the door a voice called out.
*' Wor 'appened bose 'wore 'appened /?'*
Tom struggled through the door with Frankie shouting.
*' Well I'm still 'ere aren't I ! '*
Laughing, coughing, spluttering , the cold night brought Frankie to some semblance of balance as he stumbled after Tom along the quay towards their boat.
Made it, just !

It was time to go.

As the four boats sailed from Anglesey the sky clouded over and the sea became a confusion of crests devoid of any form or regularity. Pitch black 1900 hrs.

On the Nonsuch the steward brought coffee for the Officers on the bridge, he was pleased with himself for completing the journey from the makeshift galley without any spillage.

The Commodore, Captain and the Chief Officer gratefully took hold of their pint pots and thanked the steward as the engines made cantankerous sounds, the voice pipe whistled and the Captain listened.

*' Engine problems, the Chief Engineer is cursing like hell down there, starboard engine loosing revs '*, said the Captain.

The Commodore looked stoically ahead, face streaming with spray, adjusting his feet to the downward pitch while trying to drink his coffee when a huge wave hit the forward port side sending huge sheets of spray over the craft.

The Navigators ducked.

The Commodore shouted to be heard above the sudden ferocity of the sea.

*' The engines, experimental, that's what this trip is all about. I'll get Turnbull to organise fine tuning when we get back, at least we've got three '.*

Words were lost to the elements.

The four boats plunged into the dark developing storm towards Lands End where the Irish Sea meets the Atlantic.

Aboard the Gay Viking concentration was intense as waves cascaded over the entire vessel.

The helmsman's face contorted with horror as the bows vanished into a wall of sea and the whole boat shuddered violently.

He could do little but hang on grimly to the wheel hoping that his feet would remain on the heaving deck as the Captain shouted.

*' Keep her steady man. Christ sake. Force eight. Other boats can't see other boats. Good man. Keep her steady. Keep her steady. Mister Mate get boson, get Frankie up here, get Frankie on the wheel '.*

The needle of the compass card swung wildly .

The First Office clambered and clutched, slipping down to the after deck. In an instance he was knocked off his feet and he was swept along colliding with a bollard.

Managing a handhold he pulled himself up instinctively throwing himself through the door into the accommodation where finding Frankie he ordered him to the bridge.

Frankie took the Lords name in vain and deep inside he felt a strength, a calling.

His features solidified into grim determination as he made his way up the bridge to relieve the exhausted sailor.

The sky split open with jagged, black, deep blue streaks of violently flashing lightening exploding with bolts of thunder adding awesome dimensions to the force of the sea.

In the engine room men fell over, picking themselves up and falling again , clutching at rails, mouthing obscenities, as the diesels raced, spluttered, screeched, stopped, started, spluttered and on the bridge Frankie screamed and shouted as he got to grip with the wheel and the sea.

*' Cum on lady, ya dealing with Frankie now, cum on Lady cum on '.*

The Captain glanced sidewards at Frankie and gritted his teeth as the verbal machinations mixed awkwardly with the hissing, crashing, growling of the seas.

*' Steady ya cow, don't mess with Frankie, you smart arse, ' ere we're holding Cap'n, we're holding our ..'*

Despite his foul tongue the Captain was obliged to Frankie as the Gay Viking began the dangerous manoeuvre round Lands End.

Black monstrous seas rose and fell crashing into the starboard side of the boat tossing it like drift wood in a whirlpool and the Captain and the Chief slipping, clutching, as Frankie remained upright welded to the wheel and shouting determined incoherence.

The Captain shouted.

*' Hold her for god's sake hold her '.*
Frankie, in his element was in no mood to mince words.
*' What the 'ell d'ya think I'm doing ya daft bugger '.*
The authority of Captain Whitfield's orders screamed , *' Port Mister boson , port Mister boson ',* were just heard by Frankie above the tempest who screamed back , *' Aye aye Captain, aye aye '.*
Frankie strained, stretched, exhorting his strength to move the wheel which creaked as it turned, and he shook , and for a few seconds the bridge was at right angles to the mountainous screaching waves.
Frankie screamed , *' Jesus Christ Jesus Christ '.*
It was as if the boson had seen the other side of life and for a moment there was only fear of the sea. In the accommodation Tom wedged himself tight in his bunk as he uttered an incoherent babble of prayers as the small slender boat contorted.
Through his clenched teeth he called out for Frankie to show his worth.
*' Frankie ya bastard show us what ya can do, cum on man show us what ya med of '.*
But the seas took over.
Frankie dragged every ounce of strength out of his body, defying despair as the boat was thrown up and down, thrashed, lashed, tossed and lurched sidewards and slowly, slowly she found a current which turned and brought what was left of her, out of the maelstrom into calmer waters .
The Captain shouted.
The Captain shouted.
*' Boson, good man Frankie, good man, bottle of run for you, steady as she goes, steady as she goes '.*
Slowly, slowly the buffeting began to ease and and the seas began to follow the Viking as the three other boats appeared through the mist as they entered the English Channel proper.
The wind eased, the seas died down as the boats settled into an uncomfortable formation and the crews were almost back to normality and war.

The Grey Ladies, bruised and battered, their grace tested, their pride intact, cruised sedately on a course sixty degrees east taking them to the Weymouth M.T.B. Base.

This time the  base Commander had no need for kid gloves or diplomacy as the Merchant Navy crews were confined to their boats to sleep and stayed at the base only overnight while taking on fuel. After sleep the following morning the boats departed quietly, without formality and cruised hugging the coast all aware of attack from enemy aircraft flying from mainland Europe.

Lookouts reported aircraft.

Gunners responded.

Eyes ranged aircraft.

Guns swivelled, fingers itched.

Guns remained silent.

The Commodore was pleased.

It was a sunny day.

Beachy Head.

White Cliffs of Dover.

Through the busy straits .

Heading east.

North east .

Across the Thames estuary and then North.

On the bridge of the Hopewell the Captain hummed along as the eccentric Chief Officers lungs bellowed forth a song full of sentiment which all shared.

*' And straight up the 'Umber  we'll go*
*Hurray me lads we're homeward bound*
*We'll laugh and we'll cry*
*we'll fight an We'll drink every boozer in Freeman Street dry*
*Horray me lads we're homeward bound .'*

Darkness and drizzle couldn't dampen the gut excitement of the crews as they stood awaiting to make the leap from ship to shore, from boat to quay. Frankie saw a familiar battered car come grinding to a halt out of which stepped Lask and Captain Turnbull whose beard grimly smiled as he shouted.

*' Now then Frankie how was it, a bit rough eh, piece a cake for the likes of Frankie Hebden '.*

The boson nodded an acknowledgement, though tired and in need of sustenance he managed a quick reply.

*' Aye a piece a cake Mister Turnbull, Mister Lask especially the rendezvous off the Spanish coast '.*

For a moment the three men stood looking at each other and slowly smiled as the boson went about his final duties making sure the head ropes were fast and all was secure. Lask and Turnbull went aboard the Nonsuch and in the cramped cabin discussed with the Commodore and Captain Jackson the performance of the boat and the crew. The Commodore was well pleased with the way the men had gelled together quickly and efficiently, though his main concern was the diesel engines.

Lask told of the delivery of the fifth boat which was completely modified and now had the proud name of Master Standfast.

*' Excellent Mister Lask excellent. Time to reorganise the crews over the five boats. As from tomorrow have everyone on standby after all this playing around it's almost time for the real thing. Everyone on standby Mister Lask ! '.*

Lask nodded.

Lask understood.

Captain Turnbull used his sea boots and diplomatic skills to concentrate the efforts of the ship yard engineers. Quickly they made adjustments and refinements to the diesel engines in all five boats. The Commodore noted that Lask had learned fast and his practical organisational abilities were proving to be invaluable which he thought would be a great asset for future operations .

With this in mind he asked the Superintendent for permission to take Lask to London to be comprehensively briefed on the Grey Lady operation at S.O.E. headquarters in Baker Street, London.

The Superintendent could hardly refuse.

For Lask another change.

It was late when Lask arrived home.

He was in a buoyant mood and pleasantly surprised to find the table set and supper in the oven awaiting to be served.

' Good to be home, what's your day been like ? ', he asked.

' Oh the usual, boys upstairs exhausted, tired out after larking about after school. I helped Mrs. W. organise a children's party, drank to many cups of tea, what about your day ? '.

Joan put a plate of steaming steak and kidney pie on the table.

' I don't know how you stretch our rations Joan I really don't know, aren't you having any ?'.

' No, no I ate earlier with the boys. Mind you I've had a good day for a change when I think about it. How's your day I hardly see you these days . When will it end ? ', she poured herself some tea and looked at the leaves swimming around in the cup.

' A year, perhaps a little more, then it will be all over, ' he said with quiet, smiling confidence, then he tucked into his supper.

' By the way Joan would you like to go to London ?'.

Her tea cup suddenly rattled, she coughed, fidgeted, looked at Herbert, as her face contorted into astonishment.

' What ! ', she exclaimed, ' go to London, see the sights, the bomb sights, have a holiday. Have you been drinking Herbert Lask ? '

He coughed as he choked on a piece of pie.

' Alright Joan. No I haven't been drinking, there hasn't been a raid for ages '.

But her daily anxiety was now on her lips.

' Even if there had been a raid they wouldn't tell us, I think you'd better explain yourself Herbert Lask, go on, go on '

' Alright, alright Joan let me explain. The Commodore wants me to visit the Special Operations headquarters and he thought ', but she cut him off in mid sentence.

*' I should have known, it's all t'do with this secret stuff, isn't it Herbert, isn't it ? '.*

*' Well the Commodore suggested you should come along as I'll not be working all the time, bit of holiday, daft with the war going on, perhaps we could go to the theatre. The boys can stay with your sister...'*

But as she thought, her facial expressions began to change and began to relax,*' My sister, she's enough on her plate '.*

Her stern expression began to change into a thin smile and she flicked her hair and her smile broadened and became a laugh and her laugh became laughter and she threw her arms around him.

*' When do we go Herbert when do we go ? '.*

Captain Turnbull inspected every boat as if it were his own.
On the bridge the Grey Viking he checked the compass.
On the Gay Corsair he inspected the echo sounder.
On the Nonsuch he fiddled with the guns.
The galley on the Master Standfast was to small but would have to do
and on the Hopewell he stood on the bridge like a latter day Admiral.
Lask observed his mentor.
He reckoned it couldn't be much of a life for a Master Mariner to be
torn away from the sea only to be firmly planted on dry land.
The quayside bustled noisily, a few cars hooting, dericks thudding,
winches pounding, shouts, screams and hissing of steam cranes.
Motormen, engineers, able seamen, Captains, stewards, radio men,
three star uniformed men, boarding boats with grave concern and
teeth clenched with smiling excitement of imminent departure, to
destinations unknown.
There would be no shore leave for some considerable time .
This was it.
All Officers were summoned by the Commodore for a final briefing
aboard the Nonsuch.
They crowded into the small cabin which became a murky
atmosphere of cigar, pipe and cigarette smoke which swirled amongst
the tense muted conversations which were suddenly broken by an
artificial important cough from the Commodore, bringing the men
to his attention.
He pointed to a chart stuck to the bulkhead.
He drew an imaginary line from the Humber across the North Sea to
their destination.
He coughed again, fumbling with the match, lighting his pipe.
The men looked at the chart, then at each other without expression as
their destination registered.  The Commodore spoke.
*' Gentlemen, you get the drift. First, let me explain the role of the Chief
Officers so there isn't any confusion. Their main duties will be with
military matters, to put it bluntly, fighting the enemy should the need
arise. They are very good '*, he said the last phrase with a chilling
certainty.

*' Once at sea there will be radio silence. As we enter enemy waters there will be a strong possibility of one of our number being detected by the Kreigsmarine or by the Luftwaffe .'*

*' If that happens respective Captains will abort their mission, turn about and return to base so as not to compromise the other boats. Very important '.*

*' Any problems, turn back .There are minefields to the north in Norwegian waters and  along the Danish coast to the south'.*

*' The central channel, deep waters through the Skaggerak. And vigilance goes without saying. Vigilance at all times. Drifting mines that's another thing. The line from Arendal, Norway to Hirtshals, Denmark is an established Kreigsmarine patrol route ''.*

Most of the Captains and Officers were familiar with the North Sea yet they surveyed the charts with studious attention.

*' We have to assume the Germans know of our intentions, their intelligence services will undoubtedly have examined the possibilities of such an operation. We have speed, dark nights and surprise. '.*

The Commodore sternly looked at his men and they looked at each other nervously and the silence was broken as Lask awkwardly entered the cabin with a box of glasses and bottles of rum which were seized  upon. Glasses filled and the Commodore raised his glass. With determination expressed and etched in their faces  they drank to each other

They drank quickly, then clutching their orders made their way to their allocated boats to wait the final order to sail.

With the crews aboard, anticipating departure, fidgeting in corners, feigning sleep, playing cards and telling stories which had been told before and all hoped would be told and heard again.

On the Master Standfast Captain Holdsworth checked his charts and as he could do no more made his way down to the mess room where he came across the banter of the sailors as one asked.

*' Anyone know Eddie Higgins, able seaman ? ,* the lounging sailors not all of them comfortable in the presence of a Captain, especially one who was smiling, shook their heads except one.

*' Yep I know 'im, 'e's on the Nonsuch !'.*

The sailor eager to tell his yarn laughed, nodding his head, and demanded attention and started,

*' Cheekiest bastard I've ever met. On the City of Ripon, going up the St. Lawrence seaway Eddie Higgins was on lookout, allus falling asleep 'e wuz, Cap'n, forget 'is name, 'eard 'im snoring up there on the monkey island an' didn't 'alf ball 'im out, told 'im to report everything he saw everything, else 'e wuz in trouble . Eddie reported this ship and that ship even someone fishing on the seaway bank and then 'e reported a seagulll.* ( the sailor's voice rose ) *A seagull dead ahead. The Captain went spare. He shot up the ladder t' the monkey island shouting at Eddie that he didn't want to know 'bout a bloody seagull. '*

*' Eddie snapped back saying 'e should be worried about this seagull because it was walking towards them '.*

The sailors shuffled, smiled, smirked and some began to laugh as the Captain took his leave as the sailor finished his story ,*' the seagull was walking towards them, ha ! '.*

The Captain decided he must warn Captain Jackson about Eddie Higgins.

In the hut on the quayside that went for headquarters Lask passed the telephone to the Commodore who listened, sighed with resignation then swore under his breath while looking at Lask.

*' Meteorological reports. Not good twenty four hours delay. Not good for morale. Stand the men down Lask, stand the men down. In the hands of the Gods Mister Lask, in the hands of the Gods '.*

The night was frustrating and uncertain for the Commodore and the crews except for Captain Jackson aboard the Nonsuch whose night was full of happiness and also anguish. Lask had brought him the news that he had become the father of a son. There were handshakes, congratulations but nothing more and he felt a great happiness but in the recesses of his mind was the terrifying thought, would he ever see his son. The thought was momentary.

The thought was dismissed.

Time became elongated, stretched, as an hour became two, three, then sleep. Awake and more long hours of anxious anticipation which ended quite suddenly at 16 – 45 hours, when orders were given and crews took to their stations.

Engines roared into life and the streamlined Grey Ladies sailed out of the docks into the gathering mist of the Humber.

Rounding the Bull Lightship off Spurn Point they steered northwards through the channel which cut through the minefields towards Flamborough Head and the began a stately turn to starboard bringing them onto a course of 030 degrees North by North East.

In diamond formation the five boats now faced the unpredictability of the North Sea as their destination was finally released to the crews, some of whom had made accurate guesses.

With others they were not being far off, but the port of Lysekil on the west coast of Sweden was an unknown.

*' Sweden all along, knew it all along '.*

*' Did ya 'ell ! '.*

*' Lysekil ! Never 'eard of it '.*

*' What we going for ? '.*

*' Ball bearings '.*

*' Can't do without balls '.*

*' That's a turn up for the book ? '.*

*' What's a turn up for the book ?'.*

*' Commodore, he leads from the front. He's with us. He's sailing with us ! '.*

Darkness almost complete.

Wind brisk.

Sea running high and all realised in shivering moments why all the training was necessary.

Below the decks engineers tended their diesels with a little more than nervous apprehension and almost paternal concern.

Frankie stood on the afterdeck of the Gay Viking inhaling deeply sea
air mixed with tobacco smoke,  looking into the turbulent wake and
shouting to no one in particular that it was great to be back at sea.
He looked out with a sense of well being.

The five Grey Ladies sped at twelve, fourteen, eighteen knots pushing
out bow waves forming into wakes astern with the Nonsuch leading.
On the bridge of the Gay Viking Captain Harry Whitfield, his
binoculars  in constant use kept an eye on the other boats while
keeping an eye on his own station and on the compass.

He heard Frankie speak to the sea and for a moment he thought
about the benevolent relationship Frankie had with Tom.

Whenever Frankie got out of hand Tom seemed to be around waiting
to rescue him, like close brothers. The Chief Officer interrupted his
thoughts.

*' Captain, signal from the Commodore, we are to increase speed to*
*twenty knots '.*

Suddenly the sound of the engines dropped an octave and the whistle
of the voice pipe signalled an urgency from the engine room. With
ear to pipe the Captain listened to the Chief Engineer.

*' Starboard engine. Fuel blockage, Closing her down. Reduce speed.*
*Working on it, shouldn't take long '.*

The Captain ordered a message reporting their situation to be sent to
the Commodore aboard the Nonsuch.

Now all eyes strained to keep the wake of the nearest boat in sight as
down below the engineers worked furiously to repair the fuel
blockage but now the Gay Viking was falling behind.

Another message was sent to the Nonsuch.

Captain Whitfield awaited a response but none came.

The S.O.E. Chief Officer, all to aware of their orders, pointed out
their position.

*' Captain, we've lost contact with the other boats. Do we adhere strictly*
*to orders, turn  around and go back '*, he looked at the Captain whose
facial expressions he could see where mulling over a decision
and when the Captains eye brows rose and then fell fixing his
features in a determined solidified stare, he knew the answer.

But time seemed long before he answered and when he did it was swift and clear.

*' We'll go on, we'll go on, stick to our course, bound to see the others at first light '.*

The Chief Officer half smiled and nodded his head in agreement as the bows of the Gay Viking cut into the sea sending flurries over the foredeck.

Down below the engineers worked intensely and the revolutions stuttered , crunched and then whined in predictable unison.

There was no going back as the twelve to four watch passed in ominous, weary and uncomfortable, tedium.

Aboard the Nonsuch those on the small open bridge shivered, cursed and occasionally spoke but said little as there was little to say and all scanned the seas for the Gay Viking , but there was  no sight.
Then a voice shouted.
*' Ship to port, no lights, a point to port '.*
Through his binoculars the Captain studied the vague mist shrouded shape in the emerging dawn on the horizon and he concluded.
*' Trawler, probably Danish, starboard Mister Helmsman, three points to starboard, we'll give her a wide berth, signal the others Mister Mate, signal the others '.*
*' Three points to starboard Captain '.*
*' Signal to others Captain, signal to others '.*
Suddenly the vessel put her navigation lights on.
*' She knows we're here, lets hope she's only interested in fish '.*
Short gusts of wind began to peck at the waves and the black blue sea changed to a silvery grey as dawn stretched  a line of light across the horizon between sea and sky.
The Commodore was woken by insistent knocking upon his cabin door, he sat bolt upright, rubbing salt and sleep from his eyes as Albert the burly steward opened the door, brusquely telling him that it was morning.
*' Seven thirty ! Coffee ! Sir '.*
The Commodore grunted like an old car starting up.
*' Is it, 'errrr my god, coffee, ye yes coffee ! Coffee. Bacon sandwich. Bring them to the bridge, good man, good man '.*
He swung his legs around, pushed himself off the bunk and standing up stretched, yawned, dismissed the steward and said to himself something about winning the war.
Slapping cold water on his face he growled and clambered his way to the bridge, meeting the cutting edge of the chill he shivered and found his place, acknowledging the others on the bridge.
*' Any sight or sign of the Gay Viking Captain ? ',* he asked.
*' No Commodore, no signal, no sighting ",* answered the Captain.
The Commodore clapped his hands in anticipation as the steward brought him coffee and his sandwich.

Speaking between sips and bites he assessed the situation.

*' The Viking will have turned back. Engine problems, turned back. Gone back to base. Orders were specific, loose contact with the flotilla, turned back. Nice sandwich this, nice sandwich. Captain Whitfield's turned back . An early bath. Ha ! '.*

Captain Jackson looked ahead watching the bows cut into the ice edged sea thinking of his son and turning away he ruefully said something about their position and the Commodore followed him to the chart room where they calculated their position on the chart.

From the deck  Eddie Higgins shouted ,*' Aircraft ! Aircraft three points to port. Dornier. Heinkel three points to port. Seaplane ',* and the Captain and the Commodore were quickly on the bridge where the Chief Officer watched as the aircraft increased in size.

The order for action stations was chilling.

The crew were quick to their stations.

Fingers on triggers.

The aircraft flew over then circled slowly keeping a respectful distance as the Commodore scratched the stubble on his chin, shaking his head in a shiver as he began to see the whole operation aborting before his eyes.

*' New course I think Captain, head towards the Danish coast might put the Luftwaffe off. Right Captain ',* the Captain agreed and ordered the helmsman to turn three points to port.

Without taking their eyes off the aircraft the Captain and the helmsman acknowledged the new course. Albert the steward breathed deeply as he watched the aircraft and thought of another world, another time where breakfast would be underway, with the smell of kippers, eggs and bacon wafting.

He would sit down with a mug of tea, a cigarette and a newspaper. But now he swung the Vickers machine guns round keeping the black intruder in his sights.

The aircraft's circles grew tighter.

Fingers taught.

Eyes from all boats now locked on.

Binoculars followed the aircraft as it turned away, flying into the clouds, engine noise growing feint as it disappeared.

The gunners relaxed.

The Commodore, the Captain stared at the clouds.

The Chief Officer shouted once, twice, three times for action stations. Instinctively sailors were back in fighting positions with their guns.

Out of the clouds the aircraft swooped with intent.

The whine of the aircraft became a roar as the black speck became larger by the second, flying down, levelling out and heading straight for the Nonsuch.

Albert looking out over the grey green cold sea saw mugs, kettles, plates, saucepans, ships, aircraft, swastikas as the oncoming roar opened fire sending smoke trailing lines tearing into the moderate rolling sea towards him and he thought of dolphins and the Pacific.

The Chief shouted.

*' Open fire, open fire '.*

Albert squeezed the trigger, feeling a sudden bowel movement he was engulfed in deafening machine gun fire as his shoulders began to shake violently.

*' God almighty '.*

Albert, twisted, turned, swinging the twin Vickers machine guns, blazing away at the aircraft, sweat dripping from his brows, and the aircraft roared overhead with smoke trailing from an engine and as it sluggishly climbed high Albert cheered with others and he breathed heavily as he fumbled for a cigarette and the aircraft disappeared into the clouds. Albert left his gun and shakily shivered taking long inhalations of smoke from his cigarette.

The Commodore lit his pipe puffing furiously, scratching the left side of his face making white furrows across his cheek as he spoke.

*' Damnation. They know our position, even if it doesn't make it back to base they'll know we're here. Now we'll be hunted '.*

His pipe worked overtime as his mind calculated options.

*' Even if we're reported, it'll take them time to mobilise, we're making good speed, low cloud in our favour. To go on or go back. We'll see Captain, on course for Sweden then, we'll see, we'll see '.*

The Commodore signalled the other boats to follow as the bows of the Nonsuch cut into the seas sending spray over the decks .
Albert now in the galley worked quickly and nervously to supply the aggressive demand for tea, coffee and sandwiches from all the crew. With steaming pots he climbed to the bridge smiling broadly.
*' It's all go this morning gents, all go ! '*, he said.
*' Not another bastard ! '*, shouted the Captain, and Albert backed away, pint pots spilling the brew. He shook with fear as he heard the sound of the aircraft approaching at high speed.
A twin engined Messerschmitt, growing larger by the second , passing overhead with a wind jerking, sea whipping, thunderous roar.
All watched as it rapidly disappeared and the Commodore and the Captain looked at each other with decided looks and the Commodore said.
*' They'll know our position for certain.*
*North West for a couple of hours Captain ?*
*Approach the Skaggerak from a different angle .*
*What do you think Captain ? '.*
The Captain concurred with the Commodore , both realising that Albert was still on the bridge awaiting orders.
*' Coffee. Strong. Bacon. Bacon sandwiches. Quick as you can man '.*
Albert was quick down to his galley and went about his business. Eddie Higgins looked into the galley hoping Albert would take a hint and make him a sandwich.
*' Eh Albert, all this war eh, shooting guns an' what not, meks me 'ungry, what'da ya think 'appens now ? . Bacon smells great, really great '.*
Albert didn't like intruders in his galley and he toyed with one of his knives as he spoke to Eddie.
*' I suppose that's what we signed up for Eddie , something a bit different eh a bit scary, a bit scary. Looks like we're turning, making a run through the Skaggerak, heading for Sweden, eh '.*
He took his knife, cut slices of bread and made a sandwich for Eddie and the sea became inclement.

Spray lashed the bridge as the sky grew grey and darkening.
The Nonsuch gradually began to loose speed, falling behind the other
boats. The unseen Radio Officer shouted from his shack that the
radar batteries were dead. The Commodore ordered the Hopewell to
take over radar guard for the flotilla. The voice pipe whistled.
The Chief Engineer reported the port engine was sizing up.
All hands scanned the skies with the knowledge that they were under
surveillance by enemy aircraft .
The Nonsuch sailed on at reduced knots.
Aboard the Master Standfast the Captain signals he has mechanical
problems and cannot maintain speed.
On the Nonsuch a voice shouts above the sound of the engines, the
wind and the sea.
' *Aircraft. Aircraft. Aircraft !* '.
The crew knew exactly what to do.
Swooping out of the dark clouds the aircraft now in the sight of the
gunners, twisting, turning, trying to avoid the orange and white
tracer, whining overhead, climbing rapidly, the aircraft disappeared.
The Commodore orders the boats to move in close and quick
loudhailer conversations take place in which it is established that the
Master Standfast cannot make the Swedish coast by first light and
the Captains of the Hopewell and the Gay Corsair report the engines
are running well and are enthusiastic to continue.
The Commodore considers the situation.
Engine malfunctions.
Being detected.
Probably tracked and followed.
Lack of surprise compromises the operation.
' *Not you agen, aint ya got owt better t'do than hang around 'ere* ', said
Albert as Eddie crept into the small galley. Albert offered him slices
of bread and margarine.
' *You're a pal Albert, I can't think of anything but food*'.
Albert sighed all sailors were the same, complimentary when hungry
and all insults when full.

*' Can't think of anything else '.*
*' Bet you can Eddie, bet you can ',* and pointing to the curving wake
and changing course said , *' reckon we're off 'ome this time '.*

The Commodore had made his decision, reluctantly.
The Corsair, the Hopewell and the Master Standfast followed the
Nonsuch as it completed its turn settling on a course for
Flamborough Head and the North East Coast of England.
The Commodore left the bridge, retreating to his cell like cabin and
alone went over the incidents which had led him to abort the mission.
Flotilla attacked by enemy aircraft.
Engine problems.
Radar problems.
Earlier on in the mission the Gay Viking  probably turned back with
engine problems.
He lay upon his bunk, sighed deeply.
As tiredness came  his eyes began to close.
Sleep came uneasy.

Aboard the Gay Viking Captain Harry Whitfield, Officers and crew
scanned the seas for the rest of the flotilla. No one surmised what
could have happened to the other boats and if there was a sense of
foreboding it was well hidden by all.

Tom relieved of his stint on the wheel wondered how the officers
could stand being exposed to the elements for so long and without
sleep. In the small cabin Frankie sat on his bunk darning a sock.

' Eh Frankie, 'ere we are in enemy waters, subs, aircraft, mines all
around us and 'ere's you darning a sock. While you're at it I've got a
couple of shirts ya can 'ave a go at, ya're a dap 'and at it aint ya '.

Tom took off his heavy sweaters and Frankie looked up at him
almost sheepishly, almost embarrassed.

' The Old Man is turning out 'be a bit of a lad what d'ya reckon
Frankie ?'.

' Ya rite there Tom, couldn't believe it meself when he called me onto
Bridge, pointed ta flag locker, bottom left, tek it out an' brek it
out astern, big bluddy German ensign. Didn't know where t'put meslf
with all lads jeering at us '. Tom laughed .

' Give over Frankie. Give Cap'n 'is due, it worked '.

' Tell you what Tom when that big bluddy German plane flew out a
clouds straight at us I wuz rite scared don't mind telling you !'.

' So wuz I Frankie so wuz I . With plane in my sights and us flying
German flag. Mind ya reckon Cap'n enjoyed that, like flying Jolly
Rodger, I bet 'e reads books like that '.

Captain Harry Whitfield was in reflective mood acknowledging to
himself the part played by his wife in his changing circumstances.
Previously the convoys had been long plodding affairs with days of
station keeping in fair weather and foul, punctuated by loud
explosions illuminating dark ice nights as U boats found their
targets. His wife had read his thoughts well as she encouraged and
directed him. Now with promotion he was now in a position
in which he had some say in the order of things.

He was in command of the situation.

He had appreciated the knowing look of the Chief Officer when he
ordered the hoisting of the German Ensign.

He knew the enemy had used captured British aircraft to attack
our ships off coast of Ireland, so to hide behind a Swastika seemed a
reasonable form of deception.

But he had to placate the crew when the flag was unfurled.

This crew were not servile, and they spoke their minds as Frankie
hoisted the flag

' What's going on 'ere Frankie, whats this ? '

' Captains orders '.

' Good gawd, if captured we'll be shot as spies, flying that bluddy
German flag'.

The Captain shouted harshly at the sailors.

' No joke, if German planes spot us they are hardly likely to come
screaming down to attack one of their own now are they, but just t'keep
you happy we'll keep the Red ensign handy. All right lads '.

With that he watched Frankie unfurl the German ensign and he
smiled as he waved away the shouts of derision from the crew.

' Very democratic Captain, very democratic, especially for a Master
Mariner ', said the Chief Officer with an acerbic edge to his voice.

The Captains attention was caught in a fraction of a second by a
solid shape some way ahead and when the shape sank and rose again
he realised it was just a wave then he answered the Chief Officer.

' Of course I'm democratic Chief but them lot down there know whose
boss aboard this boat, make no mistake about that '.

He lit a cigarette, paced the bridge from port to starboard,
occasionally checking the course and the compass while making
mental calculations.

They were making good

Time to alter course for the run through the Skaggerrak.

With occupied countries of Norway to the North, Denmark to the
South, the Gay Viking sped on a midway course aiming to make
the Swedish coast by first light .

A lookout shouted a warning of an approaching aircraft.

Out of nowhere !

The Chief Officer commanded and the crew scrambled to their
stations fore and aft and either side of the bridge aiming their guns at
the approaching roar.

As the words to open fire left the Chief Officers mouth they acted
and fired at the indiscernible attacking shape which streaked cannon
fire down towards the Gay Viking.

The roar of the aircraft whipped up the darkening sea and then it
disappeared into the low cloud.

With a cynical edge to his voice Frankie shouted towards the Captain
on the bridge.

' *What's that then the bloody R.A.F. ! '*, then lowering his voice he said
to Tom.

' *Scared the shit out of me firing the bluddy guns, one minute on deck
next minute shooting at that bluddy thing, scared shit out a me !'*.

Looking at his swaying friend, Tom, exasperated by his friends
outburst rebuked him.

' *Well Frankie, I 'ope ya got rid of all that shit, but I doubt it, yer just
full of it aint ya, eh ! '*.

Tom grabbed hold of the door frame as the Gay Viking violently
lurched to port then starboard, then starboard to port and on the
bridge the Captain consulted the Chief and the First Officer gave
orders to the boson who turned about the deck, shouting and cajoling
the crew with a cruel smile across his face as he gave rough edged
orders.

' *Exposure suits on, 'ear that, exposure suits on, so get t'the heads an'
do what ya 'ave t'do, then get them suits on, you'll be topside till
Sweden. T' the 'eads and suits on '*.

The sailors reluctantly understood making their way to the bows of
the boat to relieve themselves. With this accomplished they struggled
and helped each other into the exposure suits which had been
originally designed for fighter pilots baling out over the sea .

' *All sea cocks relieved and secured '*, shouted Frankie without any
humour. But when they took to their stations the Captain and
Officers laughed loudly more out of their own relief than amusement.

They then concurred, noting that they were about to cross the imaginary line between Arendal, Norway and Hirtshals, Denmark which was an established patrol course for German destroyers and armed trawlers.

The Gay Viking began to bounce and shudder as her bows dipped and sliced into the dark, wild, growling sea as a voice reported lights ahead, three points to starboard, two points to port.

*' Probably trawlers arse end of fishing fleet I reckon '*, said the helmsman breaking the Captains concentration who gave the sailor a look of disdain while looking for some semblance of recognisable shape in the distance.

He ordered the First Officer to take over the navigation who then made a course change .

As the bow began to swing the helmsman started to think aloud.

*' Probably trawlers, but then there's a lot of probability, possibility and chance in life '*.

Captain Whitfield wasn't amused, he turned and snapped.

*' What was that ? '*.

*' Sorry skipper , thinking aloud '*.

*' Concentrate, if you don't there is a strong possibility and probability that one of those dammed trawlers will blow us out of the sea. Stick to your course man '*.

The helmsman acknowledged the Captain and an eerie silence descended upon the bridge broken only by the rhythmic sounds of the engines on top of the the murmuring, ghostly hissing and crashing of the deep, dark, green seas, swirling passed.

It was cold, very, very cold.

In the radio room the Sparks watched the radar screen with hypnotic intensity.

The First Officer ordered frequent course changes and the helmsman now keeping his thoughts to himself excelled in his skill as short waves knocked the boat a degree or two off course. The now faint navigation lights of the ship passed and receded into the luminosity of the wake and now sailors on deck were appreciative of their bulky protective exposure suits.

In the chart room the Captain scrutinised charts, calculated drift, course, position and time.

Through the night at a steady speed , steering east, north, east, they sailed through the German controlled Skagerrak  into the seas of Swedish neutrality.

Captain Harry Whitfield looked at his luminous watch which showed 4 a.m.

Abreast of  Hallo island the Gay Viking slowed down and bearings fixed their position between rocks and islands as the vigilance of the crew relaxed into some sense of normality. The Chief Officer well briefed in the mechanics of diplomacy ordered the guns to be taken from their mountings to be dismantled and hidden away.

At half speed the Gay Viking cruised southwards.

Engineers and motorman appeared on deck taking great gulps of frozen air, shivering, enjoying the space away from lubricants and engines which they had coaxed through the pounding seas.

The grey rocky coastline emerged slowly in the mist.

Lysekil Sweden.

Lights flickered.

The Captain and the Chief Officer looked at each other with relief.

*' We'll have to wait until the harbour wakes up, usual formalities, courtesy flags, the harbour pilot, all looks so peaceful '*, said the Chief Officer now in his Special Operations role.

Amid apprehensive excitement the harbour pilot arrived and was quickly on the bridge exchanging cordial pleasantries .

Speaking in Swedish and English and with proceedings attended to the pilot took over navigation of the boat into the harbour and towards the quay.With fenders, spring ropes, f'ward and aft  Frankie dictated and directed the berthing operation with quick short commands and the sailors responded with easy professionalism as the boat was secured and made fast against the quay.

Curious people and officials began to crowd the quayside.

The sailors expecting to see the other Grey Ladies were disappointed Ladies were disappointed.

*' Where are they. The others. Four of 'em. Oh god no, not four of 'em.*
*Doesn't bear thinking about '.*

The bridge became crowded with Officers, Customs men, the
Harbour Master and the pilot and others who introduced themselves
as Shipping Agents.

The Chief Officer, in conversation with one, learned that the four
boats had turned back due to engine problems and were safe.

This information was conveyed quickly to the relief of all.

Captain Whitfield sipping his celebratory glass of Scotch thought he
saw flashing lights out to sea.

The shipping agents explained that the flashing lights were German
patrol boats just outside Swedish territorial waters.

Captain Harry Whitfield lit a cigarette, inhaled deeply and said to no
one in particular, *' Grey Lady, Lady luck.. We made it '.*

On the second floor of his house, not a stones throw away from
the Anderssons Kaj the German Vice Consul rubbed ice from
the window pane and was aghast to see a huge Red Ensign fluttering
from a small grey boat.
He recalled conversations with his Swedish commercial contacts.
So it was true !
The British were here.
The German Vice Consul picked up the telephone.

On the quayside of the Immingham dock  Lask, oblivious to the rain, watched as the four boats manoeuvred towards the quay and with no thought of his family he wanted to be aboard, to be one of the sailors but his rain swept introspection was interrupted by the crunching of gears and the screeching of tyres.

A voice boomed out from the car.

Lask knew.

The beard jutted out of the window.

*' Catch your death out there Lask, come in, I borrowed the car and the driver from the office over here, I don't think  they trust me ! Have a snifter '.*

*' No thanks Captain '.*

*' Suit yerself, at least one of the buggers got through, quite an achievement, sure you wont have a snifter '.*

Gangplanks clattered from decks to quay and news of the safe arrival of the Gay Viking in Sweden enthusiastically reverberated amongst the crews.  Captain Turnbull and Lask found the Commodore and in a rapid exchange of conversation, events and situations were put in place.

*' Shuttleworth had an accident. He slipped on deck with severe lacerations to his wrist. Bleedings stopped '*, said Lask.

The Commodore fiddled with his pipe finding it difficult to form a response to a minor accident and like everyone else he expected to see the Gay Viking tied up alongside the quayside. He had feared the worst.

 However the safe arrival of the Gay Viking in Sweden made Shuttleworth's accident irrelevant.

But the Commodore was annoyed with himself as his plan, the plan, was for all the boats to arrive in Lysekil, Sweden together.

Once the boats had been secured the crews were given a twenty four hour pass and some of those single, and without nearby home's to go to, ended up in the 'Freeman's Arms ' where their deep gutteral accents were met with baleful and resentful stares from the locals as the sailors ordered drinks while shuffling and hustling and making making good natured banter with each other .

*' Eh, luv, over 'ere '.' Three pints of bitter and, and..'*
*' Bit of a lark this secret mission eh …'*
*' Secret mission to nowhere eh ! '*
*' Say that again eh '.*
*' Extra pay though '*
*' Ere's to them on the Viking eh !, . Cheers lads, cheers '.*

The sailors drank their fill and their initial high spirits settled nicely into the atmosphere of the bar as they challenged four of the elderly local men to a convivial game of darts and as they played one of the sailors  noticed a wooden advertisement for ' Guinness 'on the wall which featured a large Toucan. The sailor looked at his mate and started to play with the word ' Toucan ' and he eventually he exclaimed,  *' Toucan. Toucan. Two can.  Just think what two boats can do '.*

The game of darts with the locals continued while two of the sailors quietly and efficiently removed the advertisement .

The game darts finished and the sailors conceded defeat, raised their glasses and said goodnight.

How the sailor got the advertisement back to the boat was a matter of conjecture as it was a bulky piece of wood but much later in the early hours of the morning Captain Turnbull who was out and about on business saw a tipsy sailor stumbling around the foredeck of the Gay Corsair. Captain Turnbull saw the swaying figure holding a hammer in one hand and in the other hand a piece of orange, black and green fretwork.

After the swaying figure disappeared into the accommodation Captain Turnbull took a closer look at the fretwork nailed to the bridge.

When the Gay Corsair put to sea again  she would have a Toucan for for a mascot.

In Frederikshavn, Denmark, the sun reflected sparkling diamonds on the waters of the harbour and from his office overlooking the port Kommodor Schector could see the comings and goings of all marine traffic, military and civilian.

He wondered if the returning fishing boats had made a good catch but contemplative thoughts were interrupted by the shrill ring of the telephone.

He picked up the instrument.

Acknowledged the caller.

Listened.

Grunted and replaced the receiver.

He recalled intelligence reports and a conversation with one of his Captains who told him of rumours circulating that the allies intended to begin their invasion of Europe by landing in Norway. There were also reports of the British trying to break through the blockaded trade route to Sweden and the telephone call from the Vice Consul in Lysekil Sweden confirmed this as a small British vessel had docked there.

A knock on the door interrupted his thoughts signalling the arrival of Kapitanleutnant Rudiger, his adjutant and trusted friend.

*' Ah Rudiger, what's new '.*

*' Her Kommodore the Luftwaffe reported a British torpedo boat in the Skaggerak heading for Sweden '.*

*' Ya, ya, I've just heard from the Vice Consul in Lysekil, a converted M.T.B. Crewed by Merchant sailors, flying the Red Ensign '.*

The Kommodore sat down, closed his eyes, ran his fingers through his fine silvery hair, then yawned.

For the best part of ten years he and Rudiger had worked together in the Merchant Marine, latterly the Kreigsmarine and so far they had been lucky. By chance rather than by design the war had avoided them but during the past few months the great conflict seemed to be closing in on them. Both had been transferred from their home city of Hamburg and at first their families had been reluctant to move to Denmark.

But in retrospect they had thanked God they had as the allied
air raids of July and August had engulfed their homes in a
great destructive firestorm.
He sighed wearily wishing all this war business would be over soon
but for the moment he had to deal with a small British boat.
*' Her Kommodore, the Luftwaffee reported that when the British boat
was in the Skagerrak it was flying the German Ensign, Berlin are
angry and the British are to be regarded as pirates '.*
The Kommodore laughed .
The sun flooded through the windows making intricate patterns of
light and shade upon his desk. Outside on the quayside the
fishermen unloaded their catch.
*' What do we know about this boat ? ',* asked the Kommodore.
*' An M.T.B. Converted to carry cargo of forty tons of ball bearings.
It has three diesel engines, heavily armed. The British are complying
with international agreements and have dismantled their guns. The
boats are painted grey '.*
The Kommodore roused himself and walked over to the large
map upon the wall of the coastal regions of Norway, Denmark and
Sweden which indicated positions of ships under his command.
*' Rudiger, we have the 16$^{th}$ flotilla , the armed trawlers, Schiff 7,
Schiff 47, E – boats and minesweepers so it should be relatively easy
to intercept one small boat. Better redeploy, especially as Berlin thinks
the boat is manned by pirates '.*
They studied the charts, the contours denoting deep water, shallow
water, they considered various options, positions and discussed
weather forecasts. The Kommodore listened to his friend who
suggested a more vigorous deployment of their vessels within
the parameters of diplomacy.
*' Night patrols between Hallo Island and Vaderbod and between
the Skaw and the Oslo Fjord '.*
Now the Kommodore occasionally looked at the wall as he paced
the room  circling the desk  and then passing the windows glancing
down to the quayside wishing he was aboard one of the fishing boats.
Rudigar enlarged his stratergy.

*' Her Kommodore, minesweepers patrolling north west of the Skaw*
*by day, further west by night. Patrols along the Arendal, Hirtshal line '.*
The Kommodore resumed his circuit of the desk for some long
minutes and then he stopped.
He took a cigar from his  top pocket.
Clipped the end
Placed it between his lips
and he lit the cigar with his
gold plated lighter
a present from his son.

In Lysekil the German Vice Consul took an early morning walk
along the quayside observing the activity around the Gay Viking.
Cargo was unloaded and quickly covered. Aboard the small boat the
crew were being addressed by an Officer on the after deck.
The Vice Consul's linguistic skills proved adequate to translate
despite the harsh wind and the general noise of the dockers industry.
' *Good conduct. On your best behaviour. We don't want to upset our
Swedish friends now do we* '.
The Chief Officer used his considerable personality and size to
convince some of the more wayward sailors of the importance
of their behaviour when ashore.
' *Try not to say anything. You've heard it before but it's worth saying
again, be ambassadors, understand. Ambassadors* '.
The Chief Officer looked long and hard as Frankie Hebden stepped
forward.
' *Chief, any chance of getting cleaned up, a bath while we're 'ere ?* '.
' *Yes Mister Boson you're in for a treat, can't think why. Anyway
we're being looked after at the Stadshotel where we can get cleaned
up, have a meal and a short rest. However, you'll be escorted there
and back by the local militia, just to make sure you don't go playing
the fool* '.
As if to assure the Chief Officer of their collective responsibility
the boson said.
' *All rite Chief, we know 'ow to behave ya know* '.
The rest of the men groaned, murmuring in agreement with what
the bosun had said and the Chief Officer looked on in disbelief.
As the town became used to the light of the crisp October morning
the sailors looked in the direction of ominous sounds and from a
narrow street emerged a detachment of the local militia, rifles slung
over their shoulders, marching towards them. The Corporal gave
an order and then they came to a halt alongside the Gay Viking.
Tom looked at Frankie, Frankie looked up at the Captain on the
bridge.
' *We f ' the chop Cap 'n ?* ', shouted Frankie and the Captain shouted
back.  ' *It's your escort to the Russian bath house* '.

The crew shuffled onto the quay muttering excitedly about armed guards, escorts and the importance of the mission.

The Captain waved them away with humorous disdain.

The Chief Officer , hands in his pockets, legs apart, rocked back and forth, deeply breathing, coughed and shouted fiercely to the men.

*' Belligerent, that's you lot, belligerent, Foreigners aren't allowed, but our Swedish friends have made an exception for you lot, can't think why, but there you go '*, and his voice growled into a final warning, *' ambassadors, remember, ambassadors '*.

They walked off in some semblance of order under the humorous watch of the militia and both groups exchanged half phrases, gestures, smiles and grimaces until they arrived at the Russian Bath House.

In the changing room Frankie caused some disturbance and annoyance with his singing and was severely reprimanded by Tom but all was well  when the sailors, scrubbed, refreshed and clean were escorted to the Stadshotel where they would have a few hours of sleep.

But sleep was short and at 1600hours they were awoken and instructed to assemble in the entrance from where they were escorted to Liddels Konditori.

*' What's a Konditori ? '*, said one sailor to another and the other replied. *' A place of sumptuous Swedish delights, you know this mission must be really important to be treated like this. Ambassadors '*.

*' Yeah, yeah,  get ya sen t'gether, soldier boys are waiting to escort us and it's getting dark '*.

The short walk took them to the Konditori and on entering they found themselves in a spartan yet beautiful old café.

When seated they looked wide eyed at the colourful wedges of cake bristling with cherries and cream served to them by stern looking sumptuous hostesses.Unseen by the crew Captain Whitfield, the Chief Officer and the Chief Engineer entered discreetly taking a table in the corner.

They had slept little after seeing to the unloading and loading of cargo and the greasing and polishing the precocious diesel engines.

The Captain yawned and lit another cigarette.

*' Well just look at them, they look good, the cakes I mean. No thought for tomorrow eh ! '.*

They all smiled, enjoying the atmosphere as the crew lost all inhibitions they may have had.

*' Well, we might as well enjoy ourselves ',* said the Chief Officer, *' and have a jolly while we can, cake today, war tomorrow '.*

The Captain and the others nodded in agreement as they ate their cakes with a reverence as if each mouthful was of some particular significance.

A strange quietness descended upon the crew of the Gay Viking as they digested and finished their delicacies then an ominous darkness cast shadows as they and their escort made their way back to their boat and the night closed in.

The German Vice Consul had been up since before dawn and now seated in his comfortable chair he drank his coffee. Behind him a reading lamp shone on his desk and his telephone was at hand as he kept a constant watch through the window looking down through the dark shrouded mist of the Anderssons Kaj where the British boat lay quiet in the still and the grey of the slowly emerging dawn.

Hitler was behind him framed and hanging on a wall.

To relieve the boredom of his vigil he glanced through some old newspapers.

' Volkissche Beobachter ', reported ' Terror Fleiger '.

The local Swedish newspaper advertised a film, ' The Phantom of the Opera ', starring Claude Raines, described as a spine chiller.

In disgust he threw the newspaper into the bin, it was an English language film.

In the mist of the early morning a figure moved on the afterdeck of
the British boat and slowly the Red Ensign began to unfurl.
Aboard the boat the crew turned too, fortified against the cold
by yesterdays warm Swedish hospitality they went
about their duties with added vigour, though with little humour
or conversation.
With the valuable cargo stowed and secured the Captain, Chief and
two shore based based S.O.E. men discussed departure times and
possible course permutations to avoid German patrols.
The Captain traced a finger over the chart.
' *I expect the German Vice Consul will be watching our every move*
*so if we make out we're going north he'll make an immediate report*
*and so alert German patrols. So when we're clear of Lysekil and*
*abreast of Marstrand we alter course, then head due south, making a*
*run through the Skaggerak then west to the North Sea.* '
Almost with nonchalance the S.O.E. men added a little extra to the
Captains deliberations.
' *Captain we'll make sure there is interference with the telephones*
*ashore giving you extra time* '.
The Captain half smiled.
' *Chief what are you going to do blow the telephone exchange up ?* '.
' *No no no Captain, we don't do that kind of thing, well not in Sweden.* '
' *No no, we'll just fiddle with some wires that's all if you get my drift* '.
The two shore based S.O.E. men wished the sailors good luck and
went off to practise their disruptive arts. It had been decided to
leave late in the afternoon sailing into the cover of darkness .
As departure became imminent five furtive figures boarded the
Viking and disappeared into the accommodation and at 15-45p.m.
the Chief took command of the bridge as the harbour pilot
navigated the Gay Viking out of the harbour and into the Gull Marn.

From his office the German Vice Consul watched the British
boat leave the harbour, and he picked up the telephone, dialling
a priority number.
He waited patiently for a connection.
Something was wrong.
He dialled again and again and when he couldn't make a connection
he realised with exasperation that collusion between Swedish
Officials and the British was almost certain.
With anger he formulated a formal protest which he would deliver to
the Lands fiskal, but first he would organise other means to get his
report through to German Naval Intelligence.
His report would get through.

Captain Whitfield wedged himself into a corner of the bridge leaving the navigation to the First Officer. Both waved an acknowledgement to the Swedish pilot who waved good luck from the pilot cutter as it took him back to the shore. The Gay Viking cut into the swell with spray showering the decks and bridge.

The furtive figures emerged from the accommodation revealing themselves as Norwegians as they took to the deck with the crew, all alert, all on lookout.

The Norwegians thought of freedom, exile and revenge as the clouds darkened over the sea.

There would be no respite now.

In the engine room there was no time to think of the past or the future only the present as the motormen and engineers massaged the heart and the arteries of the nervous though responsive diesels.

The Gay Viking headed north between the islands of Stora Korma and Borgmastaren towards Kungshamn and passing Brandskar, the Captain now ordered a course change and in a swift majestic movement the boat turned to starboard through thirty, thirty five, forty degrees, until the Captain ordered the helmsman to hold her steady and steady as she goes .

Sea and wind moderate.

Captain ordered the helmsman to sail due east and then blew down the voice pipe ordering the three powerful engines full speed ahead. The engines roared, the wind howled, and the sea crashed and it was dark, very dark, but Frankie picked them out.

' *Lights to the north, semi circle, fishing boats I reckon* ', shouted Frankie.

Now the sounds changed to an engine whine and a growling sea as the Gay Viking kept its course heading west through the night with all lookouts alert for lights and shapes as slowly the light of October 31st crept above the horizon.

A sailors high pitched shout woke all from the mesmerising mantra of mechanic and natural.

' *Aircraft, aircraft, aircraft, up there, high up, port, two points to port, approaching fast* '.

Through his binoculars the Captain strained his eyes , finding and fixing on the aircraft as it fast approached out of the half light of dawn.

The Chief was quickly on the bridge rousing all hands to action stations. They picked out the aircraft through the sights of their guns, waiting orders, growing nervous when none came.

The aircraft grew larger and larger towards them, then roared overhead and then was past.

Sounds reverberated over the small grey boat sending shivers amongst the crew.

' *Nearly took the bloody mast off* ', shouted the usually quiet First Officer as the aircraft flew upwards, banking to starboard, turning and disappeared into the cumulus, then reappeared and almost silently gliding down towards the boat.

The Beaufighter of R.A.F. coastal command waved its wings and as it passed the pilot could be seen grinning down at them.

The Chief Officer with a self satisfied smile upon his face turned to the Captain and said.

' *Captain, I asked the R.A.F. to meet us* '.

The Captain eyed the Chief Officer with half smiling admiration then left the bridge and the sea to his men and the sky to the R.A.F. Stretching out on his bunk, he closed his eyes and he saw the great white whale, pirates and smugglers, a fireside, a cup of tea and his wife.

Captain Turnbull had been busy amongst the debris and chaos of the Immingham docks cajoling men to work their magic on the engines of the Nonsuch. They had virtually taken the engines apart, now being reassembled but it would take time before the boat was operational. Lask had relocated crews to the three serviceable boats for the next run to Sweden. The injury to Captain Shuttleworth was serious enough for him to be replaced by quick promotion of the Second Officer who was accredited as Captain of the Master Standfast.

Two able seamen had gone missing.

Lask had a problem

The Commodore had informed him that the three serviceable boats would sail on the 31$^{st}$ October.

Lask was in attendance through the night on final preparations for the three boats but he had a need for two able seamen.

Dawn was breaking, time was short as Captain Turnbull walked through the drizzle.

' *Morning Lask, always raining in Immigham, at least it is when I'm here. Mind you it's a good morning. Everyone heard ? Raises Confidence. Morale boost with the Viking getting through, I expect her any minute. I see the Nonsuch isn't fit to sail, those dammed engines ah, I hear two men went AWOL, I'll see to them later, bastards ! '.*

He lost thread of his thoughts as his attention was caught by the sounds and the emerging shape of the sharp bows of the Gay Viking as she quietly edged towards the quay.

' *I think I can get replacements Captain* ', said Lask.

' *What's that Lask ?'.*

Men drifted out of sheds, huts and offices and began to cheer as the Gay Viking approached the quay and Lask saw the two seamen on the bows of the boat who would be fitting replacements.

' *Frankie Hebden and Tom, problem solved* ', and Lask pencilled their names onto the crew list of the Master Standfast.

' *Problem Mister Lask, what problem ?*

' *No problem Captain all three boats will sail this afternoon* '.

The jubilant sailors on the Gay Viking made fast noisily shouting
to one another about getting a move on as pints were waiting.
Officers told them they'd be on standby and not to overdo things and
as they quickly made their way ashore Frankie and Tom saw Lask
giving them a studious and serious look as he approached .

*'Good to see you Frankie, Tom, well done , did us proud,  just
the men I want to see ',* said Lask.

The two sailors glanced at each other with rigid apprehension as
thoughts of the Spanish coast came back to haunt Frankie and he
instinctively became  defensive .

*' No, no Mister Lask, not that secret mission again  !'.*

Lask had developed a mischievous authoritarian manner of asking
for volunteers to which the answer would be a foregone conclusion.

*' Two volunteers, we're short on the Master Standfast and with your
vast experience you're the obvious choice. Volunteers you understand.
There's the bonus, comes in very handy. Volunteers of course '.*

Frankie was tired and thirsty.

Tom, nonplussed and hungry.

It was raining, cold and damp as Frankie looked at Tom and Tom
looked at Lask and Lask almost felt sorry for both of them.

*' I'll arrange breakfast and a bath for you both, '* said Lask.

*' Tell you what Mister Lask if your so bloody good at organising you
can organise a few pints as well. If you can do that Mister Lask you're
on '.*

*' Right then Frankie, Tom, breakfast, bath, a few pints,,  the Master
Standfast sails at 1700 hours '.*

On the quayside two elderly retired fishermen huddled together for protection from the rain which drifted from the east .

A shaft of light played a brief dance on the serrated brown waters of the river as three Grey Ladies growled out of the docks into the rain misty darkness.

Without expression one said to the other.

*' There they go cheeky sods them lot. Still war need cheeky sods like them two in the pub earlier '.*

*' What you on about ?'*, said the other.

*' Them two sailors, remember. One of 'em called Frankie, pissed as a fart, going on 'bout yon boats, said 'ee was on secret mission '.*

The other replied.

*' No bluddy justice in this world, no bluddy justice '.*

*' What's ya on about now eh'.*

*' Seen it all before, first world war hardly finished and some madman starts another '.*

The two men stood together watching the three grey boats merge into the swirling darkness and were gone.

On the bridge of the Corsair, Captain Jackson's face was grim as he
muttered words laced with foreign embellishments known only to the
well versed seasoned mariners.
The reason for the quiet tirade was mechanical. There was a fuel
blockage. He radioed his situation to the Commodore who ordered
him to return to base.
Captain Jackson wasn't to pleased.
Aboard the Hopewell the Commodore and the Captain  looked out
over the brooding sea as the wind slowly picked up waves which
collided with the slender hull and sprayed the deck.
They had little to say apart from a reference to the Toucan mascot,
if three boats can't make it, two can which brought out a chilled
laugh from the Commodore.
Darkness now enveloped the two boats, their wakes foaming as they
sailed in steady companionship into the rolling solititude of the North
Sea. The Captain, the Commodore, the Chief and the First Officer
discussed the course which would take them round the Dogger Bank
and past any unfriendly fishing boats.
' *Helmsman, north by north east* ', barked the Captain.
' *North by north east* ', replied the helmsman whose face was hidden
under layers of protective clothing as the wind became stronger
blowing from the south west and freshening point by point.
The diesels were unusually receptive to the dictates of the oil
blackened engineers who vociferously chanted twelve hundred revs,
twelve hundred revs and it was if they believed that this mantra
would do for the engines what the manufacturers couldn't guarantee
and the crude chants seemed to work. Twelve hundred revs, twelve
hundred revs, twelve hundred revs through jagged seas.
Stern up. Bows down. Bows up. Stern down.
Spray, waves crashing, cascading.
Navigators icy cold, leaning back and sidewards like in some strange
dance keeping check on the course as engineers willed the diesels to
perform a steady speed.
Sixteen knots.  ' *Where's the Master Standfast ?* '.
' *Behind us Sir, just mek her out* '.

Throughout the cold night their position, situation and weather conditions were assessed as being favourable for the mission.

But for the Commodore unfavourably as he tried to light his pipe, but only successful on the fourth attempt when crouching behind the wind dodgers.

Intelligence reports the Kreigsmarine would concentrate their patrols in a triangle from the Danish peninsula of the Skaw to the island off the Swedish coast and down to a point adjacent with Marstrand.

Captain Stokes set the Hopewell on a course cutting through the German patrol lines heading towards Hallo Island just north of Lysekil.

A calculated risk.

But with her speed the Hopewell could probably outrun any enemy patrol craft.

The Commodore checked the time again as he tucked himself into his great coat.

A lookout reported lights ahead.

' *On course for Hallo ?* ', asked the Commodore not that he needed to ask.

' *I reckon so. I see the lights haven't exactly gone out in Eurtope* ', replied the Captain who was caught out by the depth of his own remark and he ordered a course change set for Vaderbod and from there they would sail through Swedish territorial waters to their destination.

The Master Standfast would follow.

On the bridge of the Master Standfast the Captain kept a newly
promoted eye on the barely discerable wake of the Hopewell but he
noted its change of course and followed suit. His first command and
he knew that his promotion was due to expediency and the ill luck of
Captain Shuttlworth who'd slipped and the barbed end of a steel
cable which had lacerated his wrist.

A chance accident. One man's fall another man's promotion.

He recalled a tale he'd heard in the bar of a sailor who'd survived the
North Atlantic after his ship, a tanker, had been torpedoed.

He'd been rescued. Brought home without a scratch, but then he
broke his leg when he fell out of bed in a brothel.

The Captain was brought back to the reality of cold lashing seas
by his Chief Officer .

' *Captain, the Hopewell is slowing down !* '.

' *Right Chief, half speed then, half speed*', the Captain barked his
order to the First Officer, who blew down the voice pipe and
repeated the orders to the engine room and fog began to cloud
distinction between sea and sky.

Now there was no sign now of the wake of the Hopewell.

The Captain checked the compass and the course with the Chief as
they now approached the Danish coast.

' *Christ we've lost her, what now Captain ?*', snapped the Chief.

' *Helmsman east slowly, north east, steady, steady, echo soundings,
never know around here Chief, echo soundings* ', ordered the Captain.

' *Six feet, six bloody feet* ', shouted the Radio Officer from his hut.

The Captain ordered engines to slow ahead.

As the Master Standfast lurched from side to side she was caught
between two currents, almost drifting, almost out of control and the
Captain mumbled something about rocks, but the Chief and the First
Officer couldn't see any. The Captain shouted for a leadline.

'*Six feet can't be. Leadline Mister boson. Leadline* '.

In the darkness the boson fumbled as he shouted.

' *We aint got one, we aint got one* ', shouted the boson.

The Captain screamed back.

' *Use a fucking shackle on a line, quick man, I'll see 'bout you, quick* '.

Smarting from the reprimand the boson quickly threw the
improvised lead line over the side and waited, and waited,
and waited, until the line went slack.

' *Eighteen fathoms, eighteen fathoms* '.

With relief the Captain ordered the engines half ahead and the
Master Standfast began to move on a south easterly course for
Hallo Island. Frankie Hebden, now in the unfamiliar role of able
seaman, shouted from aft.

' *Ship astern coming up fast* '.

The Captain glanced at the Chief Officer and said.

' *It'll be the pilot boat, the Swedish pilot boat, compulsory* '.

The Chief Officer responded.

' *Can't be we're outside Swedish territorial waters, can't be the pilot
boat* '.

The Captain ordered the First Officer to flash a recognition signal.
The First Officer picked up the aldis lamp, flashed the signal which
illuminated the moderate sea and the fast approaching shadowy ship.

' *It's a Jerry, a Breman built bastard* ', shouted Frankie.

The Swedish pilot boat, or the Bremen built bastard, swung across
the stern and began to run parallel on the starboard side of the
Master Standfast. The Captain grabbed a loud hailer, calling for
a pilot as the unknown ship cruised alongside showing no lights, no
sign of life or recognition, ' *What now?* ', asked the Chief.

' *Full speed ahead lets get out of here* ', barked the Captain.

The quietly swishing sea was violently disturbed by a high pitched
whistle which seemed to scratch the heads of those on the bridge,
followed seconds later by flashing, rapid, heavy staccato thudding
machine gun fire that ripped across the superstructure.

The helmsman became animated, hysterically stuttering.

' *Lalalalalalaughing death laughing death, laughing death* '.

For seconds all froze, fixated.

Apart from the sound of the engines and the swishing of the sea there
was quiet and then the quiet was shattered by the screaming voice of
Frankie Hebden, devastating in its explosive sarcasm.

' *Does that satisfy ya, it's a Bremen built bastard* '.

Clouds of acrid smoke mixed with spray animated the sides of the
German patrol boat as suddenly the  searchlight swept over the short
distance, blinding all aboard the Master Standfast as the Captain
barked orders.

*' Jesus Christ full speed  ahead. On the guns. Frankie the damage,
full speed ahead, full speed ahead '.*

Then it was stunningly black.

Stunningly silent.

Strange after images lingered in the eyes of the crew.

The ensuing silence was broken by the echo of a harsh voice.

*' Some bastard doesn't like us !'.*

Macabre laughing death started again, screeching, ripping through
plywood, smoke wafting , the radio mast fracturing in a flurrey of
sparks, sparks falling, crashing, cordite swirling, smoke,
groans, screams, fire  illuminating the Master Standfast which gained
speed as cannon shells exploded on the bridge.

Men pulsated and contorted in the blue, smoking fiery blackness and
screamed.

Knuckes white.

Eyes wide.

For a second the Captain thought of chance, accident and fate.

Then he fell.

The S.O.E. Officer crashed to the deck with thick liquid oozing
around him and as he rolled over facing the skies through a gap in
the low black clouds he saw briefly a sparkle of stars.

Laughing death laughed again.

The First Officer, screaming dived for cover into the rapidly
disintegrating bridge and the helmsman, shivering in fright,
laughingly hung over the broken wheel.

Short bursts of gunfire swept the bridge.

On the after deck Frankie Hebden swivelled the Vickers guns and
fired in the direction of the enemy.

The starboard gunner, hit badly, his guns spinning in a wide arc
spraying the deck, sky and sea with wild fire.

Enemy cannon fire devastated the remains of the bridge .

Then there was only the gentle swish of the sea, the crackling of burning timber, the scraping of metal on metal and the coughing and occasional shout of fumbling bodies.

The First Officer, feeling his sticky, pulpy left arm, dragged himself to the wrecked telegraph and slumped over it in an awkward semi consciousness of Christmas tree's, roaring fire's, momentarily feeling warm and then very cold.

The skin around Frankies eyes stretched taut to the limits of fright clamouring towards the thought of safety, mesmerised by the sweeping search light.

The sea hissed.

Smoke swirled and drifted.

Light illuminating.

Flickering fright.

Frankie, dazed, and dazzled, shouts .

' *Tom, Tom, where the 'ell are ya ?* '

But there is no sight or sound of Tom only unfamiliar threatening voices shouting.

' *Schnell. Schnell. Schnell* '.

The command echoed through the drifting smoke as the remains of the dazed damaged crew were rounded up. Those who could walked, others were stretchered aboard the German patrol ship and crowded into the narrow space of a dimly lit mess room and reality dawned on the sailors.

A medical orderly worked his way around the men, patching up, sticking, stitching wounds quickly and he tended to Tom as Frankie glared and for a moment the young medical orderly seemed unnerved.

Frankie shouted.

' *If he dies, if he dies ?* '.

Shaking his head the medical orderly struggled for some English.

' *If he dies, he lives not* '.

Frankie lunged at the man.

' *If he dies I'll, I'll, I'll* '.

A rifle butt struck him.

The German Kapitan appeared large, speaking perfect English.
' *You will do. What ?*', and he walked over to Frankie blowing cigar
smoke towards him.
' *You are seeauber, or what you English say, Pirates, breaking
International law. I understand how bad you feel. However if your
bullets had been successful, then you would be happy. Ya!* '.
The captive sailors, nervous, apprehensive, cold, looked at the
German Captain as he studiously stared for a few seconds at each
man and then he turned away.
An elderly German sailor, his uniform ill fitting, with rifle in hand,
came into the mess room. His wide eyes exaggerated the furrows on
his brow as he offered Frankie a cigarette. The older German smiled
and for a moment Frankie thought he recognised the man from
another time, another place.
' *Thanks pal, danker, danker* ', and he drew relief from the smoke.
The German pointed towards Tom.
' *Deutsche Doktor, Frederikshavn, sehr gut* '.
Frankie got the gist.
Then exhaustion took over.
Cigarette falling from his fingers.
Eyes closed  he slumped, sinking into a deep and troubled sleep.
The P.V. 1606 came alongside the quayside with the fire scarred
enemy boat in tow. The Kapitan of 1606 was first ashore to meet
Kommodore Hans Schector and Leutnant Rudiger. They all stamped
their feet in the forlorn hope of keeping out the sharp cold of the
Frederikshavn morning.
Behind them stood two men in long leathercoats wearing trilby hats.
The two Kreigsmariners saluted and the civilians raised their.
right arms as they clicked their heals.
Ambulances arrived.
A group of soldiers marched to the commands of a young Corporal
towards the boat as the prisoners came down the gangplank, heads
hung low, nursing their wounds as they began to understand the
commands of the young Corporal who physically emphasised the
position of prisoners of war with threatening gestures with his rifle.

Kommodore Hans Schector barked a command.

The Corporal flinched, his mouth twitched and then he took a more conciliatory manner and tone towards the prisoners.

' *Nich sprechan. Nick sprechan* '.

The prisoners, tired, dazed, bewildered, some in pain, made no attempt at understanding, apart from one.

' *Never 'eard of 'im* ', shouted Frankie, ' *know a bloke called Nick Neilsen, works on fish dock, allus gets ya sum 'addock if ya ask 'im nice* '.

Seaman Gunner Dobson, suspended in time and space, looked at the remainder of his trousers, then turned on Frankie.

' *Shut ya mouth you loud mouthed bastard* '.

The face of the young Corporal quickly changed colour from pale to deep crimson as Kapitanleutnant Rudiger ordered the Corporal to move the prisoners out. Tom nursing his arm and leaning on a ship mate unusually took control shouting to the crew.

' *Right lads, we may be prisoners but lets show 'em eh , lets show'em* '.

The crew responded to the words of the usually quiet sailor and in a fashion they stood to attention, all eyes looking skywards and with the mocking, stiff, clipped accent, Frankie Hebden shouted with an edge to the shuffling, despairing, sailors.

' *O.K. jolly tars, when the German chappie over thar gives his Command, move out with as much precision as we can muster, singing the song you all know, ' We're off to the wild west show, the elephants and the kangeroos, never mind the weather, as long as we're together, we're oft to see the wild west show* '.

Seaman Gunner Dobson answered, in a loud, clear, firm voice.

' *Understood Mister Hebden, march with as much precision as we can muster, but if you sing anymore, I'll kill ya, you loud mouthed bastard* '.

A thin smile appeared on the lips of the Kapitan of the P.V.1606.

' *Pity about the English Her Kommodore* '.

' *You mean the way they sing ?* '

' *Yes, yes, pity we're at war with them, but on hearing the way they sing it is just as well we are* '.

Kapitan and Kommodore smiled broadly, but only for a moment
as they watched the bedraggled bunch of British merchant sailors
march off to an uncertain future.

Kommodore Hans Schector now back in the relative warmth of his
Office was in reflective mood looking out of his window viewing the
maritime activity as he mused about the sea, thinking of his future
and what it held for his family and himself.

Kapitan Rudiger quietly entered the office.

Approaching he gave the Kommodore a small brown envelope.

The two men looked at each other.

There were no words of explanation.

The brown envelope was enough.

He knew.

He prayed.

Large beads of sweat appeared on his forehead.

His eyes moist, he steadied himself and then he sat down as his
thoughts scattered and mixed as the past became the present and the
present became the past. Conflict, destruction, seeing the Fuhrer
engineer national pride out of humiliation and degradation and
seeing him build a fine Kreigsmarine.

And now the cost.

The brown envelope told him it was his turn to pay.

He slumped over his desk.

Rudiger understood, but couldn't understand as he tried to find
words of comfort, but his speech faltered as the Kommodore raised
his arm and dismissed him.

Alone he vented his anger, fist smashing down on the desk.

He dragged himself upright and staggered to the window and looking
down at the wrecked British boat alongside the quay he shouted
despairingly about love, hate, justice, loss and his eyes narrowed and
he looked into the distance. Men on the quay went about their work.

Breathing deeply he opened the envelope. As he read, emotions
cracked, and tears, suddenly flowed down his cheeks as he heard
tortured screams of his son as the hull of the U – boat split open,
sea engulfing his creation, his hope.

Lost in action.

He looked at the photograph.

He wiped his eyes, smartened himself up and called for Rudiger, who entered with a look of concerned expectancy across his face.

*' Ah Rudiger, any information about the British sailors, the prisoners, the men of the pirate boat '*, his voice commanding, cold and calculating.

*' Her Kommodore, our Swedish Naval contacts confirm our intelligence reports, the British Operation is organised by their S.O.E. The objective of these Grey Ladies , as these boats are called, is the transhipment to England of ball bearings and special steels which their agents have stockpiled. '.*

The Kommodore yawned and tapped impatiently his desk with a pencil.

*' Ya, ya, Rudiger, I know all that I've read the reports. The British tried to break the blockade in 41 and 42, lost most of their ships, now one small boat, the Gay Viking broke through., Evaded all our patrols. Now we have that crippled hulk down there. What of the crew ?'.*

*' Kommodore I understand the Gestapo gave them a hard time, they believe they are smuggling arms, ammunition and agents into Sweden for transfer to Norway and then here to Denmark !. But there's no doubt, they're just ordinary sailors, apart from one who will be sent to Berlin for interrogation. Most of them are from the port of Hull '.*

The Kommodore impatiently shuffled papers on his desk as his eyes moved moved quick and sharp.

*' Evidence, is there any evidence of guns and ammunition ? '.*

*' No the holds contain a cargo of oil drums '.*

*' Sailors from Hull you say ! '.*

*' Yes Her Kommodore, our Swedish friends supplied us with a crew list of the boat that got through to Lyseki '.*

*' From Hull you say '.*

*' The intelligence people say its their accents. In the course of the action the young Captain and the Radio Officer were severely wounded and despite attention they died of their wounds '.*

The Kommodore rose from his chair, stretched and circled his desk
glancing at the photograph of his son.
He turned away. Moisture welled up.
His eyes began to glisten.
He feigned a cough, then he spoke.
' *I remember Hull before the war.*
*I remember the Market Place*
*and a curiously named street*
*called 'The Land of Green Ginger* '.

Constance poured the tea sensing she was interrupting an important conversation between Superintendent Watson and Mister Lask.
Her youthful features flushed as both men turned and watched her.
Their grim faces unnerved her.
Their eyes were empty.
The Superintendent spoke.
*' Thank you Constance. Thank you. Bye the way there's a package for Your Mother, a few odds and ends I'm sure will come in useful.*
*see Mrs. Nichold on your way down '.*
Constance smiled, thanked the Superintendent and closed the door behind her .
The Superintendent looked at the floor and kicked an imaginary tuft.
*' Her father, lost at sea during the first year. We do what we can !*
*Now down to business Mister Lask. I dare say you know more about the Master Standfast than I do. You might have been seconded to the S.O.E. but you still work for the Company, you still work for me '.*
Lask took a sip of tea, nervously looking around for somewhere to put the saucer without marking the mahogany table. In the past six months he had been to places and met people he never thought existed, but he always felt nervous in this office.
Where to put the saucer ?.
*' Well Sir, from our information The Master Standfast was towed into Frederikshavn. Several of the crew were wounded. Two dead, the Captain and the Radio Officer. The Hopewell safely berthed in Lysekil, We expect her to sail within the week '.*
*' Mister Lask ! ',* the Superintendent's tone was heavy with impatient annoyance, *'from what I hear some of the crews of these Grey Ladies seem to think that this operation is a bit of a jolly, a jolly romp to Sweden. I suppose by now they'll know what exactly they've volunteered for. The outward cargo, guns and agents I suppose, but that's your business, I've got enough on my plate what with the build up to the invasion .'*
Lask signalled his understanding with a nod, but now with nothing else to report, an awkward, very long silence descended between the two men, suddenly broken by an incessant knocking on the door.

' *Come in* ', shouted the Superintendent with more than a hint of irritated relief.

Mrs. Nichols came in.

' *Sorry to disturb you Sir, there's a Police Officer to see you. Says its urgent* '.

She took a step backward and ushered in a tall, elderly, weary looking Sergeant, who came to attention.

' *Superintendent Watson, Sir, you have a Captain Turnbull working for you ?*'.

Momentarily Superintendent Watson sighed with resignation wondering just what kind of racket Captain Turnbull was involved in this time.

The Sergeant took out his notebook.

' *There's been an accident. A car driven by Captain Turnbull…*'

The Superintendent interrupted.

' *Speeding again. Reckless driving. I've warned him before* '.

The Policeman asserted his authority.

' *Sir, speeding or reckless driving we'll never know as the car driven by Captain Turnbull was in collision with a munitions lorry. He can't have known much about it. We've informed his wife. It's the black out you know, 'appens a lot, more people killed on the roads than we've lost to the enemy. Anyway Sir, thought you'd like to know what with his work and all. He'll be missed by the lads at the station, he sorted many a problem for us he did, only sorry I have to tell you* '.

The Superintendent took a deep breath and looked at the grim faced Lask as both men took in the enormity of what they had just heard. They both looked at the floor for a few seconds then the Superintendent thanked the policeman who realised there was no more to say and he excused himself and made his way out of the office. The two men were silent until Lask took his leave, leaving the office with the plaintiff words of the Superintendent ringing in his ears

' *The young Captain with his first command and now Captain Turnbull with his last* '. The Superintendent poured himself a measure of diminishing fine Malt whisky.

Lask had to walk off the tension he felt and as he did he saw Captain
Turnbull on the docks kicking backsides, doing business and
collecting favours in the bar.

In the Black Boy he took his half pint and sat in the seclusion
of the empty snug recalling the night when Turnbull took him home
in his battered car, when he told him of the Operation and of his
promotion and how Turnbull drank most of his whisky whilst leaving
a pile of cigar ash on the carpet.

In The White Heart he had learned from Turnbull that official
sanction wasn't always needed to get things done.

In The George he half heartedly sipped his ale and he saw American
tinned meat broached from a cargo being distributed by Captain
Turnbull to those on his 'in need list '.

Leaving The George he walked through the ' Land of Green Ginger ',
and he felt guilty as he thought of the fate of Frankie and Tom.

His feet took him to the spiritual home of the bar, ' The Empress ',
where he knew Doris would offer understanding and sympathy but
as he approached he suddenly had a change of mind, making off in
the direction of the intimate warmth of his home.

Herbert Lask had had enough of the day.

In Lysekil on the 10<sup>th</sup> November the dawn was exceedingly cold and grey as the Officers and men of the Hopewell went about final sea going preperations.

They had learned of the capture of the Master Standfast and reality touched the nerves of every man.

For Captain Stokes sitting alone in his small cabin with his head in his hands, it seemed that one minute ago the Master Standfast was only a few cables behind, then gone, in a flurry of radar blips.

He poured himself a glass of schnapps and as he drank he looked over the charts thinking about the homeward voyage.

Earlier in the day he had befriended a Swedish harbour pilot who had promised a detailed and up to date chart of the coastal waters. Based on the latest S.O.E. reports of German Naval positions and meteorological forecasts, the Commodore and the Captain decided upon departure time.

Not to prepare food for the Officers and men of the Hopewell was a bonus for Archie Price the cook steward and to be waited upon in the Stadshotel was a luxury.

He quickly became accustomed to Lysekil and was deeply impressed by the formal courtesy shown to him by the local people.

Though he had been to many countries this was the first to have influenced him to such an extent that he began to make imaginary plans for coming back to Sweden when it was all over.

But now he was back aboard and on the 10<sup>th</sup> November the dawn was exceedingly cold and grey as the Officers and men went about final sea going preparations.

Archie attended to the provisions and making sure the equipment was in order and as he worked he talked to himself aloud.

*' Back aboard this bloody boat, can't call it a ship. Why ? Why did I volunteer, I just don't know. Bloody conned by that old sod Captain Turnbull. Captain !. I'm just at the beck and call of 'em. Better get the coffee on else they'll be screaming at me. Soups, plenty of soups they'll be needing them. If Lysekil is Sweden then I like Sweden. Waters on the boil. They'll like this Swedish bread. Civilised and so polite. '*

*' Not like 'ome with me Mam running around after the old man and 'im complaining all the time 'bout his gammy leg and at the drop of his hat he's off on his bike leaving Mam to cope with rationing , the queues.'*

*'Oh Christ 'ere we go. There goes the Chief Officer, some poor sods in for it. Strange bloke the Chief, special operations man, some special operation. Ah 'ere we go. Let go f'ward. Let go aft '.*

The engines spluttered into action, then grated and quietly settled down and Archie adjusted to the movement of the boat as tins, utensils, pans, mugs and plates rattled.

On the bridge of the Hopewell the Swedish pilot gave the Captain a folded wedge of paper.

*' Captain the chart I promised you, a diversionary route through the coastal waters and between the islands. Destroy it as soon as you're out of Swedish waters. If you are intercepted and the Germans find the chart, life will become very difficult for me. Swedish neutrality is very precarious, some of my countrymen have no liking for the Germans, but then there are the others, you understand '.*

At 20 -45 the pilot cutter came alongside and the Pilot shook hands with the Captain and wished him good luck, and then made the hazardous jump from one deck to another.Archie Price brought coffee to the bridge. The Captain clapped his around the warmth of the pint pot saying to Archie.

*' Ah coffee. Good man. Good man. Not before time, thank you, warm the cockles of my heart. Fresh breeze, salt in the air, sounds of the sea, I love it. Pity there's a war on and some bugger out there is trying to kill us'.*

As the speed of the Hopewell increased the Commodore appeared on the bridge and conferred with the Captain and the Chief Officer on the course they were taking through the coastal waters.

Dislodging himself from his fixed position on the port side of the bridge the Chief Officer studied the sea and sniffed the sea anxiously.

*' Don't like the look of it, getting mucky, in for a storm I reckon '.*

He shivered and realising he'd missed out on the coffee , shouted.

*' Where's that blasted Steward ?'.*

The bows sliced through the seas showering the decks with spray as the Hopewell responded to the turn of the wheel by the hands of the helmsman who in turn responded frequently to the commands of the First Officer. It was cold and dark.

Teeth chattered as the light stars flickered through holes in the blanket of low cloud with the south westerly wind blowing a moderate sea.

Archie Price swore as he attempted to organise himself in the moving galley.

A sudden change of course had the Hopewell meeting the sea head on, plunging downwards, gyrating and heaving and then taking a massive unexpected wave broadside.

The Commodore, the Captain and the Chief ducked instinctively, hanging on, assessing the strength of the sea, all knowing there were limits to endurance and strength.

Howling wind whipped up the seas into a storm of accelerating ferocity and the helmsman fought to hold the course as the Hopewell lurched violently to port.

Captain Stokes had worked out the equation of nature and rationality and as a betting man he took gains and losses with stoic realism and he knew when to withdraw.

Now the sea dictated any calculation.

He'd made his decision.

*' Turn her around. Back to Lysekil. Boat wont take this pounding. Two points to port. Steady and slow. Slowly '*, then he shouted, loudly above the increasing roar of the wind and sea , *' Steward, coffee '*.

Archie with an immense amount of guile, daring and imagination completed the coffee making operation without spillage.

*' They'll be cursing me now. Why I ever got involved ? War is one thing weather another, but the Captain and that big bastard Chief Officer are something else '*.

The boat shifted violently.

Archie slumped against the bulkhead.

The coffee urn left its mountings, suspended in space it took flight to starboard crashing against the bulkhead. Archie thought he was going the same way but he caught hold and the boat made steady. Slowly now, the Hopewell rolled from side to side until some semblance of stability resumed as she now headed eastwards back to Lyskil. Archie was quick to fix the coffee urn and managed to guide the liquid into pint porcelain pots.

*' I deserve a bloody medal for this effort '*, said Archie directly to the coffee urn which he'd named *' bastard . What do you think bastard ? '*. Whatever the question , the moving, semi illuminated, distorted reflection agreed with him.

*' Never understand them cretins, I go through all this for King and Country, Captains, secret agents and bloody sailors and it's all my fault.They'll never understand the difficulties of making coffee in a moving galley. Bet Rommel never made coffee on a moving tank. If I get out of this lark alive I'll tell that man Turnbull a thing or two. What do you think bastard ?'.*

Slowly, slowly the Hopewell turned, degree by degree through the chopping, jagged, surging seas with everyman with clenched fists, holding on through 180 degrees, until the boat began to steady. Archie hauled himself upwards with one hand, the other gripping mugs of coffee and on reaching the bridge he took , as he expected, the full salvo from the Officers.

' *Took your bloody time* ', barked the Chief Officer and as if it were some kind of game the First Officer joined in.

' *What's this concoction* ', asked the First Officer.

' *Least it's warm* ', added the Captain.

From behind the wheel the helmsman's voice crackled and gratingly laughingly asked.

' *Where's mine Archie, where's mine ?'*.

It was one thing for Archie to take sarcasm from the Officers but when it came from fellow crewman, there was a limit, and the Officers were taken aback with Archie's quick, ferocious, response.

*'Bloody A.B.'s. Anyone can tie a knot in a fucking rope, try making coffee with a fucking madman like you on the wheel '.*

The Commodore, Captain, Chief and the First Officer smiled hard as the cursing figure of Archie staggered across the bridge to the ladder and back to his galley to shore up his defences. Once there he wedged himself under the sink, arms clutched around his chest, shoulders firmly in the corner, feet around a supporting stanchion and as the Hopewell twisted and lurched he uttered a litany of bitterness directed towards his father, the sea and especially Captain Turnbull. Archie stuttered into a deep troubled sleep.

As the following sea increased in strength the stern rose, the bows disappeared and the gale lifted waves which crashed, swirling spray, enveloping the decks and the bridge. Captain and the First Officer ever alert, eyes on the compass watching the course varying by degrees towards Lysekil. There would be no pilot this time.

The voice pipe from the engine room whistled with apprehension.

The voice from the pipe reported, ' *Overheating. Gear box. Serious* '.

Archie Price startled out of his unconsciousness, hit his head on the draining board, swore as his vision focused and he realised the Hopewell was almost stationary. He clambered quickly out of his fortified position in the galley onto the dark shadowy deck and breathing deeply as spray lashed his face he muttered to himself thinking aloud.

' *Did I dream that storm* '.

A voice replied from a smirking face.

' *Aye lad, course ya' did. We 'avn't been out of 'arbour yet, so get the coffee going 'cos we're just 'bout to leave* '.

The smirking face laughed at Archie Price.

He began to remember the contours of Lysekil the small fishing town and he felt a sense of relief as the boat entered the harbour and edged its way to a vacant berth.

A slight air of defeat hung over the boat as she lay peacefully against the quay in the midnight shadows.

Those who could slept deeply.

The cold bitter rain lashed the coastal town.

In the small cabin Captain Stokes and the Commodore listened to the
tired, oil greased Chief Engineer who leaned against the door, sweat
rag in one hand, glass in the other as he described the consequences
of the mechanical malfunction.

' *Gear box, almost sized up. It's a yard job. Even if I could do it 'ere it*
*would take bluddy weeks and that's been optimistic. Just as well it*
*'appened where it did and not in the middle of the North sea. It's a yard*
*job '.*

In one motion he drained his glass.

Glasses were replenished as the three men lapsed into a long
thoughtful silence until the Chief Engineer departed for sleep.

The Commodore yawned loudly, stretching his frame and pushing
himself to his feet he explained to the Captain he'd be ashore for two
or three days to sort out the problem. The Captain quickly drank
from the bottle wondering what the Commodore could do about the
gear box. As his eyes became heavy he speculated if Special
Operations had a gear box within their executive, he laughed to
himself then his thoughts returned to the fate of the crew of the
Master Standfast.

The rain fell continuously for two days and two nights. The crew
were called upon to perform minor repairs which they did quickly
and quietly without rancour and without humour. The third day
brought crisp sunlight which sparkled diamonds reflecting off damp
and steaming surfaces. The crew stretched, yawned, swore and
coughed.

Lysekil was quietly busy as the seagulls swooped and squawked.

Just after ten o'clock , a noisy car pulled up on the quayside and out
stepped the Commodore who jauntily bounced on the gangplank,
onto the deck of the Hopewell making small talk with sailors about
the rain, the sun and the bloody gear box. Suddenly his senses were
alerted to important matters by the aroma of bacon frying and he
made his way to the galley.

Archie made quick the sandwich and then the Commodore met with
the Captain and the boson on deck and he told them of developments
between mouthfuls of sandwich and tea.

*' Been to Gothenburg. New gear box all in hand . Dammed good
sandwich. We'll load up the cargo then depending upon what sort of
power the Chief can give us we'll sail down to Gothenburg and get the
new gear box fitted. A few days ? ',* what do you think Captain and
without waiting for a reply he went on as he made up immediate
plans.

*' A few days in Gothenburg. Turning this predicament to our advantage
we can show the flag to the Swedes and a few Germans I dare say.
Good propaganda. I think I'll have another bacon sandwich '.*

The Captain agreed with the need for bacon sandwiches. He called
for Archie and asked where the gear box was coming from.

*' The Ministry are flying one out by civilian aircraft should be in
Gothenburg before we are ',* explained the Commodore as they
headed off to the Captains cabin where Archie delivered the bacon
sandwiches. Archie was complimented on the sandwiches and so he
took his time to clear away the remains of earlier meals hoping to
glean some odd piece of information, but he was disappointed.

The Commodore and Captain looked hard at him so Archie made a
quick retreat leaving the two men discussing diplomatic formalities
and the location of the Marine Engineering Yard on the banks of the
Gota Alv, Gothenburg.

With details considered the Commodore took his leave.

The Captain briefed the Chief Officer, the Chief Officer briefed the
First Officer and the First Officer, enthusiastic at being given some
responsibility, briefed the crew .

*' As you know lads the gear box has packed up. The Commodore has
arranged a new one. We're going down the coast to Gothenburg to get
it fixed and you can have a jolly ashore, but as Ambassadors . The
Commodore seems to like you. Can't think why ! '.*

The crew feigned a subservience and with side wards glances they
nodded and winked at each other in mischievous anticipation.

*' Gothenburg. A few days shore leave . What's the Swedish for 'er, er.
Same in any language . No it isn't !*

*' Expert are ya ' More like German than English '.*

*' Is it ?'.*

' *What is  ?* '.
' *The language* '.
' *Ow do you know ?* '.
' *Read it in a book* '.
' *Well what's the Swedish for, 'ere ya know* '.
' *Book didn't say anything 'bout that, but I suppose..* '.
' *Suppose nothing. It's the same in any language daft sod* '.

The Chief Officer appeared and coughed loudly and the amused expressions of the crew were quickly replaced by stern attention as they went about the business of making ready for sea.

The Commodore, Captain and Officers presence on the bridge was augmented by two Swedish Naval Officers and as a further display of neutrality a Swedish patrol boat would escort the Hopewell as she sailed slowly southwards.

Archie Price supplied tea, coffee and sandwiches to an unusually good natured crew. The Chief Officer took his steaming pot to the afterdeck and there sat alone and began to sing in a strong baritone voice.

' *Oh there was a little drummer boy*
*And he loved a one eyed cook*
*And he loved her though she had a cock eyed look*
*With one eye on the pot*
 *And the t'other up the chimney* '.

Sun reflected on the calm shallow water .
The Chief Officer sang on.

' *When they went to the Church*
*To say I will  the drummer got a nark*
*For her one eyed gliffed the clerk*
*With one eye in the pot*
*And t'other up the chimney*
*With a la, la, la*
*And ashore we'll have a lark* '.

With the last la, la, la, he stood up stretched and breathed deeply.

Sailors smiled, thinking of being ashore and themselves having a lark.

They looked away from the Chief Officer who wandered off satisfied with his performance and the peaceful interlude passed as gulls flew over the stern squarking with hungry anticipation.

The Captain oversaw the navigation between the small islands of the archipelago as they approached the Gota River and the Kolvsund naval base came into view.

The ice edged tranquillity was broken by a crack of gunfire and a sudden white plume of sea erupted some distance away.

The Captain, taken aback, shouting angrily at the Swedish Naval Officers just what was going on.

*' What is going on, fired on from your own base, we're complying with all the regulations. You're here to see we put into the base, to see us off load guns and ammunition, to make sure we are a Merchant ship, so why did they fire on us and don't tell me that was a Swedish welcome '.*

The Swedish Officers physically backed away, acutely embarrassed as the Commodore interceded taking the slightly confused Captain aside to explain the delicate diplomatic procedures of Swedish neutrality.

*' A gesture from the Swedes to the watching Germans understand '.*

The Hopewell eased into the Naval base.

The guns were dismantled and with ammunition packed away and diplomatic necessities attended to and with checks formally completed the Hopewell now cruised out of the Naval base and sailed further up the river.

The Red Ensign flying taut signalled that the British Merchant Navy was back and workers in shipyards responded with intermittent cheers, waves and signs, some betraying conflicting sympathies.

Archie Price, excited waved as the Hopewell approached the quayside of the shipyard.

The crew displayed a more than unusual enthusiasm and a skill in a berthing operation which was completed in record time, then they made their own personal preparations for their expected shore leave.

Shipping agents set up a make shift office on the quay with a table which was stacked with packets of currency, shore passes and street maps.

The sailors radiated enthusiasm as if they had just landed from an arduous trawling trip as they went forth with vulgar, innocent, joviality.

' That fella said the old town was the place, what was it, oh aye, Vastra Mamngaton or was it Ostra Hammer something or other '.

' Nope said it was Sodra Hammngaton '.

' What a name eh !, my old lady would give me a clout round 'ear if I told 'er I was off to Sodra Hammngaton for a pint '.

' If we remember Vasta, Ostra and Son ya then we'll be allrite '.

' Eh Archie where you off to ?'

' He knows something we don't '.

' You know what them stewards are like eh, come on lads away we go '.

As they headed for the gates of the ship yard the commanding voice of the Chief Officer boomed after them.

' Remember lads, Ambassadors. Ambassadors '.

A hurried high spirited reply echoed back.

' Right Chief, we're oft to Sod ya hammer gardens, Ambassodars, we'll remember '.

In a laughing mocking scrum they disappeared from the view as the Chief Officer stood alone shaking his head in disbelief like a benevolent school teacher. He walked along the quay surveying the converted motor torpedo gun boat and he thought of past missions in forests in Yugoslavia with guns, grenades, explosions and death as he hunted and was hunted.

He thought it was right what some sailors thought of this mission, a holiday in Sweden. He boarded the boat and in his cabin washed and shaved and laughed in expectation of the night.

Most of the crew found their way to the old town of Gothenburg and their accents loudly proclaimed their friendship to all as they sauntered along the busy Vastra Mamnergaten until they passed a group of German Merchant sailors , instantly the two groups traded insults.

113

*' Bloody jerries ! '.*
*' Englanders scheibe '.*
*' Feinlick '.*
*' Bastards '.*
*' Arshlock Englanders '.*

Gothenburgers looked on forgetting for a moment the purpose of their day and became partially involved by offering encouragement to both sides alike. Out of the crowd Archie Price appeared shouting scathing directives at his ship mates.

*' Get a grip of yer selves, remember what the Chief said. Ambassadors. Ambassadors '.*

His sudden appearance and unlikely intervention stopped the verbal acrimony between the two languages and the two groups stopped. Slowly they turned and walked away in opposite directions in search of their pleasure. But confrontation wasn't far away. In a small Konditori one of the men from the Hopewell recognising enemy sailors, became bellicose expressing an out of tune rendition of 'Land and Hope and Glory '.

A German merchant naval man took up the challenge singing deeply a pounding military song.

The Germans sang in unison.

The English sang out of tune.

The Germans sang louder.

The English sang louder.

Glass shattered on a table.

Louder and louder the singers sung.

Features became fixed, muscles hardened as the musical conflict escalated into the realms of incomprehension.

The proprietor, astonished , was taken aback but he took to his trade by producing a tray stacked with bottles of beer which he dispensed to both groups of sailors and as the volume of the belligerent noise began to die down, the proprietor began to sing in English.

*' Underneath the lanterns by the barack square I used to meet Marline and she was young and fair ', a* British sailor sang. A German sailor sang.

The proprietor began to excel in the song and the small cafe breathed a sigh of relief as normality began to resume.

A German sailor rose from his seat revealing his massive frame, granite features and huge beard. He walked over to where the sailors of the Hopewell sat. The German's features softened as he looked down at the now nervous English sailors, his sheer size and laugh suddenly became infectious.

' Ach 'ere fook 'er 'itler eh ! '.

The English smiled and laughed as one of them looked up at the beaming enemy sailor and stuttered a reply.

' R, r, rather you than me p, p, pal, but I know what ya, ya, you mean '.

The German sat down, his sheer size and with electrified enthusiasm commanded them all.

' Varno good Tommy, ya know Liverpool. Good times in Liverpool '.

' Yeah Fritz Liverpool, Scotland Road. Hamburg, Fritz, Hamburg good times ', and the English sailor remembered that the R.A.F. had just bombed Hamburg and he felt uneasy and far from home, but a nod of a head, a wink from the eye of the German and the two men understood each other.

Both men of the sea drank their drinks together.

And the German said to the English.

' Next one on me '.

And the English said to the German.

' Once back at sea we'll be trying to kill each other '.

' Tonight we'll be friends . Perhaps we'll remember '.

The Merchant Mariners raised their glasses and they looked into the eyes of each other and slowly, very slowly they began to laugh as if they had discovered some universal truth. Their laughter began to disturb the proprietor, but he relaxed when the two warring parties beckoned him for more drinks.

Some time later the two groups said their goodbyes and walked away in different directions.

To different ships.

To different worlds but still at war.

It was late when Archie arrived back aboard the Hopewell.
In the galley he made a pot of tea.
Two tired and worn out sailors emerged from the shadows.
' Ello Archie, didn't we 'av a good time , eh !, eh!, wor a time we 'ad,
and ya sen, telling us oft like that in middle of street, stopping that
barny, still it all worked out in Sod ya Gardens. What 'bout yoursen
Archie, eh, I can tell ', and the slovenly, slurred speech of the sailor
came uncomfortably close for Archie who breathed in and held his
pint pot of tea firmly in front of him as a first line of defence.
' You found yoursen a lass didn't ya, didn't you Archie ?'.
The sailor looked from Archie to his mate, winked and smiled.
' 'Ow did ya do it Archie, cum on, ya can tell us '.
Archie sighed.
' Well lads I'll tell you, it's in the eyes, its all in the eyes '.
The sailors stuttered, laughingly.
' What d'ya mean Archie, it's all in the eyes ?'.
Archie was getting tired.
' Bloody able seamen, so bloody able, ya might be good with a marlin
spike but when it comes to finesse '.
' What the bluddy 'ell is finesse, cum on Archie 'ow d'ya do it ? '.
' Told ya. The eyes. I just look into her beautiful eyes and keep saying
her name Inga, Inga '.
' And that works ?'.
' Oh yes the waitress understands and I get a plate of fresh pastries and
a nice smile '.
The two sailors looked at Archie in puzzlement, then one sighed, fell
into his mate who held him up then said .
' Yer a teking the piss Archie, yer a taking the piss '.
The two sailors ambled off arm in arm in the direction of their bunks
and Archie smiled in the direction of recent memories to a suburb of
Gothenburg thinking of Inga, Inga, Inga.
As things stood it would take a few more days before the gear box
was fixed and that meant a few more evenings, passing time in
Gothenburg.

During the day Archie was kept busy with the culinary requirements
of the crew and when his days work was finished he was away to the
quiet suberb of Gothenburg .

A rumour had taken currency amongst all the crew about Archie and
a romantic assignation, all were of the opinion that he was a lucky
man and all wished him well.

With the new gear box in place, tested and functioning the Captain
was of the opinion they should leave as soon as the Chief Engineer
gave his final approval and with this the Boson rounded up the crew
for final preparations and the Chief Officer briefed the men.

' *Everyone accounted for ?* ', asked the Chief Officer.

' *Everyone Chief, except Archie Price* ', replied the irritated voice of
the Boson.

' *That bloody steward, give him an inch and he takes a yard and to
think he was carefully selected for this mission* '.

The Boson cast an anxious eye on the quayside hoping Archie would
appear as he attempted to quell the Chief Officers growing
impatience.

' *Chief, he'll be along in a minute, not a bad bloke really* '.

The Chief Officer wasn't in a benevolent mood.

' *Not a bad bloke, he's going to miss the boat Mister Boson. It bodes ill
for him. Tight ship Mister Boson, tight ship. Understand !* '.

The boson readily agreed and when asked if the boat was ready for
sea, he replied it was and he hoped for his own sake it was.

With the Swedish Naval Control Officers aboard and with their
approval the Captain shouted to let go f'ward let go aft and the
Hopewell ebbed away from the repair yard and sedately slipped into
the river for the short trip to the Kolvsund Naval base.

There, her guns and ammunition were returned and all formalities
completed and the Hopewell's raked bows pushed into the calm seas
of the grey day and rain fell incessantly.

All swayed slightly to the whispering sea as the First Officer
enthusiastically took charge of the navigation for the voyage
northwards to Lysekil.

One of the sailors brought mugs of coffee to the bridge .

The Captain looked disdainfully at the half empty mug and then at the sailor just as the Commodore blustered his way onto the bridge taking the mug from the sailor.

*' Ah just in time. Thank you steward, oh, yes, well how are you managing the galley now our friend Mister Price is away ? I hope he can make it to Lysekil on his own steam, I really do. He makes a really good bacon sandwich '.*

The Captain looked out to sea as the Commodore told him the latest news of the imminent invasion of Europe, news from the Red Cross on the fate of the crew of the Master Standfast.

Both men looked vacantly out to sea.

The sailor, acting steward, brought the Commodore more coffee.

*' Ah thankyou. What the devil ! Half empty !'.*

*' Sorry sir, it was full when I left the galley, gawd it's all bloody go !'.*

The Commodore acknowledged the sailor then slowly turned his gaze to the sea from port to starboard then to the Captain.

*' By the way Captain I saw Lask in Gothenburg, he flew over on the aeroplane that brought the gear box, there was Company business to sort out. Lask has come a long way since he started '.*

The Captain checked the compass, picked up his binoculars and thought back to six months when Lask was  an obscure name involved in the paper work of the Company.

The rain fell as the Hopewell cruised steadily northwards and those on the bridge kept their distance from each other. There was quiet apart from the sounds of the engines, the wind, rain and sea.

With little ceremony the Hopewell arrived in Lysekil.

Stevedores appeared out of the shadows and with little direction they worked with sailors on deck and the derrick crane swung from the fore mast lifting crates from the quay over and  above and down into the hold. The extra cargo was stowed as the rain continued lending to the bleakness of the day. As the stevedores finished they had short conversations with the sailors about cigarettes and alcohol and three or four men came aboard and were shepherded into the accommodation.

Intelligence reports suggested weather conditions favourable for the homeward voyage and much to the relief of all Archie Price sauntered along the quayside escorted by two burly men and with little formality Archie Price was handed over to the custody of the Chief Officer.

Archie looked down at the deck and fidgeted awkwardly as this lion of a man, the Chief Officer, tore into him with verbal abuse which seemed to scare the seagulls.

The Chief Officer seemed to grow in height as Archie seemed to wither into a small, thin wretched soul, until it all stopped.

After a few seconds of silence the Chief Officer resumed his diatribe and he told Archie his discharge book would look worse for wear when he got back .

Archie swayed from side as he saw some of the crew looking on with apparent glee and he talked to himself.

*' Reckon the lads are enjoying this. Sneering bastards. Bunch of pratts. The Chief 's enjoying this. He's enjoying this I can tell, if I answer him back it'll get worse. Just like my old man, 'ow did I get into this, that fella Turnbull conned me. God almighty, hasn't he had enough, yes, yes Chief how can I forget '.*

The mouth of the Chief stopped moving and he stepped aside allowing Archie to scurry away to seek sanctuary in his small galley but he was accosted by a sailor who vented more torment upon the now very wary steward.

*' You bastard Archie Price I 'ad t'do ya bloody job well as me own when ya shacked up with sum lass. What wuz 'er name Inga was it ? Well Inga you'd better watch out for rest of the trip'.*

Archie, grew in size, stood his ground and the sailor left him to his pots and pans.

In his office over looking the southern harbour the German Vice
Consul for Lysekil kept a close watch on the activities on Andersons
Kaj. Through contacts he had learned of the exact nature of the
cargo in the hold of the British boat and its significance. He had very
mixed feelings about his situation which had until the arrival of the
British boats been concerned with commerce and trade that
required documentation and practical diplomacy. He had good
relations with the citizens of Lysekil and on a day to day basis his
social and working life was very pleasant. The war had seemed
distant until the arrival of these British boats, designed to carry the
small but massively important ball bearings to be used in aircraft
production in England. Now he was the first one in a chain that led to
the Headquarters of the Kreigsmarine in Frederkshavn.

The visit of the Hopewell to Gothenburg had caused considerable
embarrassment to German political, military and economic interests.
Never before had he received such direct orders from Naval
Headquarters demanding the exact departure time of the Hopewell.
He'd been ordered to watch out for fugitives, men or women, high on
the Gestapo's wanted list and he had reported what he saw, along
with the crew list and the cargo manifest. Important work, all in
defence of the Father Land. He checked on his diary for routine
consular business for November 30th 1943.

Glancing around the room he noticed that the official picture of the
Fuhrer was hanging askew on the wall and as he looked to the small
British boat alongside the quay he wondered why the British had
declared war on Germany when they had so much in common.

With his business in hand it was time for his appointment with his
Swedish contact who arrived punctually at eleven o'clock. He
touched the picture of the Fuhrer making it hang square with the
room.

His meeting was curt and cordial and through tact he managed to
obtain small items of information which was in proportion to the
amount of Schnapps he poured into the glass of the Swede who
talked liberally, with apparent authority about British intentions.

After the meeting he noticed that the picture of the Fuhrer was hanging, yet again, askew.

He looked out of the window to the harbour.

A few minutes elapsed before he realised there was a vacant berth on Andersonn's Kaj.

The Hopewell had gone.

He picked up the telephone and dialled the number.

As he waited to be connected he questioned the honesty and validity of the information he had been given.

The Commodore made mental reckoning.

So far three Grey Ladies had attempted the mission with one success and one disaster .

Now the Hopewell, a small target on a large sea with engines performing well sailing south , then changing course, due North North West heading between Sweden and Denmark then heading for the Norwegian coast.

Small. Fast. Making good time.

Darkness then blackness with an extra bite to the wind which was sufficient to provoke a rolling swell that began to turn stomachs .

On the bridge standing sentinels, watching, watching, occasionally swiped by ice edged spray they approached the Norwegian coast at 22 – 35 hours.

With menace in his voice the Chief Officer shouted for the steward Archie but the Radio officer replied, his voice just heard above the incessant whine of the engines and the sea.

' *Radar echo Captain, 'bout a mile off the port bow, about a mile off the port bow* '.

The Captain shouted a course change and the helmsman repeated the order as he moved the wheel and the bows swung quickly to starboard.

The bows plunged deep, then rose, plunged deep, then rose up then down as through the racing clouds the moon flashed , illuminating the curling, crested waves.

Stomachs groaned.

Stomachs retched.

From aft the wake spread and curved and the helmsman was oblivious to the danger as the Officers reinforced their hold on the wind dodgers.

' *Four points to port, beautiful move what do you think Commodore ?* ', and the Commodore said the move was just like that of a destroyer and the Captain said the radar blip was possibly a German patrol boat out to blow them out of the sea and with stoic realism he searched the seas through his binoculars.

The Chief Officer, his S.O.E. credentials bristling in his features was responsible for 'fighting the boat ', as he and his ilk liked to say, was about to call for action stations when the calculated stare and gesture from the Captain demanded caution.

The Chief Officer stamped his feet and his S.O.E. credentials relaxed. He then shouted above all other sound for the steward to action stations in the galley, wanting more than just a pound of flesh, he wanted a bacon sandwich and quickly from Archie Price.

Wind whipped up the waves with ominous irregularity as the slender boat plummeted in and out of the seas with all on the bridge exposed, shivering, shaking, cursing and longing to be somewhere else.

' *White rabbits !* ', shouted the helmsman which startled the Officers.

' *What was that ?* ', snarled the Captain.

' *White rabbits Captain* ', answered the helmsman.

' *Mister it's bloody freezing, we're trying to outwit the sea, let alone the Kreigsmarine. White rabbits, what are you thinking about man ?* '.

' *First of the month Captain, allus say White Rabbits on first of the month. First of December, don't know why I say it Captain* '.

' *Aye Mister, first of the month so it is. Are we in wonderland. Would you be Alice and is this the mad hatters party. Now watch your bloody course Mister , watch your bloody course daft sod* '.

The steely eyed expression of the Captain changed into what could be interpreted as a smile but no one was ever sure.

Archie brought coffee to the bridge without spillage and the Chief Officer thanked him which surprised and confused him so much he was quickly away to his galley to make the next course.

The coffee stimulated inconsequential out bursts of conversation and with seas crashing against the hull and over the decks within wind cresting waves of turmoil Archie made several trips to the bridge with relatively warm bacon sandwiches. The Chief Officer watched his every move. He was impressed.

All dodged sudden cascades of spray.

The helmsman struggled with the wheel to keep the course.

' *Did you always want to go to sea ?* ', shouted the Captain to the helmsman.

' *No Captain wanted t'be an engineer* '.

' *Well lad I'd get your name down when we get back at least they have a nice warm fire* '.

A wave crashed the port side knocking the boat violently off course.

Taking turns.

On watch.

Off watch.

On watch.

Attempted sleep.

Gyrating.

Plummeting.

Disturbing.

Briefly disturbed sleep.

Engine room working continuously, with checks and adjustments, wrenches making corrections, bodies covered in grime, oily sweaty breath. Putrid laden air.

Reasonable progress, on course.

Crossing the North Sea as on the horizon a sliver of light began to distinguish sea from sky, night from day and the voice of an alert lookout jarred the fatigue of those on the bridge instantly raised their concentration, scanning the grey, heavy low cloud for aircraft.

Black shapes moving.

Black shapes appeared, increasing in size with every second of deep breathing, deep breathing, deep breathing.

Beaufighters of Coastal Command roared low overhead and were gone.

The dawn became the day.

Cold, wet, windy, with the sun making an occasional appearance as two more Beaufighters appeared again and came down low at a leisurely pace, circling, pilots leaning out of the cockpit waving, then the aircraft climbed and waved their wings, escorting the lone Grey Lady towards home.

The Superintendent, a God fearing man, whose belief had seen him through cataclysmic seas  thought human kind was only part of the greater complexities of life. He believed in a scheme of things in which each man grew in stature by challenging adversity to all degrees and in all manner of situations and with these convictions he knew good from bad and this was reflected by the men who acknowledged him with a respectful nod of his head and others who furtively avoided his look as he walked through the clutter of the busy, non stop, working docks.

From a distance he watched the activities aboard the newly arrived Hopewell, one of the small gun boats converted to carry a cargo of much needed ball bearing from Sweden.

On the bridge he saw the newly promoted Captain and the Chief Engineer and as if by instinct he guessed the substance of their exchange .

The Superintendent was surprised to see Herbert Lask on the quay. He saw some of the crew leave the Hopewell in an agitated manner . Archie Price had had a rough ride during the return voyage from the constant verbal assaults from the crew and a sarcastic Chief Officer. Archie's frustrations boiled over into an uncontrollable rage which sought to get at the man who had persuaded him to volunteer and he shouted his demented rage as he came ashore.

He walked shouting towards Lask who was on the quayside.

*' Where's that man Turnbull, I'll murder 'im,  you seen that bastard Turnbull, conned I was. Nice little number he said. Give me convoy duty anytime compared with them sailors and that Chief Officer '.*

The name of Captain Turnbull struck sensitivities within Herbert Lask and with determination he strode towards the advancing Archie Price.

*' You  Price, Price is it ?, asking for Captain Turnbull are you ?'.*

Lasks voice booming voice startled dockworkers and sailors alike into a silent inertia. Superintendent Watson's curiosity was aroused as he witnessed an apparent radical change in the personality of Herbert Lask whose voice rose to a pitch which silenced even the squarking scavenger seagulls.

*' Asking for Captain Turnbull are you ?'*
The onlookers became transfixed and statuesque as they watched hypnotised.
Archie began to perspire.
He began to shiver. His aggression drained away and the slight frame of Lask grew larger and larger.
Archie muttered he wanted to see Captain Turnbull.
Lask lit a cigarette, inhaled deeply, then blew smoke towards the ominous scudding clouds.
From the skies his eyes calibrated, fixing upon the rapidly diminishing figure of Archie Price.
*' Why do you want to see Captain Turnbull ? '.*
Archie Price stumbled over half words mumbling about the Chief Officer and others who'd given him a hard time. Herbert Lask's eyes narrowed, his lips quivered, his voice echoed, words bounced off wrecks of ships rusting away in the dock.
*' Mister Price, sea a bit rough for you.*
*Had a hard time did you ?*
*Half a city in ruins.*
*Ships sunk.*
*Men lost.*
*Families devastated.*
*You .*
*You.*
*You little bastard.*
*Ought to be ashamed of yourself '.*
Herbert Lask stood large, still and silent, then in almost a whisper said.
*' Well  Archie Price you wont be able to see the Captain '.*
Archie Price looked up nervously, his eyes focused on Lask and he stuttered as he asked why he wouldn't be able to see Captain Turnbull.
Lask breathed in, with eyes penetrating he seemed to grow in size yet again. Touching the nerves of the not to distant Superintendent, Lasks evangelical  shouting reached a crescendo.

*' Why, why why ? . Because while you were gallivanting around Sweden, Captain Turnbull, in pursuit of his duties had an accident, his car hit a lorry. He's dead '.*

Onlookers stared motionless as if no one would break into the silence so fraught and charged until Lask was seen speaking quietly with his arm around Archie.

*' Go home Archie Price, go home, its been a long day, go home Archie Price '*, and the two men turned and walked away from each other.

The sailors and dock workers began to resume their activities around the Hopewell and Archie walked alone, isolated in his own ridicule, shuffling off the quayside to the sanctuary of the darkened buildings.

As he saw his ghostly image reflected in the splintered glass of window frames he began to exorcise the demons that played upon his senses and in his confusion he became aware of the presence of men walking either side of him.

He nervously looked up as a hand came firmly down upon his shoulder.

The gruff, yet quiet conciliatory voice of a recent tormentor spoke direct.

*' Ello Archie, "cum a 'av a pint with us '*

Archie thought of home.

His incessantly grumbling Father.

Constantly worrying Mother.

He nodded in agreement, accepting the invitation to have a pint with the sailors of the Hopewell.

Silently the three men walked quickly.

Eager thirsts to quench.

Doris wasn't one to ask questions, she was no gossip.
But customers talked to her, some revealing their innermost thoughts
from which she learned a great deal and she formed a reasonably
accurate picture of the immediate world outside her world of the bar
and the public house in which she lived and worked.
She heard secrets.
She heard confessions.
Some things heard which needed a pinch of salt.
She knew of the Grey Ladies, ball bearings and of Herbert Lask and
he seemed to have a need to confide in her and she had come to
know him well as he talked of his family, his work and the war.
Doris had been more than surprised when he told her of his
recruitment into the S.O.E. and about his mission to Sweden.
On hearing other confidential confessions she heard with a pinch of
salt but what she heard from others seemed to confirm what Lask
had told her and she needed no salt. As she went pulling pints,
clearing glasses and wiping the bar she wondered about Lask and she
came to the conclusion that he was an unlikely sort of character for
that sort of thing.
Doris had heard of the fate of the Master Standfast and she
wondered how Frankie Hebden was coping with confinement. In the
background the radio played the last verse of a popular song.
' and I know we'll meet again some sunny day '.
She heard talk from sailors sitting in a huddle around a table by the
door, drinking fast, talking loud, cigarette smoke forming a blue hazy
cloud above and she heard about the Hopewell.
She heard about Gothenburg.
She about a girl called Inga.
She heard about big Fritz and when she heard about the sing song
with German sailors she momentarily lost her concentration and
spilled beer over the glass into the trough and she scowled and
frowned but now several sailors needed attention so she smiled.
It seemed the sailors vied with each other to ply Archie with ale as if
they were apologising for their abusiveness and acknowledging his
expertise when performing miracles in the galley during the voyage.

The door of the pub clattered open as a large unshaven, wild haired, bleary eyed, intoxicated, figure of a man crashed into the bar ordering a pint as he stretched and just made the bar.

Doris, looked at the wreck and decided it would be better all round if he had his pint. He leaned, swaying against the bar, looking over his shoulder to the laughter of the sailors in the corner.

Without a word he paid for his pint, his grizzled tongue lapped the contents of his glass as he listened intently to what the sailors talked about.

Suddenly he shouted over to where they sat.

*' You lot, jammy buggers, 'eard you've bin 'aving 'oliday, eh, eh, 'oliday in Sweden, eh, eh, extra pay, jammy buggers, eh, eh, 'aving 'oliday while real men do fighting, eh. All right for sum '.*

He looked away from the stunned sailors.

His grizzeled tongue spat contempt on the floor as his features screwed taut as he shouted.

*' Teks real men t'fight war '.*

Doris suddenly fraught with anger, anxiety and tension instinctively took hold of a short handled club as she shouted at him with intent while brandishing the club.

*' Get out, sling yer hook, go on get out ! '.*

It was to much for Archie Price.

In seconds he was across the floor to the bar.

His right hand clenched into a solid mass of power which swung and smashed into the jaw of the grizzeled tongue whose body immediately collapsed against the bar, glasses shattering over the floor .

Archie suddenly froze.

Stupefied into silence the sailors looked on and then one said to another.

*' Did ya see that ! '*, it wasn't a question.

Another, silently nodded his head as his cigarette burned away to ash between his inert fingers of his left hand.

In the swirling smoke another pointed in disbelief muttering.

*' See that, that punch, I don't believe it, I don't believe it '.*

Another at the table, eyes petrified, put his finger of ash into the remainder of his ale, his lips quivering as he spoke.

*' I must be careful what to say to Archie in future '.*

Doris was angry with herself for allowing such a situation to have developed as she had a reputation of running a well ordered if noisy bar to maintain.

Looking at the slowly moving crumpled figure on the floor she thought he deserved what he got what with Frankie and the lads prisoners in Germany.

Sweeping up the glass she glanced at Archie who stood still, dazed, nursing his hand with his face fraught with shock as if he'd been the one who'd been hit. He asked grizzeled tongue if he was alright and at that moment in walked Lask.

Two able seamen picked grizzelled tongue up as he mumbled an apology to every one as he made his way to the door and then was gone.

Lask surveyed the scene with concern as Doris rapidly explained events . She deposited broken glass into a bin behind the bar and then she served Lask with his usual whisky and for a moment, she forgot herself and poured herself a large gin.

She raised her glass with Lask and toasted safe passage to another Grey Lady which was now sailing down the river Humber to the sea.

On the bridge of the Corsair the Captain ever alert ordered the helmsman to turn to starboard, for a course heading North, North East taking her past Flamborough Head with the wind moderate, fresh and exhilarating as waves crested and broke.

The last of the day was falling to night as the Grey Lady settled into a gentle undulating rhythm with bows cutting through waves with intent of purpose as the last of the dark blue flickers of light disappeared and the engines whined and time passed in monotonous regularity and the wind and sea began to talk to the Chief Officer. He leaned against the wind dodgers, standing perpendicular to the upward, downward motion, his outward calm disguised the inner turmoil as without warning recent recollections of his involvement in military action surfaced making his nerves edgy.

Suddenly his memories were gone as the Captain shouted.

' *Star shells, the navy fired star shells. Why I'll never know, I'll never know* '.

Spray lashed the face of the Chief Officer as he asked the Captain, ' *You'll never know, you'll never know what ?* '.

The Captain leaned backwards and forwards in time to the motion of the boat. He remained perfectly upright as his memories became all to realistic as he described events of not long ago.

' *My last voyage on the Fort St.James in convoy bound for Durban in the middle of the middle watch. Not like this. Different sea. Different ship. Stands to reason. Big boats. Time and space. Suddenly she exploded. Fire ball. Bits flying around. Jagged flames. A few minutes that's all it took. Just a flaming hulk. Another explosion, searing sheets of flame. Rolling blast hits us.*

*White, orange, yellow reflecting off the bulkheads. A gale of hot air scorched us followed by shrieks and screams of poor sods drowning. Five ships. Blackened patches on the sea. The escort fired star shells. We waited our turn to explode. I'll never know why. Star shells* '.

The Captains storm had finished as the Chief Officer realised the Captain was in some kind of trance but now both men scanned the moonless seas searching for anything untoward.

The Captain rocked back and forth, synchronised with the motion of the boat as the bows dipped and heaved, he lit a cigarette with expert ease and he turned to the Chief Officer.

*' Well Chief we've got speed and no one knows we're coming. Just a few drifting mines in the Skagerrak, but with our shallow draft no problems we hope. Soon be there ',* and, as he gave the Chief Officer a slap on the back, he laughed ominously, rubbing his hands, and complaining of the cold he shouted for the steward and shouted for coffee.

The Chief Officer was hungry and as he made his way off the bridge, cold crept through his sea boots and as he glanced at the Vickers machine guns, he shivered.

The Corsair was making good time and good speed for the run through the Skagerrak.

The Captain stared ahead into the darkness.

In Lysekil the German Vice Consul was infuriated when he learned of the arrival of the Corsair and this time he knew he had to make his presence more visible so he quickly walked down to the harbour with a determination in his stride and manner.

He scoffed loudly at the sight of the Red Ensign flying from the small boat.

He knew of the cargo that the Corsair brought into the country.

Oil in drums and he knew of the cargo to be loaded, machine parts and bearings, enough for the production of many aircraft.

And now he was privy to information previously thought too secret for his ears. An underground network was working to facilitate the escape of Norwegian fugitives through Sweden and on to Britain.

He was in possession of a photographic list of the terrorists, saboteurs and murderers. He thought of the possibilities. Maybe the British boats brought arms to Sweden, perhaps agents, the possibilities multiplied, perhaps the stocky uniformed man leaving the Corsair was on the wanted list but he wasn't sure.

As the British Officer walked passed, both men casually acknowledged each other with a nod of the head and the Vice Consul turned and followed at a discreet distance, but soon lost sight of him.

He then retraced his steps and approaching the Corsair he heard some British sailors shouting obscenities towards an approaching coaster flying the German ensign.

He walked towards the quay where the German coaster was to berth and he exchanged pleasantries with sailors as they made fast their boat. He did that in Swedish as here it was only a war of words.

The gangway was clanked into place from boat to quay and he made his way aboard with greetings and handshakes from the crew to the cabin of the Captain of S.S. Osterburg, and with great enthusiasm both men enjoyed a noisy celebration of German schnapps.

The Vice Consul asked about the real situation and the Kapitan told him of the constant bombing by the British and Americans and with every glass of Schnapps he swallowed his anger increased until it turned to laughter with irony at the fact that he was alive and well and in Sweden.

The Vice Consuls speech faltered as he reminded the Kapitan of Swedish neutrality and the strict formalities to be adhered to especially with the small British boat laying only a short distance away .

The Kapitan listened with feigned interest as he heard how his men would be catered for in the Stadshotel but on a different floor to the British and he warned of repercussions if any hostilities should break out.

The Kapitan finished his drink and laughed.

He laughed and laughed until tears ran down his ruddy sea beaten face.

He understood.

He told of Hamburg.

But here in Sweden there was peace and the Kapitan told the Vice consul in emphatic terms that his crew would be on their very best behaviour when ashore.

Then he smiled, winked, laughed a hearty laugh and poured a generous measure, they clinked their glasses and enjoyed a civilized conversation which would last as long as the Kapitan kept pouring the drinks.

Quietly, the Corsair sailed out of the harbour and the Swedish pilot readied himself and when the seas and the moment were right he jumped to the pilot cutter sailing abreast and as the smaller boat turned away from the Corsair the pilot waved good luck with a ' V' sign.

The seas darkened and the Chief Officer wondered about the 'V' sign but then it was the eve of Christmas, dark with a keen wind and his thoughts were taken over by the seas and the recent past. During his mission ashore he'd successfully used his skills of deception and subterfuge in a quiet and deft way and he was thankful his activities had taken place in neutral territory. His energy and nerve had been dented by his recent past when gun, grenade and knife had been his tools while working behind enemy lines. His leg shot up, but not quite the invalid and not one for a desk job, so he'd jumped at the chance to be part of this Merchant Navy operation. His mission ashore was to bring eight highly dangerous Norwegians who'd escaped to Sweden down to Lysekil and into the compact and relative safety of the cramped quarters of the Corsair.

The concentration of the Helmsman was broken suddenly when the Captain spoke to him.

' Arthur, do any Christmas shopping in Lysekil ?'.

' Aye Captain, the missis gave me a list. Tell you what the Swedes 'avn't alf been generous, lots of presents, from Lapland , for Christmas , eh Captain ', and both men laughed as the seas suddenly crashed over the bows. The Captain and the Chief Officer grabbed hold of the wind dodgers and hung on until the boat settled into a regular rhythm and then the Captain spoke with a serious edge to his voice.

' Arthur don't tempt providence, war doesn't stop for Christmas '.

Most of the crews could only guess about the Chief Officers backgrounds and so they kept a respectful distance and manner in their dealings with these gentlemen as they had ways about them which suggested shooting pheasants and drinking fine wine but then in other ways which showed decisive and ruthlessness. But the Captain's curiosity got the better of him and he ventured a cautious question about the Chief Officers on shore activities.

Chief Officer was only to eager for conversation and he explained that the newly arrived Norwegians were wanted by the Gestapo for a variety of reasons including sabotage and assassination and they were highly valued for their expertise.

*' It was more expedient for these gentlemen to escape via Sweden. Other Norwegians regularly use what is called 'The Shettland Bus '.*
The helmsman straining to hear what was being said picked up a morsel or two and the Captain was captivated by the side of war he only read about.

*' The Shetland Bus, fishing boats, sailing from various points to Lunna on the Shetland Isles. Reasonably successful I hear. Heard of a Norwegian who'd escaped to England, joined the R.A.F. as a pilot and when on leave uses the Shetland Bus to go and see his family in Norway. Just think of that eh ! '.*
The Captain shook his head in disbelief as the Corsair shuddered and lurched a wave broke over the starboard bow sending spray cascading over the decks and superstructure, lashing the faces of all on the bridge . In the forward accommodation impassive Norwegian faces with lines etched deep around sunken eyes that stared into the distance occasionally twitching and blinking dark images of their recent secret past.

In the darkness of the improvised radio shack , Sparks puked into a bucket, then washed his mouth out with lime cordial as the revolving line on the small radar screen rotated, bleeped , revealing two ships to starboard.

He reported them to the bridge.

He puked again and spat into the bucket.

The two blips receded.

The wind grew in force.

On the bridge conversation was impossible.

A huge wave violently knocked the Corsair to port.

As the vessel fell shuddering into a deep trough sailors, with thoughts of torpedoes, scrambled for hand holds. One screamed his despair.

*' What the 'ells skipper up to, thought 'e knew a thing or two 'bout sea. I've bad feelings '.*

Sailor and Boson grabbed stanchions, pulled themselves up from the angled deck as sea and wind lashed the deck and they hauled themselves to the accommodation.

The Boson scowled as he attempted to light a sodden stub of a cigarette and his voice narked, and sharp cut straight into the sailor.

*' Cap'n knows more than yer'll ever know an 'e's only a lad 'imself '.*

But the sailor wasn't impressed.

*' Maybe 'e does maybe 'e doesn't. I ran away to sea when I wuz fourteen. South Wales coaling ships. Coffin ships they called them. Christ its bloody cold. My turn on the wheel now. Bluddy 'ell '.*

He took a deep breath and climbed out onto the deck and up the ladder to the bridge to take his turn on the wheel.

The Kommodore needed to be on his own, but he managed to sum up a festive expression of convivial smiles, announcing to his guests Yule tide greetings. The telephone rang to the rescue and duty called. He made individual apologies and made a respectful exit.

At headquarters he surprised the duty staff who were enjoying their own Christmas celebrations but he hardly noticed as he made his way to his office.

He switched on the light.

Threw his coat on a chair and from bottle to glass poured schnapps and through the large window looked out over the night activity of the harbour and out to the expanse of the blue black sea.

Time was still as he stared, sipping slowly from his glass.

Minutes passed, then he browsed through papers on his desk.

Supplies. Assignments. Requisitions. Sailing orders. Intelligence reports.

Ships on station, on patrol, ready to intercept the small British boat, the Corsair. But he thought that if the Corsair evaded his patrols and surviving the inclement weather and with luck they would be half way home. Reports suggested more small boats would attempt to break the blockade of Sweden and Berlin was impatient to stop these supplies of ball bearings, small through they were, from getting through, as every cargo meant an increase in allied military production.

What could he do. Shrimps in an ocean.

His Kapitans were first class. They had spread their nets wide.

His friends in the Swedish Admiralty gave assistance of a covert nature and formal diplomatic procedures were enacted to conform to conventions of neutrality. The Kommodore smiled to himself as he put his cap on and stretched into his coat. From a side cabinet he took four large bottles and gathered them in his arms and as he walked through the outer offices the on duty staff came to attention. He placed the bottles down on a table and gestured them to make merry.With a smile of bravado he was gone. It was 10 p.m. when he entered his house and was relieved the party was still going on.

He mixed with guests, small talk, family, ships and the sea.

*' Prosit Her Kommodore '.*

*' Prosit '.*

Glasses clinked seasonal goodwill.

Now, Kommodore Hans Schector began to enjoy himself with his wife and Rudiger and family. Kreigsmarine Officers from his Command clinked glasses and laughed. A few children scampered under tables playing games, their innocence touched by the military toys and the nature of their play. The smaller children were the enemy while the older ones enacted victorious German forces.

All feasted well.

But for the Kommodore and his wife Christmas would never be the same as there was a vacant place at the dinner table and the more their guests enjoyed themselves the more difficult it was for them to hide their anguish.

Their son.

Missing.

His wife busied herself with her hostess duties, occasionally glancing with concern at her husband as he without conviction spoke small talk with a couple of submariners.

But more brandy, more schnapps multiplied his anxiety lines.

Festivities ebbed towards a musical evening as the air became thick with cigar smoke and conversations began to fade, subdued by piano music played by the delicate fingers of his wife, and slowly, very slowly, the guests paid their respects and departed.

She looked towards him.

They were alone.

Black
White
Yellow
Putrid smoke, shouting, flashing lights and commotion, the bows of
the Master Standfast crashed deep into rolling seas, soldiers shouted,
all tried to avoid the gunfire and the lash of the sea. Frankie
trembled, sweat poured from his brow and in his half sleep seas built
up for another onslaught.
Then the train jolted.
He shivered, blinking into consciousness the guards seated at the end
of the dimly lit carriage appeared with rifles slumped over their
knees. As he wiped grime from the window he could see the
countryside was full of grey rain and ominous.
Frankie talked aloud to himself, realising this brought attention to
himself  stopped and corresponded silently with his wife.
*' Ow long*
*Seems ages*
*Not long though*
*Tom said I wuz an angel at sea, a bastard ashore*
*Must be true*
*Thought I wuz for the chop when that big guard called me number*
*Don't tell ya owt just shove ya about and shout*
*God they like shouting*
*Going north I reckon*
*Thinking 'bout christmas an all*
*Never liked christmas*
*Miss it all I can tell ya*
*Sum of the prisoners are in a disgusting state*
*Meks me think*
*You call me disgusting enough*
*Suppose I am*
*Give anything t'be at 'ome listening t'radio*
*Just two of us*
*Roaring fire*
*Jug  of ale*

*Think I'll be away a long time .*
*The Superintendent will see ya get ya money*
*Doesn't like me, the Superintendent.*
*Mind you never liked the bloke meself*
*Toms with us somewhere*
*Allus looks after us*
*Bloody 'ungry*
*Gawd its black outside*
*' Eard Nazis rite bastards to Jews*
*Families rounded up*
*Shoved in railway wagons*
*Shunted off t' God knows where*
*Bloody fool t'be taken in by that man Lask*
*Volunteer he said, piece a cake he said*
*Could be 'ome*
*Pitch black*
*Could do with a pint don't think'about it*
*' Ere comes that guard mean looking bastard*
*Thank God*
*Thank God 'e's passed*
*Slowing down, trains slowing down all mixed up different languages*
*Reckon allus loved ya*
*Never thought of that before*
*If ya could 'ear me now you'd laugh ya 'ead off*
*Slowing down, clanking, screeching to a halt*
*Summuts up*
*Must be air raid*
*Remember 'em, May forty one, in shelter when bombers came, ya were just great, getting on with things as if nothing wuz 'appening, marvellous.*
*See if I can see 'owt through window*
*Search lights*
*Air raid, boots on other foot now.*

*Can 'ear rumble poor bastards under that lot*
*Trains moving*
*All clear .*
*Tired can't sleep must sleep*
*Don't forget t'put the cat out*
*Two pints of bitter Doris and one f'yer sen*
*'Ow are ya coping, I know, I know I owe ya two pound seven shillings*
*and sixpence.*
*No bloody joke*
*Bad dream*
*Food diabolical*
*Least its warm*
*One bloke with us been 'ere since nineteen forty*
*Lost all hope*
*Getting colder*
*Thinking of escaping*
*Impossible I don't know*
*Must 'av been an air raid Frankfurt 'cause one of the guards cums*
*from there, 'an 'e didn't 'alf knock 'ell out of a couple of our lads*
*Must be midnight*
*Guards changing*
*Good talking t'ya*
*Bad dream*
*Better at sea*
*Open bridge*
*Force ten gale I can tell ya, I can tell ya, I can tell ya.*

Dark, flashing jagged white crested waves undulating as the Corsair dipped, swerved and sliced through the long swell seas and for the helmsman hot tea had become an extreme desire that knotted and turned his stomach.

Lashing spray made him shiver.

A stretched line appeared on the horizon as the Captain offered a cigarette to the sailor on the wheel who nodded his appreciation at the unusual informality of the Captains gesture.

The Captain breathed deeply and from the bridge wing shouted with startling force down to the galley .

' *Steward, steward are you still with us ? '.*

' *Aye aye Cap'n '*, answered the steward.

' *When you've some spare time, bacon sandwiches, tea, coffee all round if that is not to much trouble, do you hear me ? '.*

The Captain, the Chief Officer and the helmsman waited for an answer which seemed to be a long time coming, and when it did they all smiled as if they had all won a victory.

' *I 'ear ya Cap'n, no trouble at all, coming up in a jiffy '.*

The Captain resumed his vigil pacing the bridge, swaying from port to starboard, starboard to port. The seas moderated as if resting and the cold morning brought the Norwegians and the rest of the crew out onto the deck. The steward started to bring the tea, coffee, and then the smell of bacon sandwiches provoked an uncontrollable demand from all and the steward knew he'd be working non stop now until all were satisfied.

' *Eh do ya think Germans have sensitive noses ? '*, asked one sailor.

' *Why ? '.*

' *Cos if they smell that bacon ! '.*

' *So if the Germans turn up I know I've won the war with bacon sandwiches '*, said the very jovial steward, cook , chef and gunner.

The Captain well pleased with his fill left the bridge, called into his cabin and came onto the deck with a couple of bottles of rum with which he liberally laced the tea and coffee of every man.

*' Morning, morning lads been in worse places than the middle of the North Sea on Christmas day, but never on a boat so small. Warm the cockles, get it down ya. Look out for the R.A.F. A bottle of rum to the first one to spot them '.*

The sailors and the Norwegian passengers talked easily together and drank with cautious relief as the Chief Engineer appeared on deck taking his rum with a dash of tea and toasting the day.

The engines spluttered and seemed to sigh with resignation then fell into an almost unnatural silence as she meekly allowed herself to be tethered to the quayside as the crew quickly deserted her leaving her to the mercy of the shore gang who quickly went about their business unloading the precious cargo from the Corsair in the Albert Dock.

The Commodore lit his pipe, smiled inwardly to himself, thinking that all things considered the operation was going reasonably well.

From the other base at Immingham the Hopewell and the Viking
sailed out into the broad estuary into a curtain of rain misted, rolling
sea.

With flags taken down and stowed away the wake of the Viking
churned and bubbled as the coast line of East Yorkshire gradually
disappeared and those on the bridge found shelter as best they could
as spray broke over the bows sweeping the deck and bridge.

The sea, hungry, seethed and snapped and whipped with a vicious
threatening regularity and with little inclination for conversation
each man lingered in the warm glow of yesterday's memories.

Reality and drudgery hadn't dampened the Christmas spirit and
Captain Stokes had been with his friend Captain Jackson and his
family and he still savoured the after taste of the dinner of the
chicken which two days earlier had been swarking and scratching at
the bottom of the garden.

Roast chicken, roast potatoes, vegetables, Christmas pudding, mince
pies, good conversation, a good drink and an evening around the
upright piano singing songs with infectious jollity.

The Captain laughed to himself as he recalled the high pitched whine
when everybody stopped singing, anticipating the explosion of a
bomb, until someone realised that the family dog had joined in the
singing and was whining away.

Wind turned to sleet and sleet turned to snow and those on the bridge
took refuge behind wind dodgers but there was no real escape.

In spite of the deteriorating weather conditions the Hopewell made
steady progress through the night.

Yesterday Archie Price, the steward, had worked hard at his
Christmas using his skills to make a little go a long way and he'd
delighted his Mother who'd put her feet up and even his father had
given up grumbling, even hinted at gratitude, when he smiled once,
poured himself a brown ale and wished Archie all the best.

Now aboard the Hopewell Archie had brewed coffee and made a
determined effort to deliver four steaming pots to those on the bridge
without spillage. The Chief Officer looked intently at Archie.

*' Good man Archie, thankyou. Did you have a good christmas ?'.*

To this Archie wasn't sure how to respond to the man who had tried
to make his life a misery on the last trip but he said he had a bit of a
jolly with his folks and left it like that.

Gone was the smirk, a prelude to verbal assault, replaced now with
an almost affable expression as the Chief spoke.

*' I hear you've been defending the honour of our men in the bars
around Hull. Well done Archie. When we get to Sweden try not to go
missing. Good man Archie, good man '.*

The Chief wasn't expecting a reply as he gave a quick smile and a
dismissive nod of his head.

Back in the galley Archie was bemused.

One act of physical anger that had landed on the cheek of Grizzeled
tongue had travelled by word and mouth in such a short space of
time and had changed him from one person to another.

The sounds of the engines changed abruptly, the vessel lurched from
port to starboard and flying pans clattered around him.

Those on the bridge looked apprehensively at each other .

They strained to translate the sudden change of engine pitch against
the incessant cacophony of wind and sea.

The bows swung erratically to port.

The Captain shouted to starboard to starboard.

The helmsman struggled but there was no response from the wheel .

The Chief blew down the voice pipe shouting.

*' Steering no response. Bobbing around liker a bloody cork '.*

He listened.

The staccato response of the Chief Engineer described the problems.

*' Steering. Centre engine air locks fuel supply working on it. Almost
fixed ',* and he sighed and he grunted.

The Hopewell heaved and lurched as waves shattered over decks as
the Captain swore and sighed with momentary resignation all in the
same breath.

The engineers fixed the steering.

The fuel blockage was cleared.

The Captain ordered the helmsman to keep her steady.

Then the bows took the sea and in the chart room the First Officer
was making calculations of position and drift when a surge of power
threw him and his navigation instruments against the bulkhead.
The engineers had done their job far to well for the First Officer who
lay inert and concussed.
In the galley the change in engine pitch alerted Archie Price and he
swore at the coffee urn which he called ' bastard' as it spewed
steaming coffee into waiting pint pots and when they were full he
calculated balance and weight distribution and then he navigated his
course up to the bridge. The Chief Officer eagerly took hold of his
steaming pot. ' *Took your bloody time, least its warm* '.
Archie realised that nothing really changes.
Now the bows of the Hopewell cut into the surging seas with the
Viking keeping station three cables behind on the southern side of the
Skagerrak twenty five miles off the Danish coast.
The Radio Officer reported blips.
The Captain and the Chief Officer crowded the small room peering
at the small circular screen, watching the revolving line of light which
had picked up a significant blip heading towards them and as they
approached the Skaw more blips appeared on the screen.
Back on the bridge the Captain ordered a course change to the North
East heading towards the Vaderbod navigation light in Swedish
waters.
Aboard the Gay Viking Captain Whitfield followed the wake of the
Hopewell into Swedish waters as they cruised southwards towards
Lysekel.
Just before 0400hrs the six foot six frame of Shorty Burton took over
the wheel and as he reported the course to the Captain the Captain
turned and looked at him suspiciously.
' *Shorty were you with us on the last trip ?*'.
The tall, lanky figure of Shorty Burton, happy to have been
recognised, slouched over the wheel as he answered the Captain.
' *That's rite Cap'n been with you since we started this 'er lark.*
*Caledonian Canal, remember that Home guard fella at Inverness, and,*
*and at Holyhead, Frankie Hebden really pissed he wuz, disgusting .'*

*Then on last trip when we flew German flag, told 'our lass 'bout that,
'ad a rite good laugh. '*
The Captain considered what he heard, wondered about him and
asked.
*' Tell me Shorty why doesn't anybody seem to see you around ?'.*
*' Dunno Cap'n allus the same, nobody seems to notice me '.*
The Captain shook his head saying.
*' Can't think why Shorty there's enough of you '.*
Captain Harry Whitfield began to realise that Shorty Burton
presented himself as one of lifes puzzles for which he couldn't find an
easy answer.
*' Shorty is it true that you can get hold of anything ?'.*
*' Depends Cap'n, depends on what ya want '.*
*' Just curious Shorty, just curious '.*
*' Cap'n remember Doctors plates, in Weymouth ?'.*
*' Thought that wuz Frankie Hebden'*, answered the Captain.
*' It wuz Cap'n, it wuz, but it put the police off the egg rustling , eh '.*
*' Shorty you the egg rustler ?'*, asked the Captain who was enthralled
and mystified by these revelations.
*' Lets put it this way Cap'n a lot of people suddenly had eggs to eat '.*
Captain Harry Whitfield turned to the sea, smiled shook his head ,
thinking that ingenuity emerges from the most unlikely characters in
the most unlikely situations.
*' Cap'n shame 'bout Cap'n Turnbull, nice fella, 'eard 'e crashed is car
into an ammo lorry, probably pissed poor old sod '.*
The Captain was taken aback by the familiarity, *' I take it you knew
him well ?'.*
*' Worked with 'im now and then '.*
*' Did you, well that explains a lot Shorty that explains a lot '.*
Both men looked up into the low, dark, slow moving clouds thinking
about Captain Turnbull going about his business, circumnavigating
officialdom in ways that only he knew how and as the dark clouds
merged he was gone. Captain Whitfield yawned, shaking his head
fighting off tiredness, he looked at his watch and reckoned they
would arrive in Lysekil around half  past five .

The German Vice Consul yawned, shaking off lingering cluttered images of sleep as he walked with cup and saucer in hand into his office. He put the cup and saucer down on his desk and drew the curtains revealing the dark blue of early morning which partially illuminated the room.

He looked at the clock as if to reassure himself that life on the 28th December 1943 was beginning on time.

At 7 -15 a.m. down on Andersonns Kaj he saw shadows of men positioning crane hoists over the decks of two new arrivals, two more Grey Ladies.

With irritated resignation he sighed.

He turned his back on the window and slumped into his chair, sipping lukewarm coffee he thought of the news he'd heard.

Scharnhurst, the battle cruiser sunk.

Bombing of Leipzig, Emden, Berlin and Frankfurt.

What next ?

His office had been augmented by four burly men who had travelled from the Stockholm Embassy.

Their papers informed him of their status and their purpose. Consular Officials, all legal and above board. They didn't say much but he was in no doubt about their true profession and their immediate concern was working on ways of keeping the Hopewell and the Gay Viking in port indefinitely through a legal and diplomatic framework. Later in the morning he would introduce them to sympathetic officers of the Swedish Navy.

From out of the feint misty shadows, buildings began to take form and Lysekil emerged with a crisp breeze blowing white clouds from West to East. The arrival of the Grey Ladies was a significant attraction and only occasional rain squalls would send curious men, women and children scurrying for cover as they walked the quayside inspecting the small British boats.

Most of the time the Konditori was an extension of the commercial marine offices of Lysekil and it was here that the newly arrived German Consular Officials began their plans to keep the two British boats tied up indefinitely.

A young Swedish Naval Officer wearing civilian clothes entered and exchanged civilities with the two German officials.

He sat down as coffee and pastries were ordered and their conversation began to lay foundations for their task in hand as information was exchanged.

The Germans sought to assure themselves, looking for a sign, a signal, a gesture and from the waitress more coffee and pastries were ordered.

One of the Germans placed an envelope on the table and the Swedish Officer did the same and then the two envelopes were exchanged.

For a few moments both parties examined the contents of their respective envelopes and then looked at each other with expressions of satisfaction.

Finishing their coffee they concluded their business with a conversation about oil, fish and steel.

Aboard the Viking the Chief Officer had inspected the vessel for sea damage and had little to do but watch the outward cargo being loaded. From the bridge he studied the town and the Church which sat upon a hill and he decided that if time allowed he would make a visit. From the Church his eyes casually glanced around the harbour to where a Swedish Corvette was moored some distance away.

A uniformed figure left the Corvette and walked towards the Viking and as he reached the gangplank he stopped taking a sheaf of papers out oh his briefcase quite unaware that the Chief Officer of the Viking was watching his every move.

In the radio room the Sparks leant back in his chair, feet up on the transmission desk, rolling one cigarette after another, tossing them into a cardboard box. After making five cigarettes he would smoke one while taking gulps of rum from a glass which he regularly filled from a half empty bottle.

He listened to the signals coming from the receiver. Mostly Swedish traffic. He turned the dial, changed frequencies, occasionally picking up German transmissions. He caught the flow of something which was about the deployment of destroyers in the Skagerrak, then static obliterated the flow. Hearing footsteps above on the bridge he swiftly placed the bottle and glass out of sight as the hatch above his head opened dazzling him with piercing light as the Chief Officer called down.

*' Sparks, room for two more down there, we have a Swedish Naval Officer with orders to seal up the equipment. Don't ask me why ? It's all official '.*

Sparks acknowledged with a grunt and moved out of the way to make space as the Chief and the Swedish officer climbed down. The Sparks looked on, chewing the end of his cigarette as the Swedish Officer placed a locking device over the transmission switch adding a final touch with sealing wax which he heated from his cigarette lighter. With this done he left without a word.

Sparks returned to his chair, retrieving his bottle, filling his glass and putting his feet up, he resumed his lonely vigil.

Now on deck the Chief Officer exchanged pleasantries with the Swedish Officer then watched him make his way off the boat walking the short distance to apply his sealing wax to the radio equipment of the Hopewell.

The Chief Officer climbed down to the after deck and entered the galley where the boson was making tea and without a word the Chief accepted a pint mug and as he drank he tried to ascertain the motives behind the Swedish manoeuvres.

Suddenly his taste buds became aware of the liquid he was drinking. He coughed.

He spat on the deck.

The boson casually looked up, eyes twinkling with mockery said,
' *My speciality Chief, it's the way I mek it '.*

The Chief Officer growled as he surrendered his pint pot and suddenly he realised just how important the steward was to his well being.

Though the transmission unit was sealed up the radio still received enough signals for the Sparks to hear the latest prevailing weather conditions in the Skagerrak. He rolled another cigarette and wondered how his mate Shorty Burton was getting on with his mission ashore.

On the Hopewell the Commodore appeared on the bridge furiously puffing away on his pipe with Captain Stokes and Captain Whitfield in attendance assuming attentive positions leaning against the wind dodgers.

The Commodore looked skywards.

' *Gentlemen it is now the 29th December. The engineers tell me the diesels of the Hopewell are well and truly......need a good deal of repairs which will take time. Mister Whitfield you can take the Gay Viking as soon as she is loaded, but the weather reports gales so you'll be here for a while as well. The weather seems to be in league with the Germans at the moment and they have exerted pressure accounting for the visit of the Swedish Naval Officer and his sealing wax. I'll be having dinner with the Magistrate later, so I'll see what he can do '.*

The Magistrate of Lysekil greeted the Commodore with formal
courtesy and over a dinner of poached herring the two men talked of
the ties between the two countries and the Magistrate spoke at length
of Sweden's long history of conquest and of a warrier named Russ
who planted his names in the lands to the east.

But now he emphasised that now Sweden trod a fine line, balancing
national interests between the changing fortunes and situations of the
warring parties outside its frontiers.

The Commodore diplomatically brought to the attention of the
Magistrate the Swedish Naval Officers enforcement of regulations
concerning radio transmission equipment on his boats, implying it
was unnecessary harassment .

The Magistrate explained how he interpreted the law in individual
situations and how his own sympathies tended to shape the nature of
the requirements to be enforced.

The Commodore understood, was pleased and he could ask for no
more especially after such a sumptuous dinner.

The Magistrates wife entered with a small tray of chocolate liquors
and the evening came to a relaxed and respectful conclusion.

No matter how he tried the German Vice Consul couldn't solve the problem of the framed picture of the Fuhrer on the wall opposite to where he sat. It hung at an angle out of alignment with his room and he thought he would employ a carpenter to fix Adolf Hitler at right angles but it was only a diversionary thought as his four additional consular staff discussed strategies.

His routine had been interrupted and he was irritated as two of them stood by his desk smoking cigarettes and sipping coffee while the other two walked around the office occasionally glancing through the windows towards Andersons Kaj where the British boats lay.

They agreed that their Swedish friends had been successful and their interference had caused unease and tension for the British aboard but they had been ordered to create more damaging action and limpit mines with timers attached to the boats while they were still in harbour was discussed as a possibility.

The prevailing consensus was to harass the British out of Lysekil and to have the Hopewell and the Viking move north to the Fjord at Brofjoren and keep them trapped alongside the two Norwegian merchant ships that had been interned.

The Vice Consul knew that the Norwegian ships were been used as a staging post for Norwegian terrorists on the run from the Gestapo so to keep the British penned up during the remaining long nights of winter would serve German interests and deprive the British of their supplies of ballbearings.

The Consular Officials agreed to approach their Swedish friends once more.

The Vice Consul was surprised to learn that one of their Swedish agents , a young women who had befriended one of the crew of the Grey Ladies when it was in Gothenburg had  been brought up to Lysekil with the intention of continuing the liason to elicit more information.

The Vice Consul rose from his chair and opened the window to clear the tobacco fumes from the room.

Wearing a maroon coat, a dark blue scarf and walking in low heeled
shoes she walked up the stairs of the Stadshotel carrying a dark
brown suitcase in her black gloved hand.

Archie was shocked, but sure, and he followed her quickly, catching
up with her as she reached the first landing.

' Inga, what are you doing here ? '.

The small dainty figure stopped turned and her rounded face broke
into a knowing smile as she spoke.

' I came to be with you. You happy to see me ? '.

' Inga, 'course I am, give us a kiss luv, but I don't understand 'ow did
ya know I wuz 'ear '.

She didn't answer as she continued walking up the stairs with Archie
eagerly following, happy, yet confused and as she reached the door of
her room she turned and kissed him on the cheek.

' Archie you come in we be together for a little time '.

The crisp white sheets felt good and as he stroked her slender supple
legs, time and the world seemed to stop as he lost and found himself,
entwined in a beauty he had never known before and when their love
was spent they lay half sleeping.

It was dark when he awoke.

He wondered if he had been dreaming.

Reality dawned.

He was alone.

Fearfully he eyed the suitcase on the chair by the window.

With a start he sat up.

The door opened and he relaxed as Inga came in with coffee and
bread upon a tray.

' Goddag Archie we eat a little, I tell you things '.

He watched as she poured the coffee with a delicate femininity that
aroused his passions again. The coffee could wait. Suddenly he
remembered he must be aboard the boat or face the wrath of the
Chief Officer again, but as he looked at Inga he thought he could
take whatever wrath the Chief Officer could throw at him.

She declined his overtures and he was perplexed, taken aback,
puzzled.

*' Jag alskar dig Archie, remember I love you, but I 'av to tell you things, trust me please '.*

Archie saw she was quietly crying, tears slowly meandering down her cheeks.

*' In Goteburg, my meeting with you was arranged. Germans ask me to meet British sailor from Grey Lady boat. They give me kroner. I have father who is ill. Kroner help for medicine. They ask me to find things about the boats. Father is ill, so I take kroner, I do as they ask '.*

As the words registered Archie was taken aback, felt betrayed, used and the love he had felt only minutes before swirled around touching upon hate and then the sea, the sea called him.

He laughed loudly.

He laughed bitterly.

*' You little sod, you're a bluddy German agent, at 'ome they told me 'bout you lot. Jesus Christ ! Would 'appen t'me !'.*

She threw herself onto him and with great determination she pinned him down.

*' I did it for my father. Kroner helps, but I fell in love with you, believe me, dur ar mitt libbaotnos min sockerdoccka '.*

His anger and confusion eased and though bewildered he kissed her.

*' What the bloody 'ell does sockerdacka mean, never mind, I get the drift, I think '.*

His words lingered between cynicism, humour, hope and belief as her eyes pleaded for understanding.

*' Jesus Inga I don't know anything I'm only a bluddy steward and 'ere I am shacked up with a German agent. There's a war going on out there. People get killed. I cook the food on that bluddy boat. Why choose me. I know nowt. Never thought mission was important anyway. I believe you, can't think why, but I do. What 'appens now ?'.*

Tears crept down her cheeks dripping onto her lips and Archie tasted their sweetness.

*' Germans contact me here, ask me questions, I tell them things '.*

*' Inga what can you tell them ? I don't know anything except we'll be in Lysekil until the weather changes and then we'll be away '.*

*' Archie I will tell them story '.*

Quietly laughing, he sighed staring at the white walls of the sparton room.

*' Inga I've got to get back t'the boat. Everything will be alright, I'll get back t'you as soon as I can '.*

He gave her a long lingering kiss and wondered if all this was a dream, a nightmare, but as he closed the door behind him he settled for reality. He hurried out of the Stadshotel and as he quickly made his way back to the boat he knew he must tell the Chief Officer.

On the Hopewell Archie climbed the bridge and there the Commodore, Captain, Chief Officer and a Swedish Officer were in tense conversation. Trying not to look inconspicuous he nervously awaited for an opportune moment.

The Commodore spoke angrily to the Swedish Naval Officer.

*' The entire set. Oh no !, who ordered this, the Magistrate ?, I think not !'.*

The Swedish Officer anxiously consulted his papers.

Catching sight of Archie hovering on the side of the bridge the Chief Officer gave him a long questioning look as the Commodore continued his tirade towards the Swedish Officer.

*' Its all very well Lieutenant, we've complied with all the regulations and requests and you have no authority to remove the entire set . Seems to me you just want to remove the whole set just to make life difficult. Well we'll see '.*

The Swedish Officer began to quiver as he took a defensive backwards step stuttering a reply.

*' C, commodore, do you think a simple unintelligent Naval Officer could be involved in espionage ?'.*

The Commodore's eyes bore down on him with an expression of aggressive resignation.

*' Well Lieutenant you have a very good command of English, I do compliment you '.*

The Commodore brought a studious silence to the proceedings as he slowly glanced around the harbour fixing his eye upon a particular building on the Hamngaten. He had a feeling he was being watched.

*' With great respect to Sweden and the Swedish Navy I do know that Count Joseph Matthies wouldn't have sanctioned such actions '.*
The words of the Commodore had their desired effect and the Swedish Naval Lieutenant flinched as the name registered .
He saluted the Commodore, the Captain and the Chief Officer then briskly turned and made his way off the boat.
Captain Stokes yawned and scratched his wiry beard asking who exactly was Count Joseph Matthies and the Commodore said that he was the Swedish Naval Attache in London and a personal friend.
The Captain turned away and looked towards what he could understand, the sea.
The Chief Officer looked quizzically at Archie Price who had tried to blend into the background as if he were part of the equipment and slowly, very slowly the Chief Officer moved towards him, suddenly asking him in short, sharp tones, what the devil was he doing on the bridge.
Archie shivered.
He hesitatingly told of his predicament.
The Chief listened with a detached air of authority, yet when he heard of the emotions that Archie felt for the Swedish girl he felt a tinge of envy, almost jealousy towards the steward who had encountered a side of life which he, though worldly wise had never encountered. As he listened to Archie he recalled his lonely trip ashore in Gothenburg before Christmas when he yearned for company but had to make do with an excellent, silent, dinner alone, and as the waves collided out to sea the security of the mission came back into focus.
*' Right Archie I'll have to meet this young lady of yours at a suitable time and a suitable place. As we're here for a while, Sunday, Church, yes, sometime after Church, and if you don't know where the Church is look up on the hill and you'll see the spire with a cross on the top '.*
Archie looked down to the deck shaking his head, taking it all in.
The Chief was hungry.
*' All rite Archie that'll be all for now, not a word now to anyone. As for the present, you can make me a bacon sandwich '.*

Archie Price left the bridge to carry out his culinary mission and the Chief paced the bridge thinking how to use the Swedish women to the advantage of the mission but his thoughts were partially interrupted by the sight of the illusive seaman Shorty Burton who was boarding the Gay Viking. All in place . Almost.

On the Gay Viking the Radio Officer quickly hid the bottle and the glass when he heard footsteps above him on the bridge.

He was relieved when he heard the voice of Shorty Burton.

*' Alright Sparky  only me '.*

*' Wuz wondering where you'd got to '.*

The elongated figure of the able seaman swung into the small cabin in a flurry of spindly legs and awkward arms.

*' Ow did ya get on Shorty ? '*, asked the Radio Officer.

*' Two dozen bottles '.*

*' What did  he want ?'.*

*' Pounds '.*

*' Pounds '.*

*' Hedging his bets then what's the stuff  ? '.*

*' Schnapps  ! '.*

*' Schnapps ? '.*

*' Schnapps, says it fell off the back off a German supply train on its way through Sweden to Norway, says we can 'av as much as we want '.*

*' Price ? '.*

*' Six for a pound , easily get rid of , 'av t' move fast as Viking and Hopewell are moving to a Fjord north of 'ere '.*

The Radio Officer put his hand in his pocket, taking out his wallet he carefully counted out notes and with a nod and a wink he gave them to his business partner.

The cold sun bore down on the two burly Merchant Navy uniformed Chief Officers as they walked in measured paces along the Drottinham, occasionally talking about S.O.E. Matters and their roles aboard the Grey Ladies. Turning into Stoa Kyrkogaten they caught sight of Archie Price and a young women walking towards the higher ground upon which the Church stood.

*' Ah there they are, nice looking couple don't you think ?',* said one Chief Officer to the other Chief Officer.

*' This is ridiculous you know. Sentimentality. Bloody war . Yes nice looking couple ',* replied the other.

*' I'll see them after the service, see if she's telling the truth to our lad Archie.'*

*'All seems so ordinary. I suppose the Germans hope to gain bits of information, perhaps they think they can turn Archie into a spy. I think we can feed them bits , lead them astray, spanner in their works, what do you think ? ',* asked the Chief Officer of the Gay Viking and the Chief Officer of the Hopewell agreed.

*' Walking to Church on a Sunday morning in this peaceful town one wouldn't think, would one '.*

The two men walked in silence to the entrance of the Church where they both stopped and if for reassurance or fortitude both lit cigarettes, inhaling deeply surveying the scene.

*' This Church was built in 1901, inside you'll notice the pulpit is baroque and there some interesting mosaics. Churches are a bit of a hobby of mine ',* said one Chief Officer to the other and the other thought that it really does take all sorts to carry out special operations.

Inside they took their seats amongst the congregation which was swelled by some of the crews of the two British boats .

Some hymns sung in Swedish seemed familiar and the dull words of the Lutheran priest seemed to contain sentiments and warmth to the British contingent, at least that is the way they were interpreted.

After the service all congregated outside the imposing grey granite building as they passed time in quiet, convivial, polite and diplomatic conversation.

The German Vice Consul nodded an acknowledgement
to his British counter part who then exchanged pleasantries with the
town fathers.
The Commodore appeared and had sparse dealings with the British
Vice Consul, but listened out of politeness, if not interest to his
inebriated views.
An able seaman said to another able seaman.
*' Lets slide off, Sunday eh, do a bit of exploring eh ? '.*
The Commodore overheard and coughed with irritation seeing the
two sailors walk away and he wished he could do the same.
The two Captains feigned an interest as the British Vice Consul
splutteringly drained on. The two Chief Officers looked at their
watches and made polite excuses .
Detaching themselves from the group they walked quickly to where
Archie Price would be waiting with his Swedish lady friend.
Archie introduced Inga to the Chief Officers and one took  Inga by
the arm and they walked down towards the quayside in quiet
conversation.

The weekend had gone well thought the German Vice Consul as he looked through the window down to the vacant berths of the Andersonns Kaj.

He allowed himself a smile of satisfaction, hoping that his life and position in the community would return to the quiet normality before the impudent British sailors, pirates and buccaneers came and disturbed his sedate routine and tranquil life by bringing the war to his doorstep.

He was pleased with himself and his contribution of using his persuasive diplomatic skills which had in some part resulted in the two Grey Ladies being virtually interned in the Brofjorden for the foreseeable future.

It was nearing the middle of January 1944 and soon the longer days of daylight would make further attempts by the British to break out of the blockaded Skagerrak impossible.

The Swedish Naval Offices who had accompanied the Grey Ladies to the Fjord had compiled a detailed dossier of the radar equipment which seemed to be a bonus and he could find no objections to the implementation of the limpit mine option which higher authority had sanctioned.

He shuffled his consular papers and looked at his diary.

An appointment with the magistrate for dinner.

Light began to fade as the day began to close.

On the bridge of the Gay Viking the Commodore took great pleasure in every inhalation of smoke from his roaring pipe as he looked at the shards of rock thrusting out of the deep dark waters which were disturbed only by the dancing , bubbling wakes of the Swedish Corvette, the Hopewell and the Gay Viking.

He was still irritated by the implementation of obscure Swedish regulations, but then the adverse weather conditions  would keep the boats huddled up to an interned British Merchant Navy ship in the Fjord for some time.

Days passed.

Damp and grey.

Launches brought English speaking men to the boats and amongst the crews there was talk of German agents and frogmen swimming into the Fjord to attach limpit mines to the hulls of the boats. In the claustrophobic accommodation of the Gay Viking voices whispered in Norwegian of imminent departure as on the deck sailors took positions forward and aft.

The Radio Officer made his way from the bows along the deck , passing two men fixing the Oerlikon guns to their mountings, to the short after deck.

He measured his steps.

One hundred and seventeen feet. Not much bigger than a rescue boat.

Chewing on his cigarette, he ate the smoke and looked out to the entrance to the Fjord thinking of the voyage home.

Twenty knots the engineer had said.

Through the Skagarrak and then the North Sea.

He climbed onto the bridge, then lowered himself through the small hatch into his radio room and finding his seat in the harsh contrasts between light and dark he sat in front of his equipment. He broke the official Swedish seals. He switched the equipment on, checking the frequencies, making sure that everything was in working order.

He was satisfied.

Thinking aloud of what lay ahead, his words echoed around the small room.

'Skagerrak
*North Sea*
*Piece a cake so they say . Back in dear old blighty in no time .*
*Captain knows a thing or two , a few bumps in the night, a few*
*milestones, be 'ome in no time at all , oh what a lark '.*
He checked the cardboard box and it was full enough of hand made
cigarettes for the long lone watch across the North Sea.
He was concerned about the safety of their investment in bottles of
contraband schnapps so he removed the false section of the bulkhead
behind which the bottles were hidden and the number didn't add up.
There was a piece of paper with the letters I.O.U. signed by the
S.O.E.
Angrily he tuned into the radio receiver, cursing them lot up stairs as
he knew that he was now at their beck and call .
The engines rumbled into life and the Gay Viking began to move
forward, rocking gently from side to side, towards the open sea.
Shorty Burton was on the wheel steering a course which followed the
Swedish corvette which would see them on their way out of the safe
confines of Swedish territorial waters.
On the port wing the Commodore puffed contentedly on his pipe
sending regular streams of aromantic smoke into the still cold air as
the Captain gazed thoughtfully through his binoculars to the small
village of Sandvk.
Feeling the warmth of the schnapps seeping into his body the Chief
Officer stood next to Shorty Burton and while looking directly ahead
to the sea spoke to him.
' *Keep her steady Mister Burton keep her steady. Oh by the way you've*
*become a bit of a celebrity, you were seen in Lysekil and I suppose that*
*is something in itself. And you were seen coming abroad with a large*
*canvas bag which clanked a lot, you know, like bottles '.*
The Chief Officer took a few paces forward and a few paces
backward and then a few paces forward and a few paces back, and
then resumed his position next to Shorty on the wheel.

He made nasal sounds, he coughed, and turned his head to look acutely at Shorty whose gangling frame encompassed the wheel as he concentrated on following the Swedish Corvette.

' *Well Shorty as I see it, if we deprive the enemy of anything, anything at all then its all part of the war effort, don't you think* '.

For a moment Shorty wanted to agree with the Chief but his nature got the better of him deciding to say nothing, his face expressing innocence.

' *Shorty, I reckon your secret mission with Sparks will earn you both some sort of commendation for the procurement of enemy materials* '.

The quietly mocking tone began to alternate with hard smiling authority.

' *Watch your course Mister watch your course. We don't want to run aground now do we Shorty not with all your valuable cargo aboard now do we* '.

Well clear of the Fjord the Gay Viking sailed between the islands of Bohus Malmar and Lilla Korna as the Corvette signalled its disengagement as it veered off to port and the Gay Viking turned to starboard.

Picking up speed.

Heading North.

Towards the Norwegian coast.

The silence on the bridge was broken by the Commodore.

' *Thought the Swedish Navy was in the hands of the Germans, signal from the Corvette tells a different story. Still, the Swedes are in a difficult position, adjusting to the winds and the currents of the violent climate, but we get an awful lot of vital information from Stockholm and I bet our Norwegian passengers have a few things to say.* '

His tone altered and he spluttered as he proclaimed.

' *Well, right now I don't think you need me cluttering up the bridge so I think I'll have a taste of the German schnapps which appears to be freely available on this boat. Privilege of rank, don't you know, let me know of anything untoward* '.

The Commodore left the bridge, the navigation, and the oncoming night to the Captain, his Officers and Shorty Burton.

The Captain shivered and the Chief Officer, drew breath and clenched his fists as both men agreed it was very, very cold.

*' Not good Chief, 1900 hours, everyone alert. Our Norwegian passengers can do some lookout, more eyes the better. Exposure suits on as soon as we pass Vaderbod. All hands to stations Chief '.*

The engines roared above the wind and the Chief shouted .

*' All hands t'stations*

*All hands t'stations*

*Mek a move.*

*All hands t'stations '.*

The Gay Viking cut a swathe through the coastal waters as the Vaderbod Light came into view and quickly they passed the dark rocky island as the engines reached their maximum speed.

Gunners manned the twin Oirlikons fore and aft and the twin Vickers either side of the bridge.

For safety the Norwegians huddled around the quadruple Vickers battery of guns on the deck aft of the accommodation as the Gay Viking headed North, North West towards the Norwegian coast with waves being cut into short, sharp lashings of spray.

Clouds began to black out the stars as they turned due West into the developing sea and then turning south, south west with their engines straining their bearings as the bows rose and fell, waves streaming alongside the hull which formed into a white triangular wake dispersing into the darkness as the Gay Viking began to make her run through the Skagerrak.

Sparks voice mixed with the sound of wind and seas crashing shrieked from the Radio room towards the bridge.

*' Contact dead ahead, dead ahead, contact dead ahead '.*

The Captain cursed as he read signals flashing from the ghostly shape ahead.

*' Signals challenging us Captain '*, relayed the nervous voice of the First Officer as the Captain weighed up the situation.

*' One eighty to port, try not to upset the galley '*, growled the Captain loudly.

*' One eighty to port, trying not to upset the galley Cap'n '*, answered the helmsman as the Gay Viking veered dangerously to port crashing through the swell as the crew hung on and in the engine room, engineers and motormen were thrown violently off balance.

Climbing onto the bridge the Commodore lurched, clutching at the binnacle for stability and shouting to the Captain.

*' What's happened Captain ? '.*

*' Looks like a German destroyer. We're doubling back on our course until we loose her, hopefully they'll think we're heading for Sweden. Once we've put some distance between Jerry and us we'll double back North, north west '.*

The Captain wedged himself into the starboard wing of the bridge with the Commodore to port and at midships the Chief Officer's binoculars scanned continuously the black sea.

Shorty Burton wondered why he was still on the wheel

The First Officer, in the chart room manipulated parallel rules and pencil plotting a course due north towards the Norwegian coast.

The Sparks watched the small radar screen and he shouted to the bridge twice that there was no indication of ships as the frayed line of light turned continuously around the black screen.

The Captain looked over his shoulder and gave orders to the shadowy figure of the helmsman to change course.

*' Shorty, five degrees to port and steady, good man '.*

*' Five degrees to port and steady Cap'n '.*

*' Ten degrees to port and steady '.*

*' Ten degrees to port and steady Cap'n '.*

*' Now then Shorty, take her twenty degrees to port, slowly, slowly, that's it Shorty, that's it, now steady, steady. Steady as she goes. Good man Shorty, good man '.*

Now all on the bridge were silent apart from the occasional curse when ice spray swept over.

On the wheel Shorty wondered who he could sell his share of the moonshine to and he thought of the price.

For a moment he thought he might face resistance from potential customers when they found out he was selling German schnapps but then he remembered the Chief saying that by depriving the enemy of any goods at all would help the war effort.

An ominous sound interrupted his machinations as he blurted out.

*' Aircraft up there Cap'n, I can 'ear it '.*

The Captain turned to Shorty.

*' Don't let it bother you Shorty, keep her steady, keep her steady '.*

The Captain and the Chief had words and decided to shut down two of the engines to minimise the wake making it less visible from the air. Above the low cloud the unseen aircraft circled, its engines whining with monotonous regularity, effecting the nerves of all.

The First Officer appeared on the bridge with a strong salvo towards the circulating whine.

*' Wish that bastard would piss off '.*

The bastard continued, sometimes near, sometimes far , but a constant reminder of the close proximity of danger.

Shorty began to wonder aloud what type of aircraft it was.

*' I reckon it's a Messerschmitt 110, what do ya think Chief ? '*, asked Shorty.

*' I doubt it Shorty, probably a Junkers 88 night fighter '*, said the Chief Officer and the Captain joined in the speculation.

*' Could be a Dornier, a Messerschmitt, a Junkers, but I couldn't give a dam, I just wish dam thing would piss off '.*

Shorty looked to the black sky straining his eyes and ears until he realised the noise of the aircraft was becoming feint.

*' Cap'n Jerry must 'av 'eard ya, I think 'e's pissing off ! '.*

The Captain was becoming irritated and he said to Shorty, *' And you can piss off Shorty, here's your relief '.*

The Radio Officer making regular radar sweeps reported several vessels of various sizes and speeds indicating enemy craft on the outer limits of the radar screen.

On the bridge the First Officer endeavouring to contain his anxiety was trying to emulate the stoic stance of the Captain but with limited success .

Though he had sailed in treacherous seas, experienced danger, the mine and the U – boat, the fear of the unknown , the unseen enemy ship and the aircraft fed his anxiety.

And then there was the sea.

Through the night he searched every square yard of visible sea in fear and anticipation and as time wore on he became more aware that he was in urgent need of a change of clothes.

Around the guns on the afterdeck Norwegian voices whispered the hours away until a sliver of light on the horizon revealed the grey dawn and an expanding sea.

Relief began to be expressed by all, apart from the engineers and motormen who were constantly tending the engines with oily glove and brute force but they wouldn't breath easily until the vessel approached the Humber estuary. But there was a long, long way to go for the very small boat almost immersed in the vast, cold, forbidding seas .

The Captain yawned loudly, coughed and leaned over the side and spat tobacco remnants into the flowing seas.

Stretching his arms.

Then shaking his right leg and then his left.

Rubbing his eyes, then pacing from port to starboard and from starboard to port .The First Officer relieved to be relieved as the Chief Officer reappeared to be informed about their position, course and speed.

He then climbed down to the deck acknowledging sailors and a couple of Norwegians as he made his way forward to find the boson checking batons and hatch covers. A Norwegian voice shouted ' aircraft '.

Captain Whitfield instinctively turned in the direction of the sound of distant specks and he shouted to the boson to break out the ensigns, the German ensigns.

The Chief shouted enemy aircraft.

The Captain shouted a change of course.

A north, north east easterly course.

Heading towards to the Norwegian coast.

All, apart from gunners were ordered into the accommodation.
The Captain shouts.

*' Don't think they've seen us. Can't make them out. If Shorty Burton
was up here he'd know. Flying North West, morning patrol, I hope '.*
The relief of their escape to relatively free seas evaporated as the
gunners heard in disbelief the Captains orders to wave to the
German planes should they come closer.
Now with the German ensigns flying the planes came closer and
everyone waved as the Chief made a commentary.

*' Coming down Cap'n, they're acknowledging. Now look at that, they're
flapping their wings, very civil of them, very civil. Quickly dip the
bloody ensign, dip the bloody ensign '.*
Suddenly very large the German aircraft flew over fast, flapping
their wings, on a straight course, then becoming smaller and smaller.
A course change to the South, South East now towards the Danish
coast and the Captain ordered echo soundings to be taken as he
explained his immediate course of action.

*' We'll use the fifty fathom line south side of the Skagerrak. Eco
soundings, when we're near the coast , we'll rely on our shallow draft
to get us through '.*
Partially refreshed the Commodore surfaced and the First Officer
listened attentively to the Captain. The Commodore understood but
the First Officer was unsure and he asked.

*' Captain I understand the fifty fathom, German destroyers I
understand, but I don't understand the shallow draft to get us through,
through what ? '.*
The Captain rubbed his hands together preparing for the task ahead
and then he took out his cigarettes and matches and he struck a
match which illuminated his answer.

*'Mine fields Mister Mate, mine fields, shallow draft getting us over the
minefields off the Danish coast '.*
The thought of mine fields were left behind as many course
alterations set the Gay Viking cruising on a South Westerly course
across the North Sea towards home on a gently rolling sea and
Captain Whitfield decided it was time for to sleep.

He left the bridge to the Chief and the First Officer and made his way to his cabin with its swaying picture of Francis Drake on the bulkhead.

Pouring himself a small measure he sipped slowly while thinking of home, his wife and the fireside where he would read Melville and Moby Dick.

A passage came to him.

*' I always go to sea as a sailor because they make a point of paying me for my trouble whereas they never pay a passenger a single penny that I've heard of '.*

He lay on his bunk and his eyes closed. He thought not only do I get paid but I get a bonus and I'm a pirate as well and should be flying the Jolly Rodger. He thought he must make a note to get one but before he could find pen and note pad he drifted into a deep, short, sleep.

But he was wide awake at mid day January 14th 1944 as he climbed onto the bridge taking his position on the starboard wing. He acknowledged the others with a nod of his head but nobody noticed Shorty Burton who took his turn on the wheel and no one noticed that he kept the vessel on a South Westerly course without any deviation.

Engineers and motormen had been on deck , refreshed by the keen afternoon breeze and now they oiled and greased and watched over the diesels as the Gay Viking kept a steady fourteen knots with only a slight change of course to avoid the ' Dogger Bank'.

The Commodore appeared every now and then on the bridge where he would look at the sea and look at the sky, would say nothing and when his introspective contemplation was complete he would go back down below.

The Chief and the First Mate alternated watches while the Captain kept his station as the daylight faded and the wind whipped up the seas buffeting the hull on the starboard side.

Now the night was frustratingly dreary, long and monotonous as time was measured in cigarette ends.

Beneath the bridge the Radio Officer listened to the garbled
transmissions of traffic while he sampled his special cargo .
The bottle at his elbow and the glass in his hand became extensions of
his body. Every sip from his glass made the four walls of the small
radio room more bearable as the revolving white line on the radar
screen  began to reveal the familiar shape of the coast as the Gay
Viking crept nearer and nearer and the long, long night began to be
erased  by a powerful dawn.
Into the cross currents the bows rose and fell as Flamborough Head
rose and fell.
Now, the Captain, fully alert, ordered frequent intricate course
changes as the helmsman steered through the minefield channel .
The Chief Officer out of habit, continuously checked the compass
while he muttered to himself and the First Officer felt at ease sailing
between the mines rather than over them.
The Captain went down to his cabin again to make sure he was smart
enough for when he stepped ashore onto the quayside of Albert
Dock , though he wasn't certain if it would be Albert Dock.
He straightened his  tie.
As the Gay Viking crossed the imaginary line between dark green
salt sea and the cantankerous mud brown waters of the River
Humber a fog suddenly swirled around obscuring everything from
view.
On the afterdeck Norwegians shivered as unseen gulls squarked in
the thick eerie mist. In the accommodation sailors packed their kit in
adolescent enthusiasm of expectancy.
Suddenly the Gay Viking violently jarred.
Metal screeched, wood shattered and with a dull thud the vessel
slumped backwards, jerked sidewards, then steadied herself and onto
the bridge stormed Captain Whitfield, with the Chief Officer
shouting for the boson and the boson shouting for all the crew and
the crew shouting to each other.
*' What the 'ells 'appened ?'*
*' Can't see the bows '.*

' *We've lost them, we've lost the bloody bows* ', growled the
Commodore who emerged out of a vague huddled shape on the
starboard side of the bridge.

The mist shrouded boson shouted from the foredeck.

' *Most of the f'castle's gone, hit summut, a coaster !*'.

Captain Whitfield paced the bridge peering into the fog, turning
towards the wheel at the gauping face of the helmsman who looked
distraught as the Captain speaks.

' *Ah Shorty, glad to see you're still with us. I expect your cargo is safe
and sound. We go all the way to Sweden and back, through storms and
gales, we're chased by destroyers, sail over minefields, hunted by the
Luftwaffe and not a scratch. Then in the River Humber we hit a
coaster. God give me strength* ', and he stared at Shorty who just
shrugged his shoulders.

The steward brought tea which was sorely needed as the damp thick
fog slowly began to clear and the Captain took charge of piloting the
broken bowed boat through the river channels he knew almost like
the back of his hand.

A freshening wind dispersed the fog and the Company flags flew
taught and on the quayside the Superintendent and Lask watched as
the damaged Grey Lady limped towards the lock gates.

From the quay a young lad called to anyone on the boat.

' *What 'appened t'ya bows ?*'.

A seaman answered.

' *It wuz like this lad, we wuz in enemy waters. Out of fog big bluddy
German destroyer, search lights, guns blazing, came at us. We went full
ahead and, and rammed it. Then we went full astern and left it for
Davy Jones and 'ere we are safe and sound* '.

The fresh faced young lad looked wide eyed in wonder and awe at the
able seaman on the battered boat, bristling with guns, and he shouted
back to the sailor.

' *Heroes, heroes, fighting like that, wish I'd been there, can't wait t'tell
me pals* '.

Captain Whitfield overheard and called to the young lad on the quay.

*' Aye lad wish I'd been there as well '*, and no sooner had the words left his mouth he wished he hadn't said a word .

On the evening of the 19<sup>th</sup> the Captain hung his uniform in the
wardrobe and he casually relaxed into the comfort of his armchair in
front of a glowing fire as he glanced through the newspaper, and as
he read he called to his wife.

*' I see Ada Parkinson's daughter has married '.*

*'That's right she got married to a man from Aberdeen. By the way Mrs.*
*Abrahams, at twenty eight is having problems with her cistern, being*
*on her own she can't cope with those kind of things. So if you can pop*
*around wont take you a couple of minutes. Mind you she does very well*
*for her age. Eighty four this year',* and she brought him his glass of
whisky and water.

He read of the death of Jack Cooper the manager of 'Gallaghers
Tobaconists ', near Princess Dock. He didn't know him well but he
saw him now and again in the bar talking to Doris.

He let the newspaper fall into his lap and looking into the fire he
thought of voyages he'd made on the Gay Viking and he realised the
experience had been the most exciting in his life, but slowly as the
whisky warmed he realised the implications of what he was thinking
and he was touched by guilt.

As he reached across to the bookshelf for ' Moby Dick ', the sounds of
the sea ebbed into the background as the warm, subtle, domestic
hum took over and he reclined further into his chair, sipping his
whisky and turning the pages his thoughts turned back to his own
reality of pitching skills against the enemy and the exhilaration as the
bows of the small craft rose and fell crashing through the north sea
swell.

Dodging.

The Kreigsmarine.

The Luftwaffe.

The minefields.

Poor old Jack Cooper.

Never been out Hull.

Dead.

Cycle accident.

' *I don't know* ', he said to his wife who now sat opposite him in her chair busy putting the finishing touches to a cardigan she was knitting for him.

' *You don't know what Harry ?*'.

He rose from his chair and looked at family photographs on the mantel piece as if searching for answers as he mumbled an answer.

' *War seems to do strange things to people*'.

' *Certainly does Harry, certainly does, knit one, pearl one, two together* ', as she put down her knitting she looked into the glowing embers of the fire.

She told him of people she'd known for years suddenly turning petty, greedy and selfish.

' *But on the other hand there are some who go to extraordinary lengths to help others* '.

She gave her husband a half smiling well informed look as she asked.

' *Do you know Shorty Burton ?, not a pretty sight I grant you, but with a heart of gold. He gives our little committee sacks of toys and other things for the children's parties we organise. Where he gets them from I can't imagine. Heart of gold that man, heart of gold* '.

He scratched his head and was about to tell his wife about Shorty and German schnapps, but thought better of it. Shorty and the Sparks were probably selling their moonshine and perhaps turning their profit into children's toys for children's parties.

Harry Whitfield yawned and stretched and almost by instinct she put down her knitting and then they both climbed the stairs and the night closed comfortably about them.

In one of the large rooms, in the large building in Baker Street London requisitioned by the Special Operations Executive, the Scandinavian section was engaged in planning subterfuge and sabotage.

Radio traffic, codes and signals were being invented to create the belief that Norway would play a strategic part in the imminent allied invasion of Europe so forcing the Germans to station a large number of troops there in constant readiness.

In an obscure and dimly lit, claustrophobic room a telephone rang and a clerk picked up the receiver and listened to the voice of Herbert Lask who duly reported the arrival back in England of the Commodore with another consignment of goods from Sweden.

The message was noted.

The clerk replaced the receiver.

The message was delivered.

The Deputy Director took the message and opened the door to the board room where voices of men who were more accustomed to the great financial institutions of the city than the covert operations of war, discussed dealing and double dealing with a visitor from the P.M.'s office.

*' But does he play cricket ? Lets hear from my Deputy. You know each other of course ! '.*

The Deputy looked at the visitor, examining the cut of his suit and with a convivial smile acknowledged their interdepartmental dealings.

*' Sir, the converted gunboats, commonly known as the Grey Ladies, have arrived back, or at least one of them has, with the Commodore and another cargo '.*

The Director raised his considerable eye brows and for a few moments gazed at the wall map focusing on the Skagerrak.

*' Good, thought the Commodore's luck had run out, now lets see what the situation is to date '.*

He gestured to his Deputy to expand on the operation. *' Sir , the figures, a comparison with the Air Service Operation.*

*Air Service carried out 157 flights, delivering 110 tons of ball bearings. '*

*The Grey Ladies have made four trips bringing back 160 tons, and we have one boat fully loaded, but undergoing repairs in Lysekil. Another is en route to Sweden to pick up more cargo as we speak '.*

The expression of the Director remained constant as he commented.

*' Not bad, not bad at all. The sailors are fifty tons ahead. What of the debit side of the account ? '.*

The Deputy coughed twice and his face became grave.

*' Well Sir the Air Service have lost four aircraft, with twenty three missing presumed dead. The Merchant Naval operation, one boat captured with the loss of life of the Captain. Nineteen crew taken prisoner. Our man, the Chief Officer, has been taken to Berlin '.*

For a few seconds there was silence, broken by the deep slow voice of the Director as he made a calculated analysis of the operation.

*' Good, so we're in credit taking all things into account with the possibilities of more deliveries before the end of the long nights of winter. Good, good effort by all and I should think it will be recognised with a few gongs. Now how is our new man Lask doing ?'*

The Director rose from his chair, taking a cigar, lighting it, he puffed huge clouds of smoke into the room while he stood looking at the map of Scandinavia.

Superintendent Watson looked at the cigarette which he'd automatically taken out of the packet and put to his lips and as he handled his lighter he thought of his Doctors advice. He put the cigarette back into the packet and he looked at Herbert Lask who was standing by the window gazing out over the warehouses towards the docks and the river.

*' Well Lask, the Corsair docked in Lysekil this morning I understand '.*

*' Yes Sir I heard. The repairs to the Hopewell will be completed shortly and should be able to sail along with the Nonsuch '.*

The Superintendent fondled his cigarette packet, pondering and eventually capitulated to his yearning, took the cigarette, lit it, and inhaled deeply then exhaled with deep physical relief. Turning away from Lask he examined a model of one of the Companies ships in a glass case which rested on an elegant table.

*' Now Lask, have a good look at this model. Superb craftsmanship don't you think ?. There are men using their skills making models of enemy territory, docks, installations, that sort of thing, working from photographs and all for the big day, the invasion, coming up soon I believe. Strange way fighting a war making models. Quite absurd. Superb craftsmanship, just look at those winches, so small, takes great skill. The Gay Viking was lucky Mister Lask, lucky, no I don't think luck had anything to do with it. I put it down to the excellent seamanship of Captain Whitfield and that goes for all the crews Mister Lask. They'll be the backbone of the Company when the wars over. Now Lask, tell me the latest !'.*

Herbert Lask looked at the model in the glass case then at the Superintendent in his well ordered room in which every chair, table and cabinet suggested depth, tradition and continuity and for a moment he thought back in time, not to long ago when this room was only a mystery.

*' Four successful missions Superintendent. The engines on the Gay Viking need minor repairs and as you know the bows need some attention and the repairs to the Nonsuch are almost complete and she'll be ready to put to sea in the next few days '.*

The Superintendent looked thoughtfully at Lask then abruptly
turned walked a few paces to his desk and opened his diary and in
strong clipped phrases dismissed Lask.

*' Well that's all, you be about your business, I've got a shipping
company to run '.*

Suddenly Lask became the clerk from the office down the stairs
again and as he reached the door the Superintendent called.

*' How's your Swedish coming on ? and another thing Mister Lask, get
hold of a few bottles of the schnapps that seems to be flowing around,
there's a good fellow '.*

And in just a sentence Lask was reassured of his relatively new status
in the scheme of things and he assured the Superintendent regarding
the schnapps that he would see to it.

He walked down to his office which he now shared with the amicable
ghost of Captain Turnbull with the disorganised piles of paper, the
ash trays full, the half empty bottle of whisky, photographs of family
and ships all remained undisturbed.

As Lask checked through the engineers reports he smiled as Captain
Turnbull walked through his thoughts and commanded they leave
the office to catch up with the 'were with all', with a pint or two in
the bar.

Lask decided he must act upon the Superintendents request for
schnapps and so he left the office and made straight for ' The
Empress '.

Lask walked at a brisk pace along Princess Dock and then over to
The Empress Public House and as he pushed the door open he heard
the soft, firm voice of Doris laying down the law.

*' Now look 'ere Shorty, never mind all that blather, I'm not buying
German schnapps and that's final '.*

*' Come on Doris, it's good stuff, 'onest, good stuff, even the
Commodore and the Chief took some '.*

Doris didn't look as if she was going to change her mind, or would
she ?.

*' Where did you get it from Shorty ?'.*

*' Told you, it fell off the back of a train going through Sweden on its
way to Norway for the Germans. It's a give away price ! What d'ya say
Doris '.*

Lask had heard what Shorty had to say as he sauntered to the bar
smiling at Doris.

*' Evening Doris, bit quiet I see. I expect you'll be seeing a few
Norwegians later. A pint for me and one for Shorty if you would be so
kind '.*

Doris smiled and replied.

*' Two pints coming up, I'd watch out for Shorty Mister Lask else he'll
try to sell you some German schnapps ',* and she tut, tutted as she
pulled two pints and set them down leaving Lask and Shorty to
themselves as she saw a familiar face at the end of the bar.

Lask offered Shorty a cigarette.

*' I don't mind if I do Mister Lask '.*

*' Good trip Shorty ?'.*

*' Yeah not bad. We got back didn't we '.*

The two men supped their ale.

*' Bit of an accident Shorty and you on the wheel eh '.*

*' Now Mister Lask it wasn't my fault, nobody warned me, nobody saw.
Just 'appened, 'it bluddy coaster and that was that '.*

Lask looked at Shorty who was almost crouching into a defensive
stance.

*' And you on the wheel at the time Shorty. I've also heard that you've got some German Schnapps, is that right Shorty ? I'm sure it will all work out for you Shorty. It was an accident after all and you at the the wheel. I'll have a word on your behalf and that German schnapps Shorty, if you get my drift ? '.*

Shorty realised the situation he was in.

*' How many bottles Mister Lask ? '.*

*' Lets say four or five, no make it six Shorty, make it six ! '.*

Shorty sighed with resignation and reached down and handled a soiled and clinking bag which he gave to Mister Lask saying two pounds to you Mister Lask , two pounds.

*' As I said Shorty I'm sure everything will work out for you I'll have a word with the Superintendent for you Shorty, it'll be alright, I'm sure '.*

With a defeated sigh Shorty drained his glass and his long legs took his awkward frame to the door and out into the evening,

Lask asked Doris to refill his glass.

*' Do you know Mister Lask that fella Shorty tried to sell me some German Schnapps '.*

*' Did he really Doris ?'.*

*' He certainly did Mister Lask he certainly did '.*

*' Did you buy any Doris ? '.*

*' Herbert Lask !. What do you take me for. Me buying German Schnapps with Frankie a prisoner of war, what do you take me for Mister Lask, well really '.*

All the Captains of the Grey Ladies had their false starts with their scheduled missions. Fully crewed with anticipation and away sailing down the Humber, passing the Bull lightship and turning to port, thirty degrees and into the North Sea, and then engine malfunction, sudden improvised running repair, aborting before its to late and turn back.

But not now.

Captain Jackson shivered.

He'd made full use of his time ashore savouring every moment with his family as only a man can who'd felt the pull of imminent death as his experience of the North Atlantic lurked near the surface of his consciousness.

That time a U-boat found its target aft of the bridge and the S.S. Kelso exploded and amidst smoke, steam, smoke, fire and ice, the hull cracked open and he jumped into the sea.

Frantically thrashing, he grabbed a section of broken planking which floated to his support as cold crept into his legs and body, shivering, teeth chattering and the still burning hulk awaited the last rites from the hissing, swirling, demonic sea.

Slipping away.

Below freezing.

Minute particles of strength summoned body and soul as waves battered and he screamed and lingering into lonely oblivion he sang, *' Eternal father strong to save '.*

Eyes stared, senses altered, second by second, into a whirlpool as sounds of a Klaxon sounded, with shouts of men, sounds of engines as a huge dark shape came into view riding high above the sea.

Voices, accents of men, hauling him awkwardly from the sea. Canadians. Hot tea permeated through his body, his body spluttered, shaking off his watery grave, and sleep, when sleep came it was long and sound.

And now.

Mental and physical concentration at its height as his grey blue eyes looked into the darkness of the night as the slender bows of the Nonsuch brushed away the calm of the North Sea.

The late Captain Turnbull had kicked more than a few arses to get the engineers to complete repairs and modifications quickly and now the engines sounded confident. Though graceful in line all knew the vessels were improvisations to meet the greedy needs of war.

Yet exhilaration, expectation and grim determination was etched into the facial expressions of those looking directly into the cold, dark sea.

The Chief Officer clamoured onto the bridge acknowledging the Captain and the Helmsman saying to them that he had, ' *Got the steward to bring coffee, got him to lace it with some of that schnapps, which should warm the cockles* '.

He leant against the wind dodgers looking down to the fast flowing sea as he went through the details of his own mission.

The steward brought the coffee.

The spirit dispelled the cold.

The Nonsuch edged around the Dogger Bank.

Calculations estimated they would be approaching the Skagerrak by night fall.

Darkness providing the cover for the run through with the seas clement and forecast favourable with slight southerly winds and low clouds the Nonsuch steered a course North, North East.

The Commodore needed to be back in Sweden but not on the bridge so he had slept in the Captains cabin and now refreshed he lodged himself into the port wing of the bridge and his thoughts wandered as the seas rose and fell.

Many factors contributed to the feasibility of the operation.

Every action was a small part of a plan of which the outcome was unknowable with chance the factor governing the outcome which was predictable only by unpredictability.

It was by chance that the eyesight of Captain Turnbull had failed turning him into an irksome, yet effective fixer of all things maritime on land.

It was by chance the Master Standfast had been captured and it was by chance that the Gay Viking had lost her bows to a coaster in thick fog. The factors essential to the success of the mission were low clouds and long dark nights.

The bows leisurely sliced through a mounting wave sending spray
over the bridge making the Commodore, the Chief Officer and the
First Officer duck while the helmsman and the Captain remained
upright looking ahead into the darkening seas.

Clouds low and heavy.

Hours long.

Breaking the monotony the First Officer reported a strong easterly
current which the Captain acknowledged and the Commodore
understood.

' *Thank you First, we can take advantage of the current, it'll mean
sailing within fifteen miles of the Danish coast, but it'll give us that
extra bit* '.

The Commodore, apprehensively understood the implications of the
Danish coast.

Minefields.

Minor course changes and the boat responded to the commands of
the Captain and the actions of the helmsman.

The Sparks reported blips on his radar screen which indicated
several slow moving vessels directly ahead and a vessel astern
approaching fast.

' *Fishing boats. Harvesting the seas. Industry and commerce continue
amid the slaughter* ', mused the Commodore with a bitterness equal
to the wind.

Through the dark sea mist bobbing tell tale lights provoked the look
out astern to shout.

' *E – boat coming up fast* '.

All but the helmsman turned and focused their binoculars on the
barely discernible bow wave of the following craft. The Chief barked
orders directing men to their stations and fixed to the deck as if a
permanent piece of bridge equipment the Captain towered above the
others peering into the swirling mist as the Commodore, Chief and
the First Officer breathed anxiously awaiting, awaiting commands
from the Captain which seemingly took an age, but when they came,
they were clear.

*' Maintain course, eighteen knots, following sea, six or seven fishing boats. Maintain course. Make out we're part of their escort along with the E – boat and we'll be away before they realise we're not one of them '.*

The Commodore chewed on his unlit pipe as a crooked smile crept into the dark shadows of the Chief Officers face as he climbed down to the afterdeck. With no words only his look gave orders which were instinctively known, and the sailors manned the guns either side of the bridge, foredeck and aft of the accommodation.

The adrenalin flowed at the rate of anticipation.

All ready.

Radar sweeps indicated positions of the slow moving fishing boats and the following E – boat began to alter course towards the Danish coast.

The diesels of the Nonsuch kept up maximum revolutions making distance as the fishing boats disappeared and the Captain ordered the helmsman to steer North by North East.

Stars in gaps in the cloud allowed the First Officer to make a fix.

*' Towards Vaderbod Captain '*, the Commodore asked.

*' No Commodore, no they'll be expecting us to come from the North or the South so as soon as Lysekil is due East we can sail direct, save time as well. I estimate we'll be in Lysekil by 0700 hours '.*

*' There goes the searchlights again again. Nice when it hits the window lights up the hut reminds me of christmas. Its like that outside in a morning on the way to the site were we work when sun shines 'an glints on snow, nice bluddy nice, 'an it's so bluddy cold.*

*Can never sleep shivering all time think of you 'onest, think of 'ome. So bluddy cold, 'ow are ya Doris.*

*Two pints.*

*Bluddy 'ell.*

*It's.*

*Thinking of walking inta town, 'av sum fish and chips at Bob Carvers I can smell vinigar in the rain, 'av they cleared rubble away, in old town , strolling through Land of Ginger, Green ginger, nice piece of cod, there goes the search light again, after work, nackered, bluddy cold, can't sleep.*

*After work.*

*Something to eat not much, tired play cards, sometimes kick ball 'bout outside, bluddy cold, tired.*

*We talk, there's allus talk, not much to talk 'bout. None of lads are 'ere. None of the lads from Master Standfast. Don't know where Tom is or that fella Gunner Dobbie Dobson, what a name eh, don't think 'e liked me. Funny that. I go aroung thinking everybody likes me but Dobbie Dobson doesn't. Nobody ever talked to me the way ''e did. Said 'e'd kill me if I sang and 'e called me a bastard and 'e meant it. Suppose there were others who thought same. Come to think Doris, you called me disgusting, allus thought you were 'aving us on. Allus thought I 'ad a heart of gold.*

*I knowI know, I know, I get a bit, but I'm good at sea, Tom told me that. When we sailed through great storm in Irish sea he said I wuz an angel, me an angel.*

*Some bluddy storm that wuz don't know 'ow we survived that. Mind you Tom said I wuz a disgrace ashore.*

*Meks me think.*

*Stuck in this god forsaken 'ole, 'an it's so bluddy cold, so bluddy cold. What I'd give f'me own bed.*

*Now I come to think'bout it I wuz bluddy disgusting,*

*Germans must 'av thought I wuz trouble so they split us up from rest of lads. Jerry Captain of patrol boat that captured us was alright, 'an that old German guard gave us a cigarette .*

*Wonder 'ow rest of lads are doing. Now that bloke Lask , 'e wuz a turn up for the book. Thought 'e wuz just one of them pen pushers. Bit more to him than meets the eye'.*

*' D'ya remember.*

*D'ya remember our old school, long time ago, like yesterday, freezing, remember what's 'is name, allus 'ad a snow drop 'anging from 'is nose, snotty, Snotty Bob, remember 'e caught a frog.*

*Terrible 'an we all laughed .*

*Wouldn't think people could do that .*

*Bluddy disgusting.*

*What's 'is name was in air raid shelter during air raid forty one it wuz, took a direct ' it. Everyone and what's ' is name was killed .*

*Bastards.*

*Their turn now.*

*The windows are rattling, thunder in the distance, 'ear it every night, can see red glow rising in sky see it through windows, fucking war, can't sleep, bluddy cold, can't sleep.*

*Don't know why, mebee 'cos I 'avn't 'ad a drink f ' fuckin ages.*

*Others lads 'ere mostly foreign, a few squaddies, can't get on with 'em, they say I 'ad it easy at sea, keep themselves to themselves. Bluddy Frenchman dunt alf snore, disgusting, snores 'is 'ead off, mind you 'e can speak English.*

*Wish I could sleep. I'll drift off soon I asked Frenchie if 'e'd thought of escaping, 'e just laughed. Thought 'is face wuz going to explode it went all twisted as 'e said escape to what ?*

*Frightened me 'e did*

*Big bloke*

*I didn't understand what 'e meant.*

*Then it dawned on me*

*He didn't 'ave a country anymore say's 'e's lucky to be alive as 'e insulted German Officer, he tells me he wuz working clearing up rubbish after bombing.*

*Wore a P on 'is jacket, says 'e got paid, says 'e went to work with a gang on a tram an when finished f' day came back to camp on tram. Can't believe everything I 'ear.*

*Tired now. I'll get a couple of 'ours sleep. Must getback 'ome 'av to try 'an escape' Av Get back to sea . Must sleep. Cold . Cold. Cold.*

*Must sleep, night luv, night.'*

Though the Commodore enjoyed the adventure and the notion of being a seafarer and though he enjoyed the vastness of the sea he had to admit he was relieved to be on a surface that was static as he walked along the quayside with the Captain.

*' An exhilarating voyage Captain, sailing through that fishing fleet, for a moment you had me worried. I gather from our friends here that the Germans have increased their patrols in the Skagarrak and in the triangle, Skaw, Vaderbod and here. Appears we were expected. Not a bad trip, a bit bumpy, thirty six hours and ropes made fast and secure '.*

Waves and acknowledgements from weathered fishermen as they prepared their boats for sea while others of a less friendly persuasion watched from a distance as the Nonsuch sat firmly against the quay her array of flags flying taut in the morning breeze. The sounds of a grumbling, coughing car broke into the seagull conversations as it rumbled to a halt between the two men.

*' My transport to Undevalla Captain, some business to attend t, then off to Stockholm to ruffle a few feathers at the Embassy '.*

With bag in hand and a casual salute the Commodore got into the car and departed.

With all the formalities adhered to the stevedores began to unload the cargo and the crew began to assemble for their escorted walk to the Stadshotel to be refreshed.

The Chief Officer joined the Captain on the quay.

*' You'll be about your business then Chief ? ',* asked the Captain.

*' That's right Captain, come along if you want '.*

*' Where to ? ',* asked the Captain with just a hint of curious enthusiasm as on this little jaunt he was just following orders.

*' Not far, not far, now lets see, over the road, that should be Drotting Gatan, should bring us out us onto Gamla Standgarton and there's a café near the North harbour '.*

The Captain had got used to the Chief's matter of fact attitude and accepted the invitation without a word and became conscious of curious looks from passers by.

' *Small place, news travels fast. They're friendly in a strange way, but they seem to get fed up, sombre sort of depressed, all to do with the climate I expect, they call it ' grubbla'. Apparently the further north you go the worse it gets, ah well '.*

As they passed some shops the Captain contrasted the goods on display with the starkness and scarcity of home.

Looking over his shoulder the Chief saw two men clearly following them which he pointed out to the Captain.

' *German agents Abwehhr, Military intelligence  Captain,  following us and making it obvious, they know who we are, we know who they are, almost on speaking terms. Ah here's the cafe, they'll probably follow us in'.*

The Chief led the way through the door into the small bright cafe where they took a table by the wall to the left of the counter, as few customers looked up at them with acute curiosity.

' *This is the the table that Lask specified, I think Lask likes this cloak and dagger stuff  '*, and he laughed as he ordered coffee and cake. The waitress acknowledged with an apprehensive smile.

The Captain thought about Herbert Lask  back in the Company building and wondered just what he had to do with this table in this Konditori in Lysekil on this particular day.

The Chief didn't say much, or wouldn't, or couldn't, but he did say that Lask was very specific about the table and the time of eleven o'clock when someone would come in and give him something which by implication of all the intricacies would be extremely important.

The two German agents had entered, taken their seats, ordered their coffee and made no effort to disguise their purpose of surveillance of the two British Merchant Marine Officers. The Konditori began to fill up and conversations rose amid the clinking of cups and saucers. The Chief stretched across the table, beckoned the Captain towards him and whispered.

*' Captain , there is a Norwegian whose excessive zeal when carrying out operations against the German forces in Trondheim have made him a much sort after fellow, and he is here in Lysekil. I've orders to take him back with us to England. We've made arrangements to be brought aboard the Nonsuch when the time is right '.*

The Captain smiled, nodded his head and wondered just what Herbert Lask had to do with all this.

*' Captain, Mister Lask may be a Company man but he's been requisitioned so to speak by the S.O.E. and now he works for us in one way or another. As far as I know he could be in Sweden right now. He seems to be involved in the trans shipment of goods, if you get my drift '.*

The door of the Konditori opened and a small pot bellied man with closely cropped hair walked towards them, nodded to the Chief and the Captain, pulled up a chair and sat down and talked slowly to the Chief.

As the Captain listened to the conversation which was in part English and in part Norwegian, the Captain began to wish he'd spent the morning exploring the small town.

Much to the German Vice Consuls disapproval the Abwehr agents had taken over much of his office.

The agents were courteous and polite as they flicked neat rings of fine grey cigarette ash around the ash trays upon his consular desk. It was the way they looked at him that unnerved him as if he was himself under surveillance and it seemed that when he was near to them their voices changed and became whispers.

Previous agents from the Stockholm Embassy, though secretive by the very nature of their profession at least included him in their discussions and had taken note of his opinions, but these men kept him completely in the dark, though he knew the purpose of their mission.

The Vice Consul knew he was lucky to hold his position in neutral Sweden away from the increasing devastation know been wreaked upon his homeland. He dutifully read the German and Swedish newspapers and recently he had taken to listening to the B.B.C. though in extreme secrecy but he also had bouts of patriotic fervour when he recalled the days when world peace echoed from the radio and when the Fuhrer demanded of all Germans to be brave and face the challenges of the German Empire.

Yet he felt passionate with furious hatred when he heard of the devastating air raids on his homeland, but as peace and tranquility of the small coastal town prevailed he began to lapse into indifference and didn't seem to care about the British boats that appeared at irregular intervals along side the Anderssons Kaj.

The war had seemed far away but now with the Abwehr agents had brought the reality of war into his office.

In his most anxious moments he knew that whatever happened he would still be Vice Consul, safe and secure, so long as he did his job and filed his reports.

He had deduced from overheard conversations that the agents were in Lysekil to capture or dispose of a wanted Norwegian terrorist who had murdered German soldiers and sabotaged military installations.

He then remembered with clarity the young Swedish women who had been persuaded to befriend a British sailor to gain information on the sailing intentions of the British boats.

He remembered the precise information she had managed to glean from the unsuspecting sailor.

Yet for all the diplomatic and military activities the Grey Ladies kept arriving.

He turned away from the papers on his desk.

There was commercial business to attend to.

Events had changed the tempo of the war and Kommodore Hans Schector found himself to be extremely busy and though he could see through the propaganda he had had an inner confidence which he conveyed to his subordinates.

Naval Headquarters in Berlin had issued directives for maximum vigilance during operational patrols as enemy activity was expected to increase within his sector. There were strong indications from intercepted signals that Norway would feature in the expected allied invasion of Europe.

There had been speculative talk of the Russians invading from the north and joining up with a British air born assault which would push towards Oslo and across the Skagerrak to Denmark.

He sipped his schnapps and ate pickled herring as he discussed this conjecture with his friend Rudiger. They came to the conclusion that an invasion of Norway wasn't feasible or practical.

The Kommodore had his orders.

For him eating had become compulsive diversion which took his mind off the realities of daily life and he was oblivious to his expanding waistline as he finished his pickled herring.

Both men clinked their glasses and drank to better days ahead. They discussed the innovative modifications made to the U – boat which would increase its range and perhaps turn the war back in Germany's favour. But no matter how they talked and no matter what they read in the newspapers or heard on the radio they knew it would take more than a snorkel on a U-boat to alter the course of the war.

As the schnapps seeped through his outer defences the Kommodore began to drift slowly into melancholia and he began an aimless meander around the chart table, stopping occasionally to look out of the window down to the quay.

The very mention of U-boats brought to the surface the misery of his lost, drowned, dead, son. His friend replenished his glass and within an instance of the liquid passing between his lips he was transformed and onto firmer ground.

He said the pickled herring was superior to any he had tasted, but it was a shrimp of a ship that caused him real irritation. A British converted gun boat. A shrimp on a large sea.

Every time he walked along the quayside he was reminded of the Grey Ladies as he passed the wreckage of the Master Standfast which was being repaired and converted.

It would be used by the Kreigs Marine.

Soon it would be sea worthy.

He nurtured the idea to see this boat added to his command and charge it with the pursuit, capture or destruction of other British Grey Ladies.

The shrill ring of the telephone brought both men to attention as Rudiger  picked up the receiver, listened and relayed the information to the Kommodore.

Intelligence indicated that the British vessel, the Nonsuch would be sailing from Lysekil in the next few days.

The orders which he issued were explicit.

The Bosun oversaw the cargo stored, he checked the hatch covers and made sure all was secured.

Reluctantly the crew busied themselves making the Nonsuch ready for sea as the Chief Engineer and the Captain discussed the performance of the three Paxman diesels. The voyages across the North Sea were providing the engine designers with invaluable knowledge of main bearing stress factors, synchronisation of three units, and reliability, in adverse weather conditions.

The Chief Engineer knew he was wasting his time talking about technical and mechanical details as he noticed the Captains eyes glaze over. He thought the trouble with deck officers was that they knew dam all about engines as the Captain listened and feigned an understanding. The Captain thought that the trouble with engineers was that they knew dam all about navigation as he reasoned that man had navigated the seas long before the invention of the engine and the propeller.

In accordance with regulations notice had been given to the harbour master of impending departure, but only at the last minute was the pilot was requested.

Departure wouldn't be long.

The Captain went to his cabin.

He glanced at photographs of his wife, daughter and son and for a few moments he was transported away across sea, space and time to the warmth of family life.

The cabin door opened and blue smoke  bellowed from the pipe of the Commodore who bustled in looking directly at the Captain.

' Well Captain, we'll be making a move as soon as the Pilot arrives. It's getting dark, I expect the Chief has his Norwegians aboard by now '.

' I've heard one of them has quite a reputation '.

As light faded men went about their work silently preparing to be at sea. The boson checked and then checked again.

Flags were down, neatly folded and stowed in the locker.

The First Officer checked the bridge and in the navigation room charts were arranged in order of sequence .

Harbour. Skagerrak. North Se

In his shack below the bridge the Radio Officer heard the commands to let go f'ward and to let go aft and he felt the vibrations as the engines growled into life and he heard the Swedish pilot give instructions.

The helmsman adjusted his balance as he turned the wheel and the Nonsuch slowly veered to starboard . Completing a ninety degree turn she settled on a course that would take her between the landmass on which Lysekil was built and the island rocky outcrop that was Flatholmen. As soon as the pilot transferred to the cutter the Nonsuch was on her way heading North, North, West into a moderate sea.  In the small chart room the First Officer worked their position plotting their course.

The Commodore found his familiar niche on the port wing of the bridge. Occupying the centre the Captain swayed, binoculars in constant use. The helmsman had sailed with more colourful Captains but on this voyage he preferred the quiet, confident command of this particular Captain.

On the short after deck the Chief Officer was engrossed in conversation with one of the Norwegians,  the Norwegian with the reputation. Rumours circulated amongst the crew that the Norwegian with the black beard and eyes that didn't blink, had earned himself the title of ' The Butcher of Trondheim ' and three sailors speculated with each other.

*' The one talking to the Chief  he's the resistance fighter the Gestapo's after '.*

*'Not surprised , wonder how he got a name like that '.*

*' Use your imagination '.*

*' Been there once '.*

*' Where, the butchers ? '.*

*' No Trondheim  you idiot '.*

*' I heard he was useful with his knife '.*

*' God 'elp us then '.*

*' Glad 'e's on our side then '.*

*' Still bloody dangerous '.*

Joining the Chief and the Norwegian on the after deck the Commodore steadied himself and looking out over the churning wake into the darkness spoke to the tall, black bearded, sharp eyed man standing by his side.

The Commodore chewed the end of his pipe as he formulated a choice of diplomatic words, but he couldn't mince his words, so he took a deep breath and spoke direct.

*' In your case we have a problem. If we are intercepted by the enemy it would be appreciated if you would disappear '*, the Commodore coughed, looked and waited apprehensively for a response but the Norwegian didn't move, he just kept looking into the tumultuous convulsions of the fast flowing wake.

Slowly he turned and looked the Commodore straight in the eyes and then slowly the contours of his deeply lined face altered, broadened and then he smiled, extending his hand he shook the Commodore by the hand and with a hearty, gruff laugh, he turned and shuffled off for the relative isolation of the gun emplacement.

Relieved with the knowledge that both men understood each other he made his way back to the crowded bridge where the Commodore joined the Captain, the Chief Officer, the First Officer and the helmsman . As the Vaderbod Light came into view the First Officer ordered the helmsman to alter course to the North West.

Spray began to sheet over the bows.

All calculations checked.

Compass.

Bearings.

Drift.

Speed.

The Captain puzzled over what he'd heard the Commodore say to the Norwegian and when the steward delivered pint pots of steaming tea he took his opportunity to question the Commodore.

*' Sir, the Norwegian, what exactly did you mean when you told him to disappear if we 'ere ?'.*

The Commodore looked out of his duffle coat warming his hands clasped around the steaming pint pot of tea, switching his gaze from the sea to the Captain .

*' Well Captain our Norwegian friend made himself very unpopular with the German Forces and I'm told he has information which is of great value . If we are intercepted or captured I would expect the Germans to assume that we are all implicated, so in the best interests of us all he would disappear. Over the side. It's all right Captain, he understands, but it wont come to that will it  ? '.*

The Captain acknowledged and affirmed.

He then returned and retreated into his watchful gaze into the sea as the bows cut through the swell and all aboard settled into the monotony of concentrated vigilance as the wind began to howl above the roar of the engines.

 In the radio room Sparks watched the ragged edged line revolve on the green radar screen  which picked out the presence of fast moving vessels.

He reported them to the bridge where the Captain ordered evasive course changes and the helmsman turned the wheel  and the bows veered violently cutting into the sea, sending sheets of cascading, slanting, freezing spray over the foredeck and bridge momentarily sinking the after deck in a swirling confusion of hungry angry seas. All on the bridge held onto something and many a man thought of the comparative safety of large ships on large seas.

The Sparks now became the Radio Officer as he reported the fast approaching blips were heading North West and would cut across the course of the Nonsuch.

On the bridge the Captain ordered a ninety degree turn as all binoculars were trained in the direction of the unseen enemy and the Radio Officer reported that the blips had altered course and were now heading North, North East and eventually disappeared off the radar screen much to the relief of all.

The Radio Officer lit a cigarette and became the nonchalant Sparks again as he figured the immediate danger had passed.

The Nonsuch shuddered speedily heading south.

South west towards the North Sea and the crew emerged from their bolt holds and breathed collective sighs of ease.

Most of the crew had given the tall Norwegian a wide berth except one who ventured a word to the solitary figure hunched against the gun emplacement, he spoke with stuttering apprehension.

' Hantsholm, I reckon we'll be passing Hantsholm 'bout now', he looked up at the dark silent figure.

' Eh is it true what they call ya, the butcher of Trongheim ?'.

The Norwegian broke out of his inert state, shivered, yawned and stretched his mighty frame, his eyes boring into the comparatively small able seaman.

' My friend, I do not understand this butcher, English joke ya ? '.

The sailor shivered.

'I've 'eard the Germans call you that '.

The Norwegian moved closer to the sailor and in a slow, deep, grating voice answered the sailors question.

' English friend I am a fisherman. Germans invade my country. Take my boat. Take my people to Grini camp. Fook them. I fight them. They take my boat. You understand '.

The able seaman understood the unflinching eyes.

Slowly a hint of a smile appeared on the Norwegians face and the able seaman began to relax deciding they were friends.

' Me to, I'm a fisherman. Never 'ad my own boat, deep sea trawlers, we've put into Trondheim once or twice. When we get back to 'ull 'av a pint with us in me local, ya must meet Doris , yer ya must 'av a pint with us when we get back 'ome '.

The wind howled and the spray speckled the darkness as the two fishermen shook hands shivering with extreme differences of thought.

One looked to the North and his country.

The other looked across the sea to the west and his country.

*' I 'ad to try*
*t'ger out of 'ere, escape*
*get back 'ome, impossible.*
*Seemed impossible, the one who snores a lot told me to ger a train to*
*the coast just like that, just as if I wuz going to Bridlington, anyroad,*
*ger a trtain t'coast 'e said then ger a boat to Sweden. He laughed a lot*
*this bloke, face turned blue, rite state 'e wuz, not well, no one is 'ere.*
*Another bloke one of the squaddies who likes it 'ere says its a dam sight*
*safer 'ere than out there, says if I want to escape I'll need false papers,*
*money and some food. Started to think I'll be 'ere f'ever '.*
*Met this Aussie bloke, working alongside 'im on site.*
*I laughed at 'im, 'is accent.*
*That was a mistake.*
*He hit me.*
*Didn't 'aft 'urt.*
*Told me not to laugh at 'im an 'e gave me a slap on back nearly killed*
*me, good bloke the Aussie, 'e 'as the same idea, escaping that is.*
*The coast.*
*A ship and away.*
*I wuz welcome t'go along with 'im so long as I didn't bugger up 'is*
*plans and didn't sing. Said it was better doing sumut than farting*
*around in this 'ere prison camp.*
*We wuz unloading timber from railway wagons in the siding in the*
*morning an' as we finished last wagon Aussie came up't me an said*
*this was it, asked if I wuz ready, to mek me mindup bluddy fast as we*
*wuz going on the train.*
*I asked 'bout food.*
*He said 'e 'ad 't all worked out and smiled.*
*I asked'im 'ow he knew train wuz going to coast, he said, 'e'd asked the*
*train driver an 'e 'ad. So we climbed on wagon and just hid away.*
*Seemed like ages.*

*The train began to move.*
*Aussie thinks we'll get a ship as easy as falling off a log.*
*First Aussie I've got to know .*
*Mind you I don't think I know that many people, really know them,*
*being a prisoner meks me think.*
*'E's an optimistic bastard I'll give 'im that. Talks same lingo sort of,*
*takes piss out of pommy bastards.*
*'Ope 'e knows what 'e's doing.*
*Told me to sit back 'an enjoy train through countryside.*
*Nice it is.*
*Suns shining .*
*Wouldn't think there's a war on.*
*So 'ere am I, on train, going through Germany with this Aussie fella.*
*Going through countryside looking for a ship.*
*Suns shining*
*Bloody cold, so bloody cold.'*

The Head of the Scandinavian section looked through the office window down to the hustle and bustle of Baker Street.

Soon people would be coping with the blackout which seemed to be just as dangerous though less dramatic than the air raids here in central London.

The legs of the girls never stopped moving in the show that never stopped at the Windmill Theatre and pleasure was heightened by the bleak knowledge of an uncertain future.

Turning from the window he looked down to the papers on his desk and they blurred into a mass of words, numbers, maps and reports. He knew he was tired and no amount of convivial conversations in the canteen over tea with his fellow officers or at the club with his peers could alter the fact that his mental and physical faculties were being stretched to the limit. Turning down another invitation for drinks with his wife and friends in ' The Fox and Grapes ', as duty called and dictated that he remain on station. The report compounded his wretchedness as he read of the execution of an S.O.E. Agent in the notorious Grini concentration camp near Oslo. The knock on the door seemed distant.

He contrieved a cough as his deputy entered.

*' Reports from Sweden Sir, an odd type of aircraft crashed there, pilotless. Bit sketchy, 'ere are you alright Sir ?'.*

Taken by surprise the Head of Section was annoyed with himself and he answered sharply.

*' Of course I'm alright. Anything else ?',* and he realised that just by answering the question revealed his tiredness.

*' Apparently powered by a rocket motor, oh by the way, another Grey Lady, the Nonsuch has delivered another cargo of ball bearings from Sweden and a butcher. Fastest trip yet '.*

*' Good good at least something is working in our favour. Now lets look at the Grey Lady account. The Commodore has played his hand and all in all the venture has worked out quite well '.*

Now he really wanted to be somewhere else as he coughed a couple of times then concentrated his attention on the papers in front of him and reflected as he read.

*' Calculation, risk and chance. Win some, loose some, lost some good men to the firing squad in Norway but on the other hand the Nonsuch has broken the blockade bringing us steel, ball bearings and a few agents. Many breakdwons, engines, experimental, another mission, maybe not. Nights getting lighter and then there is the larger picture '.*

He sat back in his chair, scratched his balding head, sighed , stretched and with a deep breath charged himself for the next task.

*' Another mission. Contact Mister Lask, he's in Sweden organising the Moonshine operation. Get in touch with him. Find out more about this German aircraft and pass it on. Now I've got to see this Norwegian chap, ' The butcher of Trondheim ', I believe he's called. Now how best to employ his skills and talents. I suppose he can open a* branch *somewhere else '.*

The Commodore eased himself into the comfortable deep green
leather upholstery of the chair reserved for visitors of importance.
He was tired and for a moment he thought he was unwell.
Lashing seas.
Dampness.
Improvised meals.
Bouncing and crashing across the North Sea on the homeward
voyage of the Nonsuch had taken its toll on him.
He sipped the Malt which brought back memories of sailing passed
the Isle of Islay as he congratulated Superintendent Watson as
always on his choice.

*' Excellent Superintendent, an excellent Malt. As you know we passed
the island on the trials and tribulations of the evaluation trip on the
Nonsuch. Seems a long, long time ago. An uncanny flavour, spring
water, peat, bog water. On tasting one anticipates but the final
settlement is delayed, then its beyond expectation '.*

*' Yes, yes it is Commodore, my father sends it down to me, not being
well of late, doubt if I'll see much more of it unless I go there myself.
Grey Ladies never designed for the North Sea in winter. Engineers tell
me they've done everything they can. There is a limit '.*

They all knew the demands, the dangers.
Experimental engines.
Tempting providence.

*' Superintendent, the Captains, Officers and men are a great credit to
the Company and that's not to mention some of the illegal activities
which seem to be going on '.*

Superintendent Watson wondered exactly what illegal activities were
going on apart from the day to day activities which were considered
normal if not exactly legal.
The Commodore couldn't be serious about the odd bit of smuggling,
the odd bit of broached cargo, after all it was part of the historical
nature of the maritime trade.

He made a mental note to speak to the Chief Constable on behalf of Shorty Burton who'd been arrested for selling contraband.

Burton was a good sailor.

The Company needed good men.

Hard to loose.

Hard to replace.

He'd had a word with the Chief Constable and asked him if he'd enjoyed the Schnapps which he had procured for him from Mister Burton.

He fondled his cigarette packet, resisting the urge for seconds, before he gave in and lit the cigarette, inhaling deeply the aromatic smoke of the American brand which he'd taken a liking for.

He could do with Lask to be back on home ground to kick a few arses and get wheels moving in the way Captain Turnbull used to do.

Lask, plucked from obscurity, given the chance and now at the behest of the 'odd bods' of Baker Street.

The Commodore put his glass to his lips, savouring the last few drops of the peaty malt. The dark figure of the Superintendent silhouetted in the frame of the window as the pale light of the afternoon filtered through, turned and glanced at the Commodore and spoke of the latest reports progress.

' *The Nonsuch had made the fastest round trip but her engines had taken a pounding. Repairs to the Hopewell and the Corsair ?. First week in March, three vessels, maximum cargo, three vessels ready early March , so there we are '.*

There was a knock on the door but the Superintendent, deep in thought didn't hear.

Ships arriving.

Ships departing.

Losses and additions.

The Grey Ladies and the Commodore only a small part of his concerns and it was only when the Commodore coughed repeatedly that he heard the tinkle of tea cups, then he made strides to the door, opened it and his face lit up as the bright expression of the young girl caught his eye as she entered pushing a tea trolley.

' *Ah Constance, a welcome sight. Over here, usual place. How's your mother ?'*

The young girl blushed as she answered and poured the tea.

' *We're coping quite well. Mother sends her thanks for the parcel, she's never tried Schnapps before. She has a little drink on a Saturday night while listening to the wireless if it is working. We're having trouble with the electricity, but we manage, thank you Sir, one sugar is it and the Commodore ?'*

She confidently poured the tea, remembering the important visitor liked his tea milky and sweet and with this served she made a smiling exit.

The Superintendent took  pen and paper and made a note to see one of his Radio Officers about a little domestic electrical job.

As the door closed behind the girl, the smile left his face and he explained, ' *Known her since she was born. We try to do what we can but its not easy for the widows and their families* '.

His words became lost as he coughed and shuffled papers around his desk and the Commodore understood a little more about people whose lives were entwined with the sea.

The Superintendent turned away from his desk.

Turned away from ships in glass cases.

Turned away from the Commodore who reclined in the comfort of the green leather chair  and looked upwards towards the clear afternoon sky of the late February day.

' *Superintendent, a date, could put to sea on  March 7th* '.

Doris was in sombre mood as she polished the slowly declining stock of glasses. She didn't need to, but the activity diverted tension away from her inner thoughts during a week which hadn't gone well.

But she could cope. She'd been through worse weeks.

In 1941, during the worst of it all, her fiancé, just back from a trip to South America, loaded with presents and expectations managed to find a taxi, no mean feat in itself, and he had the driver sound the horn as they came down Chiltern Street.

It must have been the last of the raiders.

A straggler.

Dropped a bomb.

Mutilated wrapping paper.

Splattered red.

Broken flowers.

How did he get flowers ?

Aftermath of the raid.

A kind man.

Made things out of nothing.

Celebrate anything.

She thought and often said, that his life was one endless party and she enjoyed every minute of their time together.

She was bitter.

But there was another man in her life and when he sank with his ship she lost all hope and part of her died.

After a while she knuckled down to life, just as others did.

It hadn't been her week.

The unexpected air raid on Wednesday had caught her in the confusion of the looting that followed. The Police were heavy handed and it was only the intervention of a Company man, one of her regulars, that had saved her, not only from embarrassment, but from prosecution and a possible prison sentence.

She just walked into it.

It felt bad to be caught up in the air raid and worse to be caught in the behaviour that followed.

The air raid brought it all back.

The taxi. Her man.

All seemed possible, then, the exploding finality.

She could hate.

The glass she polished glinted, reflecting memories.

She hated Frankie Hebden because he slurred his words, slurped his beer, wasted his money and neglected his wife and him now in a Prisoner of War camp in Germany.

As the bar filled with large, loud, rough edged sailors and associated shipping men her thoughts of what might have been were finally buried in moments of the present.

Doris pulled two pints for the two eager young Captains who then negotiated their way through the crowd of drinking men towards the dart board and with darts in hand played their game and Jackson smiled with self congratulation as his arrow struck double twenty.

Ginger Stokes frowned at the dart board as Harry walked in.

*' Thing about you Jacko you always find space to throw your darts. Fastest trip I hear and what's all this about a Norwegian butcher ? '.*

*' Good t'see ya Harry, not a bad trip, talked to the Chief quite a bit, he told me what he gets up to in Sweden, all manner of things '.*

Jackson gave way, as Stokes threw his arrows who laughed in disgust at his score as Jackson told of what he knew.

*' There's a few things I don't understand. The manifest always says oil drums, but I've wondered, its the way things are handled over there it's, well, 'ere I don't know. That's not bad, three double twenties. Anyway, Ginger tell Harry about the parrot, go on '.*

Captain Stokes didn't need encouragement.

*' You must have heard it .The parrot, I bought it in Rio. Tried to teach it to talk. Pretty polly pretty polly. The dammed thing lunged at me. Bit my nose. Wouldn't let go. Flapping wings. I went berserk couldn't get bloody thing off me nose hurting, shouting like hell . Second engineer couldn't stop laughing and the Chief, they just stood there talking about the mechanical difficulties of getting a parrot off a nose '*

Captain Jackson had heard the story before and he knew he would hear it again but he smiled as Harry howled with laughter.

*' Well how did he get it off ?'.*

*' The Chief called one of the stokers. A huge bloke. The stoker lit a cigarette, shoved it up parrots arse ! '.*

Captain Jackson laughed more at the sight of Ginger and Harry coughing and choking until all settled into quiet occasional smiles . They all stared at the dart board until the silence was broken when Captain Harry Whitfield announced that *' March 7$^{th}$, would  be the date for the last of the missions '.*

Superintendent Watson noted a good percentage of marine traffic was being taking up with preparations for the invasion of Europe, he also noted that Lask had been busy reassigning the crews to the serviceable Grey Ladies.

As he had business to attend to in Immingham he took the opportunity of crossing the river aboard the Gay Viking as she led the Nonsuch and the Gay Corsair to their operational base where they would load their outward cargo for Sweden.

The river was at its smooth, sun glinting , silver best .

On the bridge of the Viking Captain Whitfield looked at the gangling frame of Shorty Burton who hung over the wheel like some debauched relic of the fraught and frantic night before. The Captain was about to ask him about children's parties, smuggled watches and schnapps when the Superintendent looked away from his picturesque thoughts and spoke in ominous tones to Shorty.

*' Mister Burton, if you do any more smuggling use your imagination. A few bottles of spirits is one thing but selling watches on the black market is another. Black marketer's !, you know what people think about that don't you and rightly so. Stick to what you know ! More importantly look where you're going.'*

Shorty knew that he had been saved from the real court room and acknowledged the advice with a confessional expression as the Superintendent turned and winked at the Captain.

Shorty turned the wheel and guided the Gay Viking towards the quayside, in the Immingham dock.

The Superintendent turned to the Captain.

*' Well thanks for the lift Captain, you'll be away on the afternnon tide about 16oo hours I believe. Oh Shorty put me down for a half dozen bottles of your finest '.*

Shorty Burton acknowledged and smiled to himself as the dockers came aboard and began loading the cargo.

Drums of oil was written on the cargo manifest .

The crews quietly busied themselves with final preparations for sea with self conscious zeal as the Superintendent looked on with a world weary ' I've seen it all before ', look.

Satisfied he made his way off the boat and slowly walked off the quayside to attend to business and seemingly for a moment all was right with the world as rain began to fall .

The rain gave way to bright sunlight in a near cloudless sky as the two elderly fishermen stood on the shore watching the Gay Viking, the Gay Corsair and the Hopewell purr their way through the smooth golden waters towards the estuary of the Humber.

' *Three of 'em this time, cheeky sods them lot* '.

The other spoke.

' *No justice in this world ! Know anyone on yon boats eh ?* '.

His companion breathed deeply.

Eyes squinting furtively.

He scratched his abundance of grey whiskers upon his chin.

In deep thought.

His brow began to furrow and suddenly he looked from right to left as if he was a party to great state secrets.

He was unsure of divulging his recently acquired information.

' *You'll not tell anyone will  yer* '.

' *Don't be daft stupid sod who am I going to tell* '.

' *Well, first one the Hopewell, that's flag ship. Commodore he's on it. Important man the Commodore. Captain, young fella called Stokes, 'Ginger that's what they call him 'cause 'e's got 'ere ...*'

' *Don't tell me. Don't tell me* '.

' *Second one. Gay Corsair, Captains called Jackson and they call 'im...*'

' *Jacko !* '.

' *Suppose you want to know 'bout the third one, that's the Viking, the Gay Viking, Whitfield is the Captain, 'Arry to his friends . ' Av you ' ' 'eard 'bout Shorty ?* '.

' *Shorty Burton ?* '.

' *Yeah Shorty Burton on the Viking with 'Arry* '.

' *Thought 'e'd been caught by police, 'ow do ya know all this then ?* '.

The other looked into the distance assuming a look of superiority, raising his head towards the sky, the way he'd seen royalty do on the newsreels at the cinema.

His companion looked at him, then towards the sea and he coughed and spat upon the grey, green grass of the foreshore.

*' Aye  bet ya don't know what's the purpose of  the mission  of yon boats sailing down river ?'*

*' Purpose of mission, course I do, course I do '.*

Again he assumed his air of superiority .

*' Real purpose !. Real purpose of the mission, do I know it ? Of course I do. Teking cargo out, guns, bombs for resistance blokes in Denmark and Norway '.*

*' Ger away with ya, been at the moonshine agin 'avn't ya '.'*

The two old fishermen watched the three converted gunboats grow smaller and smaller in the late afternoon light and one said to the other and to the distance.

*' Aye whatever they're up to I wish then well '.*

And the two old men retired into their memories, memories of sailing on the afternoon tide to the fishing grounds .

As they walked away from the foreshore towards the pub called 'The Poacher ' they continued their reminiscences as the afternoon faded into shadows.

Hopewell, Gay Corsair and Gay Viking  sailed abreast.

Cutting into the unusual calm of the North Sea.

Fifteen knots.

Cold.

Slight breeze, exhilarating.

Hopewell.

Engines roared.

The sea spoke an untranslatable language as it hissed and gurgled along the hull.

Stern low.

Bows high.

Flying spray, swirling, joining the flowing bow wave, forming a spreading wake of rapidly receding luminosity.

The Commodore huddled on the side of the bridge.

Captain, Chief Officer, First Officer stood apart in silence occasionally glancing through binoculars looking southwards as they passed  ships fishing over the Dogger Bank.

For Captain Stokes shore leave had been long.

Rain hadn't helped making the grey drabness of the town, damp and dismal and after so long the sea called him.

Land was something to sail towards and then to sail away from.

He'd wandered around so many bars, drank so much, told stories, tales, repeating himself sometimes during the same evening. He knew he'd imposed himself more than once upon friends and their families and he knew there were limits. When the taste of drink began to offend his palette and brain, and when the sound of his own voice began to bore him he knew it was time to be on the bridge of a ship, any ship, in some vast spacious sea, on course for another land.

But he had pleasant  memories of the chaos of the Jackson family home when the whine of a bomb provoked panic until it was realised the high octave sound was the whine of the singing dog called Prince.

That was good, but now he felt better .

Breeze on his face.

Calm dark sea before him.

Stars, navigators beacons sparkling above in clear black blue sky.
Gay Corsair, Gay Viking and the Hopewell on course together.
Intimate solitude.

Sleep came easy to the fortunate few as the boats sped quickly and
smoothly through the slowly moving calm sea.

An occasional bump was no comparison to the muscle wrenching
pounding of previous trips.

Now at one with the elements the Captain smoked, coughed and
paced from starboard to port and in passing would look at the
compass oblivious to the man on the wheel and oblivious to the
hunched statuesque figure of the Commodore on the port side.

Like the Captain, the Commodore enjoyed the reflective solitude of
clear sky, dark sea  as he stared into his innermost thoughts.

The Chief Officer, a hard man, a man who said little but when it
mattered, said a lot. He suffered from cold in his feet yet he'd been in
more hot water than he cared to remember. Archie knew him more
than most and when he brought mugs of steaming coffee the Chief
was more than grateful and the Commodore broke out of his exile
into urgent words which brought the Captain to his side.

*' Captain, Captain, I remember reading an accident report of a
collision at sea '.*

The Commodore on seeing the Captain's expression wished he hadn't
began his attempt conversation, but he persevered.

*' The lookout on a P & O Line ship sailing  in the Indian Ocean
reported a low flying cloud. No one took any notice. Then....'*

The Captain annoyed at the invasion of his mental space looked
expressionless as the Commodore paused as he tried to get his facts
together and then continued.

*' The ship collided you see, and the master realised the low flying cloud
as reported was an island, 'ere shrouded in cloud  '.*

The Commodore laughed half heartedly then looked introspectively
forward as the Hopewell cut through the swish of seas with the whine
of the diesels and gentle pitch of the boat ensuring confidence.

He smiled to himself reflecting that his age had barred him from his want to be active in the service of the Royal Navy yet here he was on the bridge of a boat, a Commodore to boot with the enemy lurking. But he knew that his knowledge of Scandinavia and the steel industry was invaluable and it was over dinner with influential people that he had proposed buying up large quantities of Swedish ball bearings knowing that they were difficult to transport to Britain then at least the Germans would be deprived of them.

Operations in 41/42, using freighters sailing through the Skagarrak brought success and failure .

His innermost thoughts were invaded by voices of sailors surfacing from the accommodation, grumpy and hungry as the first shards of light heralded the dawn.

And now as he looked aft he could see the bow waves of two other boats with success and failure down to the fickle nature of circumstance and chance.

Time passed into hours towards the dawn .

Gay Corsair, Gay Viking and the Hopewell keeping perfect station as the engines produced fifteen knots steady which would take them to the entrance of the Skagerrak by night fall.

The ominous, repetitive, calm of the day to contend with and with every hour thoughts of Inga became more real for Archie Price who concentrated his energies on breakfast making in the minute galley. With guile he performed miracles occasionally looking at his own reflective conscious image in 'Bastard ' the coffee urn.

' Bastard', looked him in the eye, steady, confident and resolute.

Archie knew there'd be no complaints from the crew but he couldn't be sure about the Chief Officer whom he knew would be suffering from the affliction to his feet and was likely to alleviate his discomfort by verbally lashing out at whoever was nearest.

The Chief Officer enjoyed an enduring, tetchy relationship with Archie.

Breakfast over.

The Bosun turned out the sailors.

There was no need, but they scrubbed the decks as a breeze developed into a freshening wind and the white caps rose, glinting in the pale sun.

It was Eddie Higgins aboard the Gay Corsair who heard them first.

On the Gay Viking it was Shorty Burton who identified them.

Aboard the Hopewell it was the Chief Officer who called for action stations .

There were two of them.

Black, twin engined aircraft, Dornier D.O.17's came swooping down to sea level about four miles east and closing fast.

No mistaking their intentions.

Sailors donned helmets, loaded magazines, swivelled Vickers Oerlikons, fixing sights.

Captains shouted .

The boats broke formation.

The first Dornier opened fire, shells hitting the sea, sending plumes, in a deadly line running towards and raking across the stern tearing chunks out of the deck of the first Grey Lady.

Fire, red, white black smoke thickly erupted, swirling as Vickers and Oelikons opened up with a devastating hail of fire as the two attacking German aircraft shrieked passed.

The down draft picked up the sea and the sea fell back as the smoke cleared and the two aircraft banked, quietly climbing, flying into the distance becoming specks and then seemed to hover, then turning, heading back towards the Grey Ladies.

Captains ordered course changes to face the oncoming aircraft.

Chief Officers ordered gunners to withhold fire.

Nerves grated.

All quiet.

Then ear splitting roar of engines as cannon shells tore into the sea , plumes erupted and raced towards the boats.

Chief Officers gave the order.

Quadruple Vickers cannon opened up belching smoke and flame as the large black shapes closed fast into the circular gun sights .

The first aircraft roared overhead, turned, gained height and came around again.

The second aircraft came straight towards the Hopewell and all aboard ducked as the huge black aircraft screaming cannon fire swept over head  and kept on towards the sea.

Wing tip touched the sea.

Cartwheeled.

Wings breaking off.

Disintegrating in an awesome explosion of red, yellow, sea, metal, white and black. With the attention of crews diverted,  the second aircraft  was on them with a vengeance.

Attacking broadside.

Shells ripped into the armoured box bridge of the Hopewell.

Captain Stokes was lashed across his face with blood.

The First Officer flew passed him in a ball of smoking screams hitting the wing of the bridge, arms, legs distorting falling over the side.

The aircraft was over them guns blazing at the Gay Corsair .

Shells converging, metal screamed, fire, smoke, white heat and the boson broke up into exploding pieces.

Now the Dornier roared guns blazing towards the Gay Viking .

Shorty Burton squeezed the trigger on his gun swearing violently, willing the bullets towards the enemy.

As sweat ran down his contorted features he kept his guns blazing as the black shape headed straight towards him.

Swivelling and firing round after round, with shell cases  ejecting in white hot smoke the Dornier screeched over head and Shorty's guns jammed. Slowly he breathed deeply, watching small sections of the aircraft break away then fall to the sea as the main frame of the aircraft climbed into the afternoon light, smoke trailing from its fuselage and port engine. It climbed high.

Weaving and dipping its wings.

Apart from the sound of the engines and the swish of the sea there was quiet as all looked up to see the aircraft climb to the limits of its endurance.

For long, long seconds it was stationary, a solitary black smoking
speck in the sky.
Suddenly falling like a stone.
Engines, scratching through sky, reaching a crescendo as it hit the
sea in a beautiful, violent, eruption of ascending and descending
jagged white sheets of white which quickly merged with the sea until
all was calm and settled.
Sailors, motormen, engineers, officers all looked on.
Looked on to where only a patch of debris and oil floated.
A collective stare empathised with the Germans, victims of their own
attack.
Slowly.
Slowly the boats resumed their course.
Aboard the Gay Viking Shorty Burton wiped cold sweat from his
brow and  unwilling tears meandered down the cordite grime on his
face as he thought of children's parties.
Aboard the Hopewell the Chief  Officer stamped his feet and thought
Russian boots might offer better protection for his feet.
Ten.
Fifteen.
Twenty minutes elapsed.
Nobody counted time.
Nobody noticed how every weather beaten face had aged just a little
turning a slight shade of blue into violet and grey.
The swishing sea and wind whispered an oration to the dead and the
living, and slowly, very slowly time and the sea resumed their drift.
Debris was cleared, thrown overboard, hammers nailed, short pieces,
long pieces fixed and fitted, all was sea worthy if not ship shape and
the engines purred, occasionally grating. The Commodore, Captains
and all aboard the three boats knew that the Germans would be
making  efforts to find their aircraft and exact some sort of revenge.
The Commodore ordered the two other boats to close in on the
Hopewell and as they cruised together he shouted orders through a
megaphone to the other two Captains.

They would plot their own course, sail independently through the Skagerrak aiming to rendezvous off the Hallo light at 0700hrs the following morning. The Commodore wished them Gods speed, the wind whipped up the seas, and the engines growled.

As the last of the day died the three small boats sped eastwards and within a few hours they parted company for the two hundred mile run through the Skagerrak.

Bitter cold and after shock effected Harry Whitfield on the Gay Viking as he shivered off the darting lashing spray that the bows threw up.

It was as if he wasn't in command, realising the arbitrary nature of life, he breathed deeply and his lungs took in the cold night air and his resolve returned.

He wondered if Shorty Burton was alright as he hadn't seen him since the engagement with the enemy.

But Shorty had a reputation of blending into the background.

In the darkened room beneath the bridge the Radio Officer looked up at the threatening piece of jagged cannon shell shrapnel stuck in the bulkhead in line with his head.

He mused that a different angle would have caused him acute discomfort.

He wasn't religious.

But he thanked God.

The frayed line of light revolved around the black circular radar screen slowly revealing the Danish coast.

To the north the Gay Corsair ploughed through the calm sea.

Captain Jackson, on the bridge, heard dull rumblings in the distance but wasn't sure if the noise was only in his head but he didn't want a second opinion.

His stoic, expressionless stance disguised and contained screams, of North Atlantic cold, torpedo, explosion , nerve end fear.

Fear would come and go.

Memories came and went.

As he looked towards the bows he could still see the boson, the boson disintegrating into small pieces, vanishing into the quick of smoke, spray, fire.

So quick.

The boson in the right place at the wrong time.

Out of intuitive reason he promoted Eddie Higgins who was in the right place at the right time.

He became boson without a word or hint of expression as actions were all rolled into one as the war seemed bizarrely distant and he began to organise sailors who accepted him as if it was the natural order of life and in a way it was  as he gave them orders but they didn't obey, they just did what he asked  of them.

The sea was calm .

Navigators instruments remained static on the tiny chart table as the First Officer worked on approximate calculations of their position on the sea chart of the Skagerrak .

He manipulated the parallel rulers across the chart and drew a direct line .

For the Captain on the bridge it was a little too quiet, ominously quiet, as he looked through his binoculars scanning the seas, and as the wind picked up, the bows heaved and plunged deep into the sea sending showers of spray lashing across the decks and bridge.

On the chartroom table instruments rolled to the edge .

In the galley hanging from hooks pans veered from port to starboard and starboard to port, colliding with each other, making  macabre music .

The seas rose and the boat pitched and rolled.

In the cramped accommodation belongings, cases, bags, fell from lockers inflicting more than one with minor irritating injuries.

Ordered to wear exposure suits, sailors remembered to have their last piss before putting on their suits.

Eyes quick and sharp looked out over the rolling seas knowing that they were being hunted.

Wind began to howl .

Waves began  to buffet the boat with intent.

On the Hopewell, Captain Stokes nerves twitched as the after images of the action reverberated through his senses, but his relationship with the sea remained the same, only his relationship with his fellow man had changed.

The Chief Officer stamped his feet thinking about Russian boots that were made to survive the harshest of winters. Enemy aircraft, cannon shells, bullets, stench of death, all part of war he could accept, all in a days work but the continuous gnawing pain in his feet was something else.

The Corsair slowed down.

Bearings taken, it was 05 -46 a.m.

Captain Jackson saw the Hallo navigational light blinking reassurance and the small flickering lights of a country at peace .

He blew down the voice pipe and asked the Chief Engineer to join him on the bridge.

It was still dark.

Some of the sailors took advantage of being in Swedish territorial waters and slept soundly, others talked, smoked and relaxed as the Corsair cruised towards Lysekil .

The Chief Engineer staggered onto the bridge throwing himself awkwardly onto the wind dodgers for support and he heaved and spewed over the side. The Chief Officer shook his head in disgust but the Captain was aware of the machinations which afflicted the Chief Engineer. As soon as the Gay Corsair was in Swedish waters the Chief Engineer was at the bottle.

The Captain knew the Chief was a good engineer and he looked at the drunken man with more than a little understanding as memories surfaced.

After effects.

In the North Atlantic along with himself the Chief had been at his station in the engine room when the torpedo struck.

Drowning.

Almost.

Encased. Ship sinking. Oil black. Cracked split open. Eternal minutes.

Black hole.

Screaming men.

Dying drowning.

Sea gushing, rushing and in a flurry of bubbling oil up, up, and onto the ocean surface thick with fire.

Both men owed their lives to reaching hands of Canadians .

Dark time ago and no matter how hard he tried, memories returned with noise, screeching, oil, smoke and the smell of cordite, the striking of a match could start him off and would take the Chief Engineer straight to the bottle.

The Captain knew but was annoyed.

The Chief Engineer coughed, spluttered and tried to speak but could only make nonsensical sounds as he jerked his frame from hand hold to hand hold but he realised he was safe when he saw the shoreline and the sky.

Secure he tried to speak but could only laugh .

Though irritated and angry the Captain understood.

The Chief Engineer began to slur out phrases of incoherence until laughing words formed sentences of little sense.

*' Capt'n good man, good man Cap'n, that's me trouble can't bloody forget, sorry Cap'n can't put to sea tell ya why 'cos engines like me, pissed an broke, get it Cap'n, pissed and broke, can't put sea, pistons broke'.*

Loudly laughing, spluttering, coughing he swung his head over the wind dodgers.

Cold gusts brought some sense back and he focused on the disapproving Captain.

According to the book the Captain should fine a man in his condition or worse, but as far as this Captain was concerned there was no mention of a situation like this in the book.

He shouted for the nearest sailor to take the Chief Engineer to his bunk to sleep it off where there would be no Luftwaffe, no Kreigsmarine.

The urgent voice of Eddie Higgins ever alert to his new position called .

*' The others, it's the others , its the others Capt'n '.*
And through his binoculars the Captain saw the Viking emerge from the north and then the Hopewell from the west.
In the grey dawn, the ladies made their rendezvous and all the crews were relieved, happy and sad at the same time.

It was usual for the German Vice Consul to be up by 6.a.m. everyday even Sunday. He prided himself on his regularity and his discipline. But this Sunday his wife suggested he lay in bed a little longer and at first he resisted the temptation of breaking his routine which had served him so well.

But his wife was so persuasive.

For both of them it had been to long since they'd said yes to each other and no to the greater cause.

Her eyes told him and he knew it.

With a new found vigour he hummed a tune as he walked down the stairs to his second floor office. As he opened the door the picture of the Fuhrer fell from the wall and the glass splintered over the floor. He swore vehemently, but wasn't sure if he swore at the Fuhrer or at the thought of clearing up the broken glass.

He looked at his dairy.

March 9th 1944.

Church was later on and apart from a coaster which would arrive later in the day he had no official business, no urgent telegrams or Abwehr agents to complicate his day.

The morning light was shining through the window and he decided to take a walk around the harbour. He asked his wife to accompany him but she declined as she was making pastries for the Church function which he had almost forgotten about.

He buttoned up his coat, breathed in the cold fresh air and with a glance towards the southern harbour walked north along Drottinggaten saying ' *Godday* ', to acquaintances who passed him by as they went about their business. He became aware of people heading towards the southern harbour more than usual for this time of day.

People walked if not fast then with an urgency suggesting something unusual, but he continued to walk north with memories of his wife still in his mind.

Feeling younger, he walked briskly and on this fine morning all was right with the world and he decided to walk as far as Gallenberg Point to view the island of  Stora Skeppsholmen.  -

More people walked with purpose in the opposite direction.

On this sunny cold pleasant morning with an unexpected bright start to the day he only wanted a quiet and restful place to order his thoughts and his feelings.

To look into the dark deep green seas as they crashed onto rocks would serve him well, but from passers by he heard snippets of conversation, talking of invasion.

Curiosity forced him to slow his walk.

He looked southwards.

After a few moments deliberation, his instincts got the better of him. He turned and walked back and he felt the excitement of the people as they began to congregate of the southern harbour, perhaps fifty or sixty or more. He'd only ever seen such a gathering outside the church on a Sunday and as he looked across the waters of the Gullmarn he realised why as a small grey boat bedecked in an abundance of flags and then another small grey boat and then a third small grey boat came into view.

Unmistakable, a line of Grey ladies, all decked out and flying huge red ensigns of the British Merchant Marine.

People talked unusually rapidly, enthusiastically, all looking, pointing, shouting at the colourful invasion as the boats sailed slowly in line, crews waving to the crowd and the crowd waving back to the crews on the boats as if they were all taking part in some nautical pageant. He watched. Puzzled by his own reaction.

A few months ago he would have felt a deep and righteous indignation at the sight of just one of these boats and would have done his utmost to terminate their mission.

But now he felt a sense of admiration for these enemies who waved from the decks of their small boats.

The graceful weather beaten Grey Ladies headed for the quayside .

He had to admit, they looked impressive.

Perhaps it was the colour of the flags.

Perhaps it was the people, the voices calling to each other.

The war seemed a long, long way away.

He thought of his wife and children, for so long in the background as the dictates of war demanded and now feeling an affirmation of something unfolding before him which he found difficult to comprehend.

He watched for a short time then turned away from the harbour thinking perhaps he could arrange a few days holiday with his wife and children but his thoughts were interrupted .

A young women in a frantic hurry brushed past him and for a moment he thought he recognised her.

Same features, same expressions, same height.

And she wore a maroon coat.

He wasn't sure, but if it was, then one of the British sailors was in for a pleasant surprise.

The German Vice Consul walked away sedately towards his house with the emblem of the Reich upon the door.

Seated at his desk  Kommodore Hans Schector read through a communique from one of his Kaptains detailing  sightings of ships in the Kattegat. He listened as Kapitanleutenant Rudiger read the daily reports.

*' Her Kommodore two of our aircraft lost to enemy fire,  from those irritating Grey Ladies. The aircraft crews were fortunate, they were picked up by a Danish fishing boat '.*

The Kommodore gestured impatiently with his hands and facial expressions and Rudiger understood .

*' The explosion in the harbour caused extensive damage to an armed trawler, the work of the same group of terrorists who were responsible for a recent attack on a troop train outside Aalberg and on rail lines around Aachus according to military intelligence.  But this report Kommodore of empty oil drums found on the shore near Randers is unusual because they were cut open suggesting they had been carrying something else other than oil and they had English markings .Then there is report of a Wehrmach patrol arresting two Danes driving a lorry with a load of oil drums which contained not oil but guns and ammunition which leads me to think about the Grey Ladies and their cargo '.*

The Kommodore stood up and now felt there was something to be done.

*' Rudiger what was the cargo on the captured Master Standfast ? '.*

*' Her Kommodore, it says oil, in drums on the Bills of Laden,  all in order for civilian trade '.*

*' Rudiger where are they now ?'.*

The Kommodore didn't need an answer.

He picked up his telephone and ordered his car.

Both men put on their great coats and caps and walked quickly, acknowledging salutes of startled subordinates in the outer office, then they walked down the stairs and out of the Headquarters into the awaiting car for the short drive to the ship repair yard.

The Kommodore remained in the warmth of the car as Rudiger sought out the foreman .

After a curt exchange of words and directives the two men walked some distance around sheds to where the foreman pointed to a stack of drums.

Rudiger ordered them to be opened .

The foreman grudgingly summoned workers who inserted probes into the first, second and third drums, prodding and stirring to no avail. More drums were opened and as the foreman probed and stirred he became agitated.

Heavy duty cutters removed the tops of drums which after a messy retrieval revealed packages and after awkward manipulation were unwrapped and unfurled revealing short barrelled machine guns , ammunition and explosives.

On drive back to Headquarters the Kommodore looked at his trusted friend and spoke to him in hushed tones.

*' Rudiger, this dammed war isn't going our way. The allies have carried out a massive air raid on the Schweinfurt ball bearing factory and that will slow down production. These raids put the British and the Grey Ladies into sharp focus. There is a duality here, these boats bring in arms hidden in these oil drums which are smuggled to the Danish resistance . Then the Grey Ladies take ball bearings back to England. Priority from Berlin is to capture the Grey Ladies with their cargo intact as soon as they leave Swedish waters, if they leave Swedish waters . Our agents might incapacitate them while in Swedish waters.'*

The two men arrived back at Headquarters and immediately set about reassessing and reorganising patrols with orders to be transmitted to Kapitans of destroyers, E – Boats, armed trawlers and submarines.

*' Mister Lask, this int real, it's a story, all med up, a dream, a night*
*mare, well Mister Lask, ya want to know what 'appened, well as far as*
*I can remember train travelled North an I slept a lot.*
*During day.*
*Sun shone.*
*Beautiful skies.*
*Cold winds.*
*High sides of wagon sheltered us.*
*Huddled in corner, slept, felt good.*
*The Australian might 'av told me ''is name but I forgot, I forgot.*
*He didn't talk a much*
*Big bloke, blond 'air, blue eyes*
*Powerful*
*I asked 'im where 'e came from, didn't tell me. Didn't talk much.*
*Powerful bloke*
*Quietness unnerved me.*
*Never met anyone like 'im before*
*When train came t'a stop I wuz scared*
*I wuz scared I'b been scared before but now something else*
*Australian told me t'look confident*
*'Ad a nerve 'e did*
*Got off train med our way from goods yard walked through gate it as if*
*we owned the place.*
*'Alf expected to see soldiers everywhere but there wasn't any*
*Town we arrived wuz a port you'll know that Mister Lask.*
*Seagulls.*
*Ship horns*
*Steam an noise med us feel better as we walked streets just like 'ome*
*Different*
*Difficult t' look confident*
*Clothes falling off*
*Needed a wash.*
*It wuz late afternoon and the sky had turned murky and overcast.*
*'e knw what 'e wuz doing*

*'e knew what 'e wuz looking for I'll give 'im that.*

*We came across a group of men working , clearing up rubbish on bombed out building*

*Reminded me of 'ome*

*We just pitched in with them, shifting bricks and timber 'e really got stuck in*

*Funny bluddy hysterical two escaped prisoners on the run.*

*In Germany out in the open clearing up bomb damage our lads had done.*

*The Australian didn't say much just grunted now and then and by this time I'd learned to do everything he did.*

*Asked 'im what wuz 'appening as I 'adn't a clue.*

*He did*

*Said if we played our cards right, then 'e winked knowing like and that wuz all.*

*Reckoned we were somewhere on the Baltic*

*Looked f'signs*

*Blokes we worked with wore a 'P' on their jackets and I remember the snoring bloke back at the camp the bastard who kept me awake all night long.*

*Mister Lask, Mister Lask, when ya ask me 'ow I escaped, you'll never believe me, I know 'cos its not real, we just mucked in with these workers, they 'ad ' P ' on there jackets, and when we finished work we caught tram back with Polish workers 'an found ourselves in a camp. Daft Mister Lask, daft.*

*There wuz a guard on the gate of the camp,'an old man who couldn't give a toss, and the Australian 'ad a way with gestures and I wuz glad 'bout that, 'e knew what t'do , 'e 'ad sum nerve 'e did. I 'adn't a clue, me Frankie Hebden not knowing what t'do, that's saying sumut Mister Lask !.*

*Spent night at camp*

*Couldn't understand what blokes were talking 'bout.*

*But 'ad a good nights sleep.*

*Wasn't cold as Poles 'ad wood for fire in stove in middle of room.*

*Next day went back to work on tram, same site, clearing rubble 'a I wus*
*beginning t' feel more confident .*
*' There were guards like, old blokes, they just seemed t' go through*
*motions, didn't seem t' be bothered.*
*The Poles shared there food, they seemed to understand.*
*Then the Australian disappeared, the Poles shrugged their shoulders,*
*smiled and winked.*
*I kept on working.*
*I started to worry. Really worry.*
*Bluddy selfish bastard I thought.*
*Bringing me all this way.*
*When I could be ….*
*Dropping me in it.*
*Leaving me with all these blokes who didn't speak Englsh.*
*What the 'ell wuz I gunn a do.*
*I kept working.*
*Started to rain.*
*Up to me neck in muck, everything different at sea.*
*He could 'av been captured.*
*Not 'im !*
*Bastard came back.*
*Later we just walked off the site.*
*The Australian, a Pole and mesen, just walked off site an', you'll never*
*believe this Mister Lask, we went to a cafe.*
*Mister Lask, Gods trueff, we 'ad watery soup and bread. Not bad either.*
*The Pole paid for it. How ? I'll never know.*
*The Australian said he'd got us a ship to Sweden .*
*Bluddy marvellous.*
*A Swedish sailor came into cafe an' sat with us.*
*Daft, funny, scary when I look back.*
*An Australian, a Pole, a Swede and me all sat around a table in a cafe*
*somewhere on the German coast 'and any minute the R.A.F. About t'*
*bomb 'ell out of the place. But they didn't.*
*The Swede helped me onto the ship.*

*All I 'ad t'do wuz act drunk, an that Mister Lask wasn't as easy as you may think.*

*' Av to laugh.*

*Me !, pretending t'be drunk.*

*We staggered t' docks in driving rain. At the entrance to docks, guard wanted to see passes, but Swede acted really drunk, come t' think of it, 'e wuz, gave the guard a hard time 'an the Swede was big bloke.*

*Guard got really angry and shouting.*

*Told us t'get to our ship an we staggered off in pouring rain all way to ship.*

*Aboard I wuz taken to engine room.*

*Told to hide under boiler . Bluddy 'ot I can tell ya. One extreme to another ,*

*Not much room.*

*Spent a long time there I can tell ya Mister Lask on me own I wuz frightened.*

*Closed me eyes.*

*Tried to sleep.*

*Couldn't stop thinking 'bout me wife, an' Doris in The Empress and the Grey Ladies '.*

*That wuz sum storm we 'ad in Irish sea.*

*Round Lands End.*

*Best storm I've been in.*

*In the Skagerrak, Bremen Built bastard, shooting, explosions, Germans an prison camp, locked up, shouting, ordered about, always cold, so bluddy cold, not much good except 'board ship.*

*Thanks to that Aussie, the Pole and the Swede I found meself back at sea underneath bluddy boiler of ship.*

*So bluddy 'ot Mister Lask.*

*So bluddy hot.*

*Lost track of time.*

*Swede came t'get me, took me on deck, it wuz night at sea and 'e pointed to land ahead an' 'e told me I wux free.*

*Didn't say much else.*

*I asked why he 'elped me 'an 'e said he liked the Australian, I asked 'im if 'e liked the English he shrugged 'is shoulders 'an laughed.*

*Anyway, that's what 'appened Mister Lask, I know it sounds daft but I couldn't mek it up, anyway what are you doing 'ere.*

*Stockholm isn't it.*

*Last person to see*

*Anyway then we docked.*

*Car came for me.*

*Embassy ? Isn't it Mister Lask.*

*You were going t' tell me what your doing 'ere '.*

Herbert Lask sat listening with belief and disbelief to the events described by Frankie Hebden, now in the security of a quiet reception room in the British Embassy, Stockholm, neutral Sweden.

*' Well Mister Hebden, you are a very lucky man. Now I have a few arrangements to make before we can travel back to England '.*

Frankie, tired, slumped backwards into the comfortable chair and was about to nod off when thoughts of home reinvigorated him and he sat up and asked.

*'Eh, Mister Lask, you 'avn't told me what you're doing 'ere in Stockholm. Last time I saw you wuz in Immingham docks with Captain Turnbull '.*

*' It wuz you that hood winked me t'mek trip on Master Standfast so what yer doing 'ere Mister Lask, I know Company looks after its own but I can't believe you've been sent 'ere to tek me 'ome '.*

Herbert Lask rose from his chair and as he walked around the room he thought of Captain Turnbull deciding to tell Frankie of his death later.

Lask effected a slight smile as he replied.

*' That's right Frankie, the Company sent me over to bring you back, you see we're short of a boson '.*

Frankie croaked a sigh of despairing resignation.

*' Ah, Mister Lask I thought there'd be a fucking catch. All this special treatment. I suppose you arranged for the escape as well '.*

Herbert Lask stayed silent, smiled and made for the door thinking about pilotless aircraft, the new weapon in the enemies armourary, but he called back.

*' Mister Hebden we're going back tomorrow, so get some rest '.*

*' How are we going t'do that Mister Lask ? '.*

*' The Grey Ladies Mister Hebden the Grey Ladies ! '.*

And with that Herbert Lask closed the door leaving Frankie to drift off into a warm comfortable sleep.

Aboard the Hopewell the Commodore poured Schnapps into glasses as the three Captains crowded into the small cabin. Apart from ' good health ' nothing was said until the liquid lubricated their vocal chords and then they talked about their individual voyages through the Skagarrak , the battle, the injured and the dead.

The Commodore told them the injured had been taken to the local hospital and he spoke gravely of the death of the First Officer of the Hopewell and the boson of the Corsair, saying he would break the news to the next of kin. He asked of the morale of the crews. The Captains expressions were in the affirmative. Captain Jackson made no mention of his Chief Engineer who was still sleeping off excessive consumption of rum.

The S.O.E. Chief Officers worked in conjunction with the friendly Swedes organising the unloading of the cargo of oil drums and then when that was done the loading of their homeward cargo of ball bearings which would be completed by the following afternoon.

The Commodore instructed the Captains to be ready to sail as soon as the hatches had been battened down. There would be two passengers and he thought it would be fitting if they sailed on the Gay Viking though he didn't explain why.

Glasses emptied, briefing finished and with a few hours of shore leave beckoning most of the crews would head for the hospitality of the Stadshotel. Some trying to remember what was needed at home which wasn't difficult as everything was needed and  decided to seek out shops.

Archie had hoped to see Inga again but he knew it would be highly unlikely .

As the Hopewell had touched the Andersonns Kaj his
senses were shocked when she appeared out of the small crowd that
had gathered.

Light played tricks.

Impossible, possible, not a second time.

She was there, pushing her way through the crowd, shouting for him,
and as he left the boat he heard the voice of the Chief Officer
shouting a slightly mocking warning to him not to miss the boat.

The welfare of Archie Price was high on the Chief Officers list of
priorities.

Reunited, Archie and Inga hustled their way through the crowd and
words came out in a torrent as Archie knew there was little time.

Elated, excited, confused.

He asked how she knew.

How she knew he would come back and as they turned right from
Drottningaten into Korsgaten her answers came quickly and as he
looked into her eyes he thought he understood.

She told him that her father had died and so there was no reason to
stay in Gothenburg so she'd come to Lysekil in the hope that Archie
would come.

He asked about the Germans.

She was silent and as they walked the narrow street she blushed with
embarrassment as she recalled the way she'd been used.

They came to a bakery where she worked and lived and as they
walked  up the stairs to her room she squeezed his hand, looking at
him with apprehension as if to reassure herself that it was really him.

She opened the  door.

A collection of small glass ornaments sat on a table.

A wardrobe.

A hand basin.

An occasional table and a bed.

The room, though sparse, a small home.

She held him tightly and his fingers ran through her hair and in their
embrace they found each other again.

A veil of mist drifted off the sea and as it reached the harbour and the Anderssons Kaj it began to envelop the three small boats in eerie silence.

Captain Whitfield welcomed the two passengers aboard the Gay Viking and those who recognised Mister Lask were more than surprised to see him.

Some thought they recognised the other man, but the mist obscured their sight as he was spirited away. When asked who he was the Chief Officer would only say that he was an escaped prisoner and wasn't one hundred percent fit and he needed rest.

On the Hopewell the Captain called for the boson to let go f'ward and to let go aft. The Chief Officer peered anxiously into the swirling mist along the quay and just as the Hopewell began to move he heard the voice of Archie Price and then he saw him running frantically towards the boat and with a leap of utter disbelief jumped and landed and stumbled on the afterdeck. He picked himself up and looked apprehensively with expectation towards the bridge the bridge and sure enough the Chief Officer glared at him with disapproval .

Archie grinned and said .

*' I didn't Chief ',*

*' You didn't what Mister Price ? ',* barked the Chief,

*' I didn't Chief, I didn't miss the boat '.*

As the boat left the quayside the Chief waved him away and told him to get to his galley and make him a bacon sandwich.

The Hopewell followed the Gay Corsair and the Gay Corsair followed the Gay Viking and the Gay Viking sailed slowly through intermittent patches of fog in the dwindling light of the late afternoon.

The three boats sailed North, North West leaving Swedish territorial waters . Their intention was to break formation and sail independently and the cover of the sea mist would provide extra security or so the Commodore hoped.

The night clouded over and it became dark, very dark.

The Gay Viking disappeared from the view of the other boats.

On the Gay Corsair the First Officer checked and Captain Jackson double checked their course . It became apparent the compass reading was out of line with their course and position . They reasoned that the hold full of steel bearings had effected the magnetic compass which wasn't showing true. So with vague visual references from the radar of the Norwegian coast they made adjustments to the compass readings and calculated their course.

Looking astern Captain Jackson could just see the bow wave of the Hopewell about two cables astern. He picked up the Aldiss lamp and flashed a message to Captain Stokes informing him of his compass problem and requesting the Hopewell to overtake so he could follow in their wake .

As the Hopewell responded and began to increase speed to overtake the Gay Viking a dense fog descended restricting visability to a few yards.

Voices mutated as they carried on.

The eerie mist merging with the sea whispers.

From the Gay Corsair the high pitched voice of Eddie Higgins chilled every man to the bone.

*' Torpedo track starboard coming straight at us ! '.*

The Captain ordered full speed ahead and the engines roared and the boat surged and the Captain ordered hard a port and the Helmsman wrenched the wheel and the bows cut deep into the sea sending spray over the entire boat as the mist thickened in the black night.

Voices shouted.

Shouting voices.

Metal scratching, voices shouting, wood screeching, voices screaming, shuddering, scraping, shouting voices, halting, unseen rock, men breathing deeply, no explosion, no fire.

The Captain shone a torch into dense fog.

The beam illuminating a gaping scraped gash in the side of another ship as confused voices came from here and there.

*' What 'appened ? Torpedo '. Collided . Torpedoed.*

' *The Hopewell . Jesus Christ ! Sinking. Commodores on that .*
' *Commodores on that* '.
The harsh frantic voice of Captain Stokes shouted through the dense swirling misty fog .
' *Jackson, you hear me, we're badly holed, taking water fast, we've no chance, stand by* '.
The voice of the Captain of the sinking Hopewell gave the order to abandon ship then his voice was lost in the cacophony of rushing seas, shouting sailors, roaring hissing engines, steam, mist and thick swirling fog. In the confusion of erratic movement of torch beams, men broke out inflatable rafts throwing them with themselves into the black swirling sea.
The Chief Officer had to make sure the Hopewell would sink and he had to activate the scuttling charges. He talked to himself, directing himself, swearing and cussing himself as he grappled his way to the switch which would set off the charge that would sink the boat .
' *God me feet, can't see dammed thing, torch where's my bloody torch, end of cord, tied to my belt, got it, the bridge, dammed plug, where's dammed plug, never thought I'd be doing this, bloody cold, time running out, here we are, switch , turn handle, bloody boat, get out, to old for this lark, dropped torch, on cord, cords tight, can't move, cut bloody cord daft sod, cut cord, jump, no life jacket, bloody leg, jump, go on jump* '.
The Chief Officer immersed, thrashing, stretching every sinew of muscle taut as he swam into troughs away from the crippled boat. Cracking, exploding, ear splitting, surging sea, head cracked , sea bright, illuminated, deep, deep, dark, end.
A hand moved, he felt a hand, he felt a feeling as never before, he heard a voice, a hand hauled him up , voices yelled.
' *Got ya Chief, ya med it, cum on get a grip, there's the Corsair, thank God, cum on dingy is sinking, cum on* '.
Fog drifted away.
Moon lit the sea.
The Hopewell sank.

They saw the approaching damaged bows of the Gay Corsair and a hard edged voice shout.

*' Eh Chief, you there I 'ope ya 'avn't ruined me Russian boots '.*

The crew of the Hopewell were hauled from the dingies , hauled from hanging on wreckage and from thrashing in the sea  and all the crew were saved and were now in a commotion of  excited shivering, smiling, revelry, relieved  to be alive.

As the new arrangements were made some semblance of order descended upon the small , sea drenched, wind battered, over crowded boat.

When the Commodore found some dry clothes he climbed to the bridge and his tone was tense and nervous as he spoke to Captain Jackson.

*' The mission is to get ball bearings back to Britain, , you should have gone on. Mind you, glad you didn't '.*

Captain Jackson , features taut, grim, eyes looked with intensity as he shouted without intention back  in reply to the Commodore.

*' So fast, torpedo tracks sighted, changed course, sunk your boat, all crew safe, so fast, why ? God knows '.*

And as his nerves settled he commanded checks and reports to be made on the state of the boat, from the engine room to the cargo in the holds and the galley.

Now all the crews were grim faced and determined.

Captain Whitfield on the starboard wing, solid and quiet, stoically enjoyed the sensation of icy wind on his face as the deep green seas raced towards him only to be brushed aside by the slender bows of the Gay Viking as she sped across sea routes sailed by sailors for centuries . The Chief Officer and the First Officer were on the port side ever vigilant as Herbert Lask climbed onto the bridge.

*' Morning Chief, First, Captain ! '*, said Lask with an irritating boyish enthusiasm as if he was going to set sail on the boating lake in a park.

*' Hardly call it morning Mister Lask, how's our famous boson doing, the one that got away, they'll be making a film about his exploits what d'ya reckon Mister Lask ? '*, asked the Captain with a smiling smirk .

*' Don't know 'bout that Captain,  he's still sleeping,  talks in his sleep, saying he can't believe it. Never seen a man change so much in such a short space of time '.*

*' Really Mister Lask you do surprise me '.*

Mister Lask  and the Captain stood side by side swaying in motion watching fading stars between racing clouds as the wind freshened and picked up the gathering sea as they sailed in a south westerly direction as the day began to dawn in the East.

The Radio Officer checked behind the false panel to see if all his contraband was intact, carefully counting the bottles stacked one on top of another and when he was satisfied, he secured them and fixed the panel.

He was surprised to see Lask aboard .

He was curious about the other passenger closeted away out of sight. Almost silence now.

Broken only by the rustle of wind and sea and the engines whine.

A blip of the revolving line on the black circular screen made him sit upright, focus his eyes, concentrate, anticipate, visualising the shape of the blip and without moving he shouted to the bridge.

*' Echo, strong, echo strong, get that, echo '.*

He raced through his memory of images, size and speed of the radar blip as he chewed his cigarette into a nicotine mush, and he shouted much louder, much louder with words which had an edge cutting through the incessant whine of the rapidly rising sea.

A few minutes elapsed then Captain and Chief manoeuvred awkwardly through the hatch into the radio shack. They stared, watching the frayed line of revolving light picking out the blip which was travelling from the edge towards the centre of the screen.
The Radio Officer was transfixed by the rapidly approaching blip. The Captain and the Chief hustled their frames up and out onto the bridge.
Those sleeping were roused, eyes opened, bodies responded to ominous commands calling for action stations which reverberated through the small boat like electricity.
Half dressed, half asleep, knowing exactly what to do, quickly in their gun positions, muttering obscenities under their breath, a voice said.
' *Thought it was to good to last, in the wars again* '.
Suddenly a deafening explosion high above accelerated the on coming dawn, to day, as the sea became an undulating white bright awesome expanse of beauty, lasting seconds.
' *Like the Northern Lights* ', said Lask still on the bridge and staring at  the sky until he was told in no uncertain terms to get off the bridge, to make himself scarce.
' *Star shell Mister Lask now get off the fucking bridge* '.
The star shell burnt out and the emerging dawn became black , then as eyes adjusted into the grey dawn, with everyone alert, at their stations,  the blip on the radar screen turned into the reality of a fast approaching enemy destroyer.
Captain Whitfield barked quick orders down the voice pipe to the engine room.
' *Open her up Chief, many revs as you can muster . What ?, gere it fixed, open her up* '.
He swore, knowing  roughly the speed of the destroyer as the vague shape grew more and more distinct by the minute. Another star shell burst turning men into flickering images as they stared in disbelief at the beauty of the exploding light.

' *God's that something, never seen the likes of that before* ', remarked
the helmsman, as if time, place and situation had mysteriously
changed.

The light began to fade and the short aesthetic excursion viciously
ended with a massive explosion, an eruption of sea, throwing the
small boat lurching sidewards and in an unnatural, whirling
movement seas came crashing down partially submerging the
forward part of the boat. In the blackness, the Radio Officer thrown
against the bulkhead fumbled for a handhold, vomited and the hatch
above his head was torn away.

Incoming wind spray shook him seconds before unconsciousness. The
Captain slipped down the up ended bridge trying for handhold,
foothold on the slippery surface.

Now the Gay Viking, pitching, heaving was completely out of control.
The helmsman, blood gushing from his head, fought his way to the
wheel which rotated dangerously from port to starboard.

The Captain shouted in staccato bursts.

' *Helmsman. Get a grip. Get a grip of that dammed wheel* '.

The helmsman exerting every ounce of strength, fought for control of
the wheel when a huge high pitched ear splitting explosion on the
starboard side lifted the Gay Viking out of the sea , then it fell back
with such a force that in the engine room the diesels visibly
moved in their mountings.

The boat, twisted and warped, as rivets, nuts and bolts possessed of
some catastrophic demon, rattled a deranged tune out of twisted steel
and screeching wood, found a trough into which she slipped and the
Gay Viking steadied herself sufficiently for those still conscious
to find their footing.

Captain Whitfield screamed to be heard.

' *Damage, casualties, you hurt Mister Mate ?* '

A sodden heap of a First Officer reached out, grabbed the wind
dodger and hauled himself up as he replied.

' *Bloody head hurt Capt'n, bloody head* '.

The sodden heap pulled himself around and finding binoculars said
he wanted to see the bastards who hurt his head.

The Captain relieved, breathed deeply, almost smiled and through the grey spray and cresting waves he made out the shape of the destroyer in the near dark distance accelerating towards them.
The Chief Officer screeched.
*' We're a sitting duck for that what'll we do Cap'n ? ',* and it wasn't a question.
The Captain ignored the Chief as the boson climbed onto the bridge reporting injuries.
*' Broken arm, few gashes, bruises, nothing that can't be fixed, starboard engine dodgy, otherwise O.K, '.*
The Captain nodded his head and for a second he had a great desire to be somewhere else but these thoughts vanished as quickly as they had formed.
*' Boson. Men at their stations. Not over yet, we're getting out of 'ear as fast as we can '.*
The Captain looked through his binoculars towards the German destroyer which seemed to be slowing down. He shouted for a radar report. A quick reply said that it was out of action, beyond repair, but the Gay Viking began to gather speed and make distance.
The Chief Officer reported that Mister Lask was the worst for wear.
The First Officer reported they were approaching the Danish Coast.
The Captain realised why the destroyer was slowing down.
*' Mine fields, like the last trip eh, the destroyer wont take the chance, but we can, blessing in disguise. All eyes looking out '.*
Captain Whitfield smiled.
*' First Mate, you're in charge of navigation over the minefield, over the North Sea, Flamborough Head, up the Humber and home. Get on with it '.*
The dawn became day .
The sea slowed becoming a shimmering, sparkling surface as the cold March sun emerged against the last of the dark night clouds.
Lask appeared on the bridge.
Yawning and scratching his head.
The Captain acknowledged him with a grunt rapidly followed by an invitation for Lask to try his hand at steering the boat .

Like a boy with a new toy he took the wheel much to the amusement and watchful eye of the helmsman.

He got the hang of it.

He wondered what his wife would say if she knew he was messing about in a boat in the North Sea.

From the accommodation a thinly disguised figure emerged mumbling to himself and the immediate world and those who heard, deciphered the mumblings of the man.

*' Bremen built bastard I told you Bremen built bastard '.*

But it wasn't Frankie Hebden the boson with the notorious reputation.

It was Frankie but not Frankie.

Everyone knew that Shorty Burton was illusive, yet no one could understand why he wasn't to be seen considering his considerable size.

They had a good look out for him.

The Ministry was pleased.

The operation was deemed to be success.

The gains outweighed the losses and casualties were minimal.

The war had progressed until now, with vast amounts of hardware and vast armies of soldiers being assembled for the greatest invasion ever.

Steel and ball bearings kept the wheels turning and the supplies brought by the Grey Ladies, though seemingly small, were of great importance for aircraft production and this was recognised by the upper echelons of power.

The information Lask had brought back from Sweden of the crashed pilotless aircraft, some sort of rocket propelled bomb suggested the Germans were far from finished.

The S.O.E was also pleased with the way Lask had operated when helping to set up the supply route through Sweden for the transshipment of weapons to the Danish resistance.

Lask himself wasn't sure if he was pleased with himself or not, but he did know that over the past year he had seen more of life than he could have imagined and it showed as he relaxed in the deep green leather chair in the inner sanctum of Superintendent Watson's office.

Measures of Malt were poured.

The Superintendent thought the Commodore didn't look at all well , seemed to lack some of the bounce, confidence and enthusiasm he was noted for, and as it happened, the Commodore really didn't feel like himself at all and at that moment he knew exactly why he'd been rejected  by the Royal Navy. The homeward voyage from Sweden, the collision of the Hopewell and the Gay Corsair, the ever present threat of death and death itself and also the casualties had taken its toll, mentally and physically.

 He enjoyed the Malt which began to dispel the dark memories as he asked Lask to give an appraisal  of the operation in real terms.

*' Supplies of ball bearings and steels invaluable to aircraft production. It had been said that Mister Churchill took a special interest and there is some sort of decoration for the men. '.*

The Superintendent became impatient and told Lask he knew all the details.

Lask did say that Frankie Hebden had come back from his short captivity a changed man.

*' Aren't we all Mister Lask, aren't we all '*, and the Superintendent coughed as he lit another cigarette and rising from his desk he walked to the window and surveyed the silhouettes of war.

He turned, knowingly said to the Commodore and Mister Lask.

*' From what I've seen and heard the Gay Corsair and the Gay Viking took a bit of a pounding. Rough crossing '.*

He knew it was an understatement.

Suddenly he remembered the telephone calls he had to make and the messages he must convey.

*' Mister Lask, your wife keeps calling, I think she wants to know where you are, you better get off home, I expect you'll have some explaining to do '.*

Lask slowly rose from his chair and with a certain formality and anxiety made a fumbling departure.

The Superintendent and the Commodore sat in their chair looking at the floor as the afternoon began to fade into a peaceful, quiet gloom. They sat silent.

For some minutes.

Until the Commodore said he would like to see the crews of the Grey Ladies before he travelled back to London.

The Superintendent said it could be arranged and invited the Commodore for an early dinner.

Lask drove his old battered Company car through the dark streets occasionally swerving to avoid scattered debris.

He realised he was extremely tired.

He guided the car along the street bringing it to a shuddering halt three doors away from his house. Unintentionally he slammed the door and he cursed as he knew half the street would know he was back and sure enough a few curtains twitched.

Lighting a cigarette he lingered, inhaling the smoke deeply.

Feeling relaxed enough he summoned up enough courage and he strode towards the door and in one motion he was in the hallway.

*' I'm home '.*

Joan emerged from the kitchen, looking weary and angry.

*' Herbert Lask were the devil have you been. Worried sick I've been. I phone the office they tell me nothing. Never see you, they boys are forgetting they have a father, by the way they are staying at Chris and Dericks for a while. I don't feel safe any more. Its all the fault of that cigar smoking, whisky drinking Captain Turnbull, it was better before'.*

He breathed deeply, thoughts reacted, he remembered how pleased she was with his pay rise, the telephone and the car and how she was so full of herself when telling neighbours of his important war work. For a moment he wished he was back aboard the Viking on that dark morning of exploding shells.

Her face set in defiant, anxious, defence of herself.

*' I bet there's another women ! '.*

Just standing, bemused by the onslaught, so taken aback, he didn't contradict her and as she began to cry, he threw his arms around her and held her. She clung to him. Tears became sobs.

Remembering and forgetting.

Forgetting and remembering.

He thought he knew, but he didn't realise just how anxious Joan had become looking after two children going about their daily business with war all around, not knowing where he was or when he'd be home.

He felt a deep guilt as if he'd been out in the world, in the war and enjoying the experience all at the expense of his wife.
Tiredness became confusion.
Not knowing what to say.
He recalled the Superintendent saying that the Company was his family and how he and Captain Turnbull looked after those in need.
He thought of Joan going about her domestic routines while the fabric of life and the familiar was slowly falling apart.
Buildings, neighbourhoods and people changed and sometimes disappeared overnight.
Before Turnbull his life had been regular weekly work , important clerical work which hardly seemed to make any outward difference to the war. He was home every evening and always on a Sundays.
Now he did feel more alive, more worldly wise, a changed man  and he knew his boys told other children of their fathers exaggerated secret missions. All because he was away. He knew he had changed.
He was glad to be home. He kissed her and she wiped the tears away from her eyes saying she was getting soft and she needed a cup of tea.
Both sat quietly, sipping tea, and slowly  he began to tell her why he'd been called away so often. He told her more than he'd told her before though he didn't tell her everything. He couldn't resist telling her about Sweden and on hearing of this she scowled.
She said it would have helped if she had known more and he realised she was right as  he saw the look in her eyes which he'd not seen for a considerable length of time, and he knew he was really home.
He suddenly remembered he had something else to do.
He had to go out.
He had to go to the The Empress and he said it couldn't wait, it had to be tonight and with trepidation he told Joan of this with faltering trepidation.'
' Joan I've got something important I must do tonight, back at the office, important, very important, it wont take long I promise '.
She got up quickly and then she sat down, deflated and a long moment passed before what he'd said registered.

Then her green eyes flashed, he facial expression became rigid as furrows  appeared on her brow.

Looking into the embers of the fire she said softly ,

*' Well Herbert if you must, you must but please don't.....',* and her voice trailed off .

He grabbed his overcoat,  he shouted a goodbye as he opened the front door and was gone into the night.

In the vast board room panelled by a painted history of the
Companies ships, the Superintendent and the Commodore enjoyed a
silver service dinner of roast chicken served by Constance and when
the men had finished she cleared away with her customary efficiency
and guile and left them to their cigars , brandy and the last of their
conversation.

*' Commodore, you'll be wanting to see the men before you go, you'll
find them in 'The Empress'. By way of warning, you'll be on your own
in there, if you get my drift '.*

The Commodore was puzzled by this and the Superintendent
suppressed a smile.

*' In that bar you'll be a equal amongst equals. Rank counts for nothing
there. I'm sure you'll be alright after all you've sailed with them, and
over minefields I understand '.*

The Superintendent slowly began to laugh until his laughter turned
into a cough as the inhaled cigar smoke conflicted with air and
humour. When the burst of coughing ceased he picked up a
telephone and ordered a car.

The Commodore collected his coat.

The Superintendent opened the door and the two men walked slowly
down the dimly lit stairs to the entrance of the building.

As the car pulled up the two men shook hands and went their
separate ways.

 Driving through the darkened streets the Commodore saw the
hideous half buildings, empty plots, piles of rubble left by the
concentrated bombing of this North East City and by the time the car
came to a halt he was in sombre and reflective mood.

The driver interrupted his thoughts.

*' Ere we are Sir. beggin your pardon Sir are you sure this is the place,
perhaps you got the wrong pub '.*

For a moment the Commodore was taken aback, doubt crept into his
mind, but he knew, or at least thought he knew, he was in the right
place.

*' Yes driver, this is the pub where I want to be. If you could pick me up
in a couple of hours please, a couple of hours that'll do nicely '.*

The diver looked at him with astonishment.

*' A couple of hours I'll be 'ere. Good luck to you Sir, you'll need it in there '.*

With a wry smile the driver accelerated and drove nosily away into the night leaving the Commodore feeling slightly apprehensive as he pushed the door open.

The bar room was a forest of swaying limbs shrouded in clouds of bluish smoke. The Commodore hustled his way to the bar pushing aside men slouching, standing and swaying in groups, some huddled around tables and he heard rough snippets of conversation.

*' Invasion coming up '*

*' Eard they are running out a sailors ',*

*'Lot of 'em in t'night '.*

*' Aye off Grey Ladies, that there secret operation '.*

*' Jammy bastards if you ask me ? '*

*' Keep that t' yourself if I wore you, last fella who said that came a cropper, flatened by that fella over there '.*

*' Teks all sorts '.*

The Commodore reached the bar and catching the attention of Doris ordered a large pink gin.

It wasn't so much his manner but his voice that caught the attention of those around the bar who didn't know him.

Quickly the noise of the bar subsided as all eyes looked towards the man whose accent had ordered a drink which was quite out of place.

Doris looked on and without a word mixed him his drink and as he placed some silver on the bar she smiled shaking her head from side to side,

*' On the 'ouse luv. I've 'eard all 'about you Commodore and your secret missions, not to mention Moonshine '.*

He thanked her, chortled a bit, raised his glass, looked sidewards to see Lask appear by his side and the two men exchanged greetings as if they were members of an exclusive club, and they were.

The curious eyes of men looked on and a voice was heard above the steadily rising volume of conversation.

*' He's the one I told you about. Commodore, leader, bossman, up front with us all the way '.*

And the man the voice belonged to pushed his way through the crowd to the bar.

*' Good t'see you Sir. Glad ya came down  t'see us, that wuz sum mission eh, Doris, drink,  for, Commodore '.*

But the Commodore wouldn't hear of it.

He proposed that all drinks be on him and the men around him readily accepted the proposal and within seconds the Commodore was surrounded as conversation ebbed and flowed from man to man.

*' Don't mind telling you ....'*

*' Scared stiff I wuz '.*

*' Archie is it true you met a Swedish lass '.*

*' She a spy ? '.*

*' No not really a spy '.*

*' Was she a spy wasn't she a spy'.*

*' For us, spying for us she wuz '.*

*' Good that's all right then ! '.*

*'You'll be back to Sweden when it all ends then ? '.*

*' See Mister Lask '.*

*' Yeah he's the man to see '.*

*' Shorty Burton was lost so they say when that German destroyer attacked Gay Viking off coast of Denmark '.*

*' He'll turn up allus does '.*

*' Suppose so, anyroad he's a good swimmer '.*

The semi circle grew as sailors, motormen, engineers, Captains and Officers came in talking seriously, loudly, quietly, all enveloped in bursts of near and distant laughter.

The Chief Officers appeared, merged, shook hands, spoke a few words to all around then sought out Mister Lask  forming a closed circle around him subjecting him to intense questioning and then suddenly they left the bar leaving Mister Lask befuddled and wanting another drink.

Doris worked furiously, but her customers, though thirsty made few demands, they were patient and when their glasses were full they savoured every mouthful.

Someone noticed the door open and a familiar figure, muttering to himself pushing his way straight to the bar saying,

*' Doris, Doris I 'owe ya £2 7s 6p, all time away, didn't forget '.*

Her face lit up.

Surprised.

She couldn't hide her emotion.

Tears ran down her smiling face.

Embarrassed she wiped the tears away, quickly taking hold of a glass.

*' The usual Frankie ? '.*

*' No Doris, not tonight. Lemonade. Lemonade, then I must be off, promised the wife I wouldn't be late, just came to say 'ello '.*

There was a silence.

Doris poured the lemonade.

Men looked at each other in disbelief,

They stared and muttered to each other.

*' That's not Frankie Hebden '.*

*' Looks like 'im '.*

*' Not Frankie '.*

*' Lemonade , I ask ya, Frankie 'an' lemonade ?'.*

*'Going 'ome t'see 'is wife '.*

Ignoring the apparent apparition, conversations carried on about the past, the present and the future, and the future was all about the coming invasion of Europe and where their destinations would be.

One man did venture to ask Frankie, just how he managed to escape.

*' Cum on Frankie tell us,'ow did ya escape, 'cum on Frankie tell us ? '.*

Frankie drank his lemonade in one gulp and he looked, slowly, deeply at the lined and cracked faces around him and he smiled a demented, crooked smile.

*' Well lads I wuz in this 'er prison camp, 'bout 'undred miles south of Baltic. Me and me mate, Australian fella got dressed up in uniforms, we med 'em our selves.'*

*' I wuz this fella ' Itler and Aussie was that other bloke, forgotten 'is name, ya know the bastard. One morning we marched up t'gate, guards saluted us, opened gates and we walked through.*
*Got inta German staff car.*
*Drove off '.*
*Me in back seat waving I wuz like 'im seen in the newsreels with the Australian driving we got clean away, bluddy crazy driver. There wus a box of wine on back seat so we 'ad bluddy good drink '.*

Doris and the captive audience listened and watched in almost awe, though with a few winks to each other and quick smiles which didn't distract  Frankie as his eyes flashed in all directions as his story unfolded.

*' We 'adn't gone far when we ran inta lots of traffic, tanks, lorries full of soldiers and they cheered as we drove by. Suddenly there wuz explosions all around us . Planes overhead. Tanks firing guns. Then at a road block we wuz arrested. Thought German soldiers were going to shoot us but they just laughed at us and  put us in a lorry. '*
*' Drove us t' airfield and threw us inta plane. 'A General came to see us, made us put  on parachutes. In perfect English he told us that we'd be more use to the Third Reich if we both created havoc in England. He smiled and waved us off and the aircraft took off. Bit later they pushed us out and 'ere we are '.*

All looked at Frankie in stunned silence, then they began to murmure and slowly expressions broadened and then one began to laugh, then another, and the laughter grew until the bar echoed with a rich, rough, cacophony of pain, tears and the laughter rose in pitch, then eased, until men looked in all directions. Then in a shuffling commotion cigarettes were lit, ale drained from glasses and Frankie Hebden looked at them as if they were total strangers.

Suddenly he announced he must be on his way to be with his wife and with that he turned and pushed his way through the crowd and as he reached the door, he turned and looked at the men looking at him and his faced twitched in apparent confusion.

Then he was gone.

There were those who swore it wasn't Frankie.

No one had ever heard Frankie mention lemonade.

No one had ever seen Frankie drink lemonade before and they all knew he came back aboard the Gay Viking with Mister Lask, the man was an imposter.

With Frankie gone, quiet descended upon the gathering and collectively the men seemed to have a desire for privacy, to be at home, in their own homes and they all seemed to have had enough of the sea and all who sail on her, at least for the moment.

After shaking the hand of the last departing sailor, the Commodore said his farewell to Doris with a polite kiss upon her cheek and then he made his departure in the wake of the sailors .

Now the bar of 'The Empress' seemed so vast with only Eddie Higgins remaining. He had no where else to be, and in silence he helped Doris  clear the glasses away.

Torpedo tracks had been on his mind. He was sure he'd seen torpedo tracks. But thinking about all the swirling fog in the dark he wasn't so sure. He told Doris about it all and she listened sympathetically as they finished the cleaning of the bar.

Doris locked the outer door and they climbed the stairs together.

Lask got into his battered car and he slumped into the seat but he was unable to move , he was frozen, as events and people appeared in the misted reflection of the windscreen until all became hazy and blurred.

He shook his head.

Got out of the car.

He decided to walk for a while .

He remembered the night when Captain Turnbull barged through his office door, disrupting his carefully well ordered routine and the drive home in his battered Company car when the Captain told him of the Operation and his promotion. He recalled how he drank most of his whisky and his cigar ash fell in a neat circle upon the carpet. The night was intensely dark and the streets and alleys were full of shadows and seeing passing pubs where he'd learned so much, so quickly from his mentor.

In ' The White Heart ', he'd learned from Captain Turnbull that
official sanction wasn't always necessary to get things done and in
' The George ' he saw the illusion of American tinned meat which
had been broached from some merchant ship, being distributed by
Captain Turnbull to those on the Superintendents ' in need list '.
Walking through the ' Land of Green Ginger ' he felt guilt when
thinking of the fate of Tom.

He slipped.

Falling to the ground he hurt his arm.

Suddenly he thought of his wife Joan. Now it was late very late.
In the mid of night he shivered as he made his way back  to his car
and with haste he drove towards home.   Turning left, down his
street, he brought the car to  a standstill .

He was out of the car and quickly through the front door of his
house. There was no sound. The house was still.

In the kitchen an official envelope addressed to him was propped up
against the sugar basin. He opened the envelope and read the
contents which was all direct, polite and matter of fact.

Where to report.

When to report.

Who to report to.

Travel documents included.

Not much time.

He couldn't understand.

He was just a Company clerk.

As he climbed the stairs to their bedroom he wondered what he
should tell his wife.

What kind of story could he make up.

With every step his thoughts took different turns.

When he opened the door he found the bed was empty.

On a pillow lay a note.

He lay down upon the bed.

With the end came quickly sleep with dreams of ships and the sea.

**THE END**

*About the Author*

*Peter Thomas Jackson*

*Born in Kingston Upon Hull, England, U.K.
Peter Thomas Jackson spent a few years of his
youth in the British Merchant Navy sailing to
many countries experiencing different climates
and cultures of the world.
Leaving the Merchant Navy he travelled to North
America and for a while lived and worked in
northern Manitoba, Canada.
Then he wandered around Canada and the
United States eventually travelling back to the
U.K. where he found himself in London and
attended the Central and Wimbledon Schools of
Art. Following on he settles down to a fine life of
family, teaching, painting and writing.
He now lives in Yorkshire where he continues.*

*2020*